THE ARTIST'S DAUGHTER

CATHERINE LAW

B
Boldwood

First published in 2013 as *The Flower Book*. This edition published in Great Britain in 2024 by Boldwood Books Ltd.

Copyright © Catherine Law, 2013

Cover Design by Head Design Ltd.

Cover Images: Shutterstock

Interior image: David Bryant

The moral right of Catherine Law to be identified as the author of this work has been asserted in accordance with the Copyright, Designs and Patents Act 1988.

All rights reserved. No part of this book may be reproduced in any form or by any electronic or mechanical means, including information storage and retrieval systems, without written permission from the author, except for the use of brief quotations in a book review. This book is a work of fiction and, except in the case of historical fact, any resemblance to actual persons, living or dead, is purely coincidental.

Every effort has been made to obtain the necessary permissions with reference to copyright material, both illustrative and quoted. We apologise for any omissions in this respect and will be pleased to make the appropriate acknowledgements in any future edition.

A CIP catalogue record for this book is available from the British Library.

Paperback ISBN 978-1-83751-631-5

Large Print ISBN 978-1-83751-632-2

Hardback ISBN 978-1-83751-630-8

Ebook ISBN 978-1-83751-633-9

Kindle ISBN 978-1-83751-634-6

Audio CD ISBN 978-1-83751-625-4

MP3 CD ISBN 978-1-83751-626-1

Digital audio download ISBN 978-1-83751-629-2

This book is printed on certified sustainable paper. Boldwood Books is dedicated to putting sustainability at the heart of our business. For more information please visit https://www.boldwoodbooks.com/about-us/sustainability/

Boldwood Books Ltd, 23 Bowerdean Street, London, SW6 3TN

www.boldwoodbooks.com

This book is dedicated to the memory of my grandparents:

Sydney Charles Law, Nellie Law née Marsh, Albert Butler Smith and Miriam Annie Smith née Robinson, who were all born before the First World War.

Here in your book, the buds and blooms you collected ever since you were a little girl speak to me now.

Our very own language of flowers.

— ASTER FAIRLING

PROLOGUE
ASTER

Cornwall, 1918

The clock struck seven times and they still hadn't told her to go to bed.

Outside, the summer evening sky was radiant; the light inside the drawing room soft and luminous. Aster heard the clock chiming in the hallway and shuffled further back into the armchair, scented by her father's tobacco. His newspaper lay folded on the arm with a half-filled-in crossword and sleepily she traced his scribblings with her finger.

She gave an eye-stinging yawn and peered around the wing of the chair to watch her grandmother at the card table with Great-Aunt Muriel. Both had their backs to her, their identical grey, wavy haired heads poised, their spines in long, smooth gowns as straight as rods. Muriel deftly shuffled her cards, flicking them out across the table's melted-toffee surface. The ladies must have forgotten about Aster, curled up in the deep armchair. Or perhaps, Aster thought, she was allowed to stay up because her father was home.

The low sun intensified another degree, pouring gold across the parquet. Aster heard her mother talking in the garden, her voice drifting through the open French windows. A comforting whiff of her father's cigarette wafted with it. She heard his quiet response, his rumbling words. They tickled

Aster, seemed to settle inside her. Jess the cocker spaniel lay in a furry pool beneath her feet, guarding her and sighing with responsibility.

With a wink of excitement, Aster felt drawn back to the playing cards flipping from Muriel's fingers over the table. Her grandmother watched the cards, too, as if they held a peculiar magic, drinking her steaming tea, pursing her lips. A glance at Muriel and a hesitant shaking of her head. Muriel lay the last one down with a flourish, and then hastily mixed the cards over the table and clawed them back, together, whispering, 'We shouldn't be doing this now, Eleanor. We really shouldn't.'

She didn't say why, and Aster wanted to ask, wanted to know why she felt that something terrible had happened, and was happening, and will always be happening.

Her grandmother, suddenly remembering her, turned her sharp gaze on her.

'You're not still up, are you, Aster?' Her grandmother's voice sounded a fraction below anger. 'It's getting late. Time that little girls were in bed.'

'But the garden is still light,' Aster said, sinking back into the chair. 'The birds are still talking. And Daddy is here.'

'Grannie is right. Time for bed.'

Aster looked around in surprise at the voice velvet-deep in her ear. Her mother had come back into the room and knelt at the side of the chair. Her dark hair was rolled in a great smooth puff over her forehead, wisps escaping to touch her ears. Aster loved the russet-brown depths of it, but her mother's green eyes looked cloudy, hiding something. Tears streaked her apple-round cheeks. She flicked something from her eye and declared, 'And high time Aunt Muriel put the cards away.'

'Where's Daddy?' Aster asked.

'He's taking a stroll. He will come up and tuck you in,' her mother replied, a graininess in her tone. 'He won't be long.'

'You spoil that child, Violet,' Aster's grandmother said. 'She should have been in bed an hour ago.'

'Today is different, Mother, you know that.'

Aster's mother sounded weary and her grandmother's scowl too severe to do battle with. With grave obedience, Aster shuffled out of the chair and, on tiptoes, planted a kiss first on Great-Aunt Muriel's powdered cheek, and then on her grandmother's. She took her mother's hand and crossed the ocean of parquet, the cool stone-paved hallway and began the long climb. Her mother smelt of the sea, of fresh air and lily of the valley. Aster wanted to bury her face in the smooth cream skirt that clinched her tiny waist and the blouse that puffed lace over her shoulders and arms.

'Hotch in, that's it.' Her mother pulled down the sheet. 'It's too hot for blankets tonight.' Aster thought she looked broken and tired. 'Didn't you have a lovely time at the harvest? You and Harry, and little Kate, riding in the back of the wagon. Such a jolly time.'

She pulled Aster's bedroom curtains and shut out the balmy dusk, to snuff out the memories of the day. But Aster clung to them. She could still feel the sun on her arms, the scratchy straw between her toes. She still sat with Harry and Kate, the birds still sang in the corners of the field where she'd gathered the wildflowers and took them to her mother. But Harry and Kate had gone. A car from the Big House had arrived earlier, around teatime, when her parents were out. The car from the Big House took her friends away.

Aster's legs twitched with unbearable tiredness, her head thick and drowsy. She could not form the words to ask her mother why they had to go. The house felt appallingly quiet, the sheet cool and heavy, a scent of the linen cupboard; the candlewick bedspread a wide expanse of dusty pink.

'Soon be morning,' soothed her mother, her face a pale oval in the half-light.

'But Dad?' Aster barked, rudely, deep in her throat.

'Be patient, darling, he won't be long.'

Aster fought it, wriggled against it, but sleep quickly found her.

* * *

She woke, briefly, peering through a crack in a dream, and sensed that night had moved on. It was dark, so very dark, the air cooler in her nostrils. In the silence, she heard the sea. Waves hissing in over the flat sand half a mile away, beyond the garden, beyond the woods. She must be dreaming. For how could she possibly hear it; it always took an age to get to the cove, down the ferny path, with her grandfather slashing at undergrowth with his stick,

Jess racing ahead and grandmother dawdling behind with her mother. How well she knew that long sloping path that merged into the dunes, breaking open to the sea. But her father was never with them. In the darkness, he wasn't there.

Aster called out for him. She wanted to get up, to run, to find him. She sat upright in the pitch-black and her hand touched a wall where one should not have been. She reached again to the other side. Another wall, hard and impossible, imprisoning her in blank darkness.

She screamed. The door opened behind her, letting in a triangle of lamplight where she had not expected it to be.

'Oh, what now? You've turned round in bed. You're all of a tussle.' Her father hauled her up and plonked her the right way round.

'Are you not going to come back?' Aster asked as he pulled the sheet over her shoulders. 'Great-Aunt Muriel said.'

'Hush. Sleep tight. I'm here now, Aster.' A kiss on her forehead but she could not see his face. 'Look after Mama for me.'

Her head sank into the cool puff of the pillow, no longer able to fight sleep. He shut the bedroom door behind him.

* * *

Aster woke again in cool grey early light to the noise of an engine pulsing on the lane outside. She ran to pull the curtain aside and saw a peculiar vehicle parked, a man in army uniform, waiting behind the wheel. She heard strangers' voices from the path below, a violent hammering on the front door.

Her father emerged from the porch beneath her window in his cap and brown uniform, his awful, scratchy brown uniform and a man in neat khaki and the policeman from Looe walked with him up the path to the car, as if he wouldn't know the way. One of them made him stand still and he attached something heavy and metallic to his wrists. It shone in the strange peeling radiance of daybreak.

Aster heard the front door again and her mother ran out along the front path and through the gate. Her father turned to face her, still and stiff, as if on duty and her mother stood staring at him with such intensity that her head quivered. But he looked at the sky, at the ground, the trees, never at her.

Aster saw her mother reach her hands out towards him as if stretching across a fire, but the men took hold of him and made him get into the car. The engine revved, a slip of tyres on the stony lane, and it vanished around the corner.

Moment followed empty moment, the silence unbearable as the light increased and chased darkness from under the trees. And Aster's mother stood alone and stunned as if she had been planted into the ground.

He'd said last night in the darkness, *I'm here now, Aster, I'm here now. Look after Mama for me.*

But he did not say when he'd return.

PART I
VIOLET, CORNWALL, 1914

1

AS MANY MISTS IN MARCH AS THERE ARE FROSTS IN MAY

On certain nights, if the wind is right, you can hear the sea from Old Trellick. So the legend has it, although Violet had never caught the sound of the waves and her parents would not even try.

As a child she'd stand at the open French windows and implore them to be quiet, to stop what they were doing and to concentrate with her, to catch this magical and elusive sound.

'We're far too far away,' her father, a doctor and cynical beyond measure, would say. 'Even if the breeze was coming right off the sea, we'd never hear it from here. And anyway, my girl, it's broad daylight. Isn't it supposed to happen during the night?'

And her mother would tell her not to be so silly. 'If you want to hear the sea, Violet, then go down to the cove,' she'd say, not understanding.

But at night, Violet would lie in bed longing to hear it, imagining the rhythmic hum echoing from the cove up the steep ferny path, meandering over the hillocky meadow made rough by cattle, blowing up the lane to Old Trellick, the old stone house, snug in the crook of the valley. She longed for it to come right through her window and into her room. She wished to be rocked to sleep by the waves' consistent sighs and intangible whispering. But, in the long empty darkness, Violet knew that if the sea would not come to her, then indeed, she must go to it.

***

It was the first time this year that Violet had been down to the cove. The tide would be full, the waves heavy and she hoped to find early sea holly sheltering in the dunes, the marram grass already robust and vivid. She walked down the steep path, worn into a gully, sheltered and silent for now. But at some point, the pristine air would change in a blink and the sound of the sea would at last reach her, suddenly, forcefully, like the turning on of a tap.

Violet paused, letting her young cocker spaniel sniff around the roots of the hawthorn, and lifted her head to listen. Her nostrils tingled, catching the fragrance of sea spray. She could hear the wind rattling the branches, birdsong, and from over the stone hedge, the bawling of a newborn lamb.

'We're not there yet, Claudia,' she cried, 'not quite yet.'

Her friend, a little way behind peering into the bushes, acknowledged her call with a wave to say: wait for me.

'Just looking for where the best elderflower bushes are,' Claudia called, forever searching hedgerows so her mother could make jam, pickles, preserves and a particularly good elderflower wine, which she sold at Looe market.

Violet perched on a mossy pile of stones that had tumbled long ago from the wall and pulled the puppy's lead close. The dog quivered under the impact of the moving, breezy, scented world around him. His snout twitched furiously. She reached down with her finger to smooth his worried little brow.

'All right, Jess, sit. Sit, I say. Now we must both stay here and wait for Claudia.'

Violet watched her friend's narrow frame as she walked towards her. Her angular elbows had worn her blouse, her skirt an old school one she'd first had at fifteen, the hem let down many times.

'Come autumn, we won't be able to move in our kitchen for bottles and demijohns,' Claudia said, reaching her. 'And there'll be some good blackberrying here, come August,' she said, her eyes luminous with the thought of it. 'Mother said specifically that I was to look, and note, and remember. Some lovely thick brambles pushing through up there. Jam galore.'

'I will look forward to it.' Violet met her smile, admiring the unchanging fairness of Claudia's smooth cheeks, dashed with freckles. Her friend's fine silvery blonde hair made Violet's look a darker, duller brown than it needed to be.

Violet nudged her puppy's flank with her toe. 'Not sure this one is up to the cove,' she said. 'Look at him shaking. He will be overwhelmed, will be dive-bombed by seagulls, carried off. Never to be seen again.'

Claudia grimaced in mock horror, then peered past Violet's shoulder. 'Are we nearly there?'

'A few more yards, I think.'

'Let's try it.'

The two girls linked arms, their giggles tight with anticipation. They took long strides, walking together down the path, matching each other's pace, the little dog scurrying by their feet. And the moment met them. Was it a turn of a corner, a dip in the hedge, the change of the wind? Whatever happened, and it felt different every time, the rushing, blasting voices of the sea suddenly hit them.

With a glance, a nod, a full understanding, together they cried out 'Now!' and ran, hurtling down the path, letting gravity pull them on, their ears now full of the heave and swell of the waves. The damp ferns retreated, and the gorse wore fiery yellow. The rocky ground gave way to short, shining grass and then sandy clefts, shifting dunes. And they ran in unison, their laughs hardly able to break out of their bodies as they hit the beach, the sparkling rocks and shallow cliffs now their cauldron and the sea before them an enormous and generous old friend.

Violet threw herself onto the silver sand. It shifted, lightly and dryly beneath her, her palms pressing on fragments of shells, tiny crystalline pieces of pebble.

'Jess, where's Jess?' she panted.

'He's here, I have him,' cried Claudia. Her voice seemed far away, snatched by the wind.

They laughed now, heartily, as the sea spray moistened their throats. Claudia thumped down beside her and they rested their heads together. The sea was grey, not yet its summer blue, but perfect. Violet wound the lead tight around her wrist as Jess cowered between them, offering minute yelps of terror.

'Poor little thing,' said Claudia. 'He doesn't know what's hit him.'

'God above,' said Violet, 'will you look at the state of your skirt?'

'The gorse got me,' Claudia said, tugging at the torn hem. 'This is never going to mend. Oh hell, Mother will kill me.'

Violet glanced down at her own skirt, new that season, a fine linen of periwinkle blue.

'Yours is intact, not a mark on it,' said Claudia. 'Thank goodness. You always have such nice clothes.'

'I want you to have it,' said Violet. 'I have another, identical. I don't see why you should have to walk around in your old school skirt. You're a grown-up lady.'

'Well, we're both eighteen but don't behave like ladies much, do we,' giggled Claudia. 'Not today, anyway.'

Violet lay back into the bed of sand. Pewter clouds bowled across the sky, stirring a hunger for freedom inside her. She felt Jess shuffle around her, inspecting her, pressing little dabs from his wet nose onto her cheek and her ears.

'You're right. I'm not sure I'm quite ready to behave like a lady,' sighed Violet. 'Not every day, anyway.' She glanced at her friend. 'We might have gone to different schools, Claudia, but we always stayed close, didn't we? So glad we did,' she mused. 'I did wonder if we might have drifted apart when they sent me off to that blessed Exeter Priory.'

'No, never. That's why I stayed your friend, because you still liked to chat with me, and share with me, and come to the cove with me. Me, the little ragged girl from the farm who went to Chapel Street School in Looe.'

'I don't think going to the local church school did you any harm.'

'No, but look, I'm still wearing the blessed uniform! I used to like your school uniform, that lovely emerald green.'

'Ugh, but the boater. Give me strength. I stuck out like a sore thumb whenever I came back on the bus for holidays and the odd weekend they let me out. Like being set free from a zoo.' She shuddered. The very idea of her old school made Violet feel dull and dragged down.

'And what about the time you ran away?' Claudia teased her. Sitting up, she drew a wriggling Jess onto her lap, planting kisses on his silky ears.

Violet laughed. 'Not one of my finest moments. We don't like to talk about that.' Even so, the memory of her crawling out of a dorm window as dawn broke and running, running, into short-lived liberty, still gave her a tingling thrill.

'The deadly dreary lessons really did for me.'

'Oh, but you liked nature studies,' Claudia reminded her. 'You love your wildflowers, your trees. Even the weeds. And you have your precious journal, your *Flower Book.*'

'But the teacher made us use the Latin names when all I know is coltsfoot, eyebright, and cranesbill,' Violet said. 'She asked me to bring the book to the lessons, so that everyone could have a look. How *dare* she?' It had been as if her teacher had asked her to show everyone her diary. 'I kept forgetting it on purpose and then told her I'd lost it. But I especially loved the time we studied the poisonous plants.'

Claudia laughed, 'Look at you – you enjoyed that!'

'Deadly nightshade, of course, so obvious, plus hemlock and tansy.'

'Do you mean bitter buttons? I know that one. Those horrid little yellow flowers. My mother swore by it to bring herself on when she was expecting me. She made a tea with it. Worked a treat. I was late and lazy, she said.'

Violet teased her that some things never change. 'Whereas, I'm rebellious and ridiculous, according to my mother.' She shivered. 'It's getting a bit too chilly to be lying around in the sand. Shall we go?' And what's more, in all honesty, weren't they both a little too old to be playing like this on the beach?

'Well, all things considered,' Claudia said, easing herself up onto her elbows, 'you running away from school might have thoroughly vexed your parents, Violet, but also would never have best pleased that gentleman over there...' She squinted into the low sun, wrinkling her nose. 'Mr Penruth. Unmistakably him. I can tell by his silhouette. Look at the way he walks. With his dogs. Must have come round the head. The tide's on its way out.'

Violet sat up. Weston Penruth indeed approached from the far side of the cove. She pulled at Claudia's arm.

'And why would it not best please Mr Penruth that I may or may not have run away from school?'

Claudia glanced at her, blushing, giggling.

'*Everyone* knows, Violet.'

'Knows what? *Claudia!*'

'Come *on*. My mother told me years ago. You must realise we all know...' Claudia paused, relishing the nugget of gossip '...that, in his wisdom, Mr Penruth, our very own Lordy over there, paid your school fees.'

The breeze took away Violet's shout of surprise. 'But how did you know! I only found out by chance a few years ago when Papa let slip. Something about a bursary and me not needing one. If that wasn't bad enough, at least I assumed it was kept within my family. Heavens, Claudia. You can't *all* know!'

Violet looked over at the distant figure of Weston Penruth, squire of Charlecote, the Big House, and the biggest landowner in this corner of Cornwall. Landlord to Claudia's father, and of Old Trellick and, seemingly, benefactor wherever he picked and chose.

She had not seen him for a while, but reminded herself of what she always thought of when she did: aloof, rather annoyingly fine-looking, and exactly ten years her senior. That is, she thought, absolutely ancient. And ever since the elder Mr Penruth had died, a few years before, more formidable than ever. He always walked, she noticed, with a peculiar air, wincing and stiff-backed, as if his jacket was far too tight across his shoulders.

He stopped to bellow at his dogs, two boisterous lurchers bounding over the breaking waves and seemed to release a great sigh, as the wind whipped at his collar. He drew a flask from his greatcoat pocket and took a nip.

'Still a drinker, I see,' whispered Claudia. 'Good God, he's seen us, and me with this awful, ripped skirt.'

'He can hardly miss us here on this otherwise deserted beach.' Violet got to her feet and brushed herself down. 'We better be polite, pass the time of day.'

'Why is it I feel so *sorry* for him...?' Claudia uttered.

Weston Penruth took his slow measured pace towards them across the sand. Violet plucked Jess from the ground and held his quivering form, feeling the tick of his heart, fixing a pleasant smile on her face. Claudia beside her mumbled in trepidation.

'Good afternoon, Mr Penruth,' Violet called as soon as he came within earshot. 'How do you do? What a lovely day.'

He nodded, and took off his hat, revealing dark ruffled hair.

'How do you do, ladies?'

Up close, his features appeared wind-reddened, his eyes brightened by the blustery air. It seemed to Violet that the breeze must have blown away his smile.

'I see you have one of the Churchtown puppies there, Miss Prideaux,' he said, his conversation as stiff as his frame. 'A good choice, although cocker spaniels are always hard work. How are your parents? How are Dr and Mrs Prideaux?'

'Very well, sir,' Violet replied, wishing immediately that she hadn't called him that when Mr Penruth would have sufficed.

She tilted her chin in defiance, to prove to herself and him that she did not feel intimidated.

'And you, Miss Ainsley?' he asked. 'I trust you are well?'

'I am, I am...' Claudia blushed and threw a dazzling smile, concentrating on tickling Jess around the snout as he strained to exit Violet's arms.

Weston gazed beyond them, his eyes focusing far out to sea where the light broke through milky clouds to sit in pools on top of the water. Then, as if remembering, looked suddenly at Violet, and spoke quickly, 'How rude, I have not asked you, Miss Prideaux, how you yourself are—'

'Here come the dogs,' Violet cut in.

He turned to face off the brutish onslaught of sopping wet lurchers with a sharp shout of a command. They ducked to the sand, panting.

'They're good dogs, Mr Penruth,' Violet said.

'Trained them myself.' He looked at Violet as if he wished to say something more, ask her again, how she was.

But he planted his hat back on his head and exhaled a ragged sigh. 'Well, I must be getting on,' he said.

'Of course,' said Violet.

'Good afternoon, Mr Penruth,' Claudia bobbed, and gave a coquettish giggle.

He stalked off, calling his dogs to heel, and Violet felt they'd better leave, too, for how strange it would be to flop themselves back down onto the sand and loll about like schoolgirls with Weston Penruth still walking on the beach.

'Did you not notice? He has such a soft spot for you,' teased Claudia as they hurried back up the path, letting Jess scoot ahead of them, their giggling breaking free again once they were inside the seclusion of the gully. 'No wonder he paid your school fees.'

'Well, I wish he hadn't. And I wish he didn't,' Violet muttered. 'Soft spot? That man is as hard as granite. He couldn't wait to get away from us. Didn't know how to speak to us. Could barely look at us. We are just silly little girls to him.'

'Oh no, no,' Claudia teased her. 'He likes you. You could do worse.'

'I could also do a lot better, Claudia.'

'He is always alone...' Claudia pondered. 'Somehow, that's quite appealing.'

'Alone with his dogs, yes,' said Violet. 'And I think that tells us a great deal, does it not? Not sure *appealing* is the right word.'

'Just think,' Claudia laughed, linked her arm through Violet's and began to tug her up the slope, 'if it wasn't for that gentleman, *in his wisdom*, and his social conscience, you'd be in an old ragged school dress right now, just like me. Oh, what's that you have there?'

Violet drew a sprig of gorse out of her pocket, a flash of intense yellow.

'This shall be duly pressed,' she said, 'and mounted in my *Flower Book*. It will be entitled, "Ides of March, 1914, first walk to the cove. The gorse that ripped Claudia's skirt."'

2

IN THE LANGUAGE OF FLOWERS: NARCISSUS, EGOTISM

After three days of sea-blown rain, the forsythia that had brightened the front of the house since February wilted, leaving only crumpled daffodils and shredded crocuses around the quince tree. Violet stood at the parlour window admiring the blaze of sunshine catching raindrops clinging to every bud. Sodden and sopping, the earth was warming up and pressing out its shoots, the season turning a corner.

Her father walked his bicycle over the granite slabs of the front path, bicycle clips clamping his tweed trousers. On fine days, he preferred to cycle, leaving the motor car in the old barn. It proved to be unpredictable, its function sporadic, he said, and he would rather rely on two wheels not four. Once through the gate, he hooked his leg over and rode off down the lane with his doctor's bag stowed in the box on wheels behind him, his whistle faint but tuneful.

'Papa's off to Lansallos.' Violet's mother, taking coffee by the small fire in the grate, shook out her newspaper. 'They think little Benjamin Davey has pneumonia. This is the time of year for it. Weather warming up, all the coughing starts. Deathwatch beetle tapping away. Papa will be gone all day, no doubt, and probably half the night. But not a lot he can do for the little lad.'

This, then, would be the last spring the little boy would see. The beauty of the day turned sour, and Violet sat on the window seat and turned her back on the view, thinking about her father's dedication. People from the likes of the Daveys, fishermen from the damp cottages behind Lansallos quay, to the families of the big houses, the Penruths included, respected her father, turning to him in their time of need. He helped at births, deaths, and everything in between, including ironing out disputes and witnessing legal documents, refusing payment.

But, Violet thought, with a sting of irritation, her father had no qualms about accepting money from Weston for her schooling. No wonder Weston seemed so awkward with her, unable to look her fully in the eye. And, worse, according to Claudia, this rather demeaning snippet about her was all over the neighbourhood.

'You're looking a little cross with the world, Violet,' her mother said. 'Seen something out there you don't like?'

Unable to express exactly what rankled her, Violet shrugged and slumped down in the other armchair.

'Well, my girl,' her mother pressed, 'what are you going to do today?'

What indeed, thought Violet, was there to do for a gentleman's daughter of moderate means?

'Thought I'd take Jess out for a walk along the valley and teach him some more ground rules,' she said. 'He is still not very good off the lead.'

'You're a braver soul than I. Where is the little fellow, anyway?'

'Padding around the lawn in the back garden. I'll call him in in a minute. He was just paying a visit.'

'I hope he will keep out of my herbaceous border and won't go lifting his leg on the delphiniums. Papa has only just put them in. You know, he will have to learn to stay quiet in the boot room at night. I can't stand his whimpering through the small hours.'

'He will improve, Mother. Allow him, and me, some time,' said Violet, reaching across for *The Times*. As she moved it from the table an envelope fell to the carpet. 'Oh, is this a letter from Auntie Muriel? Is she well?'

'Yes, read it if you like. These days she is spending an awful lot of time at Selfridges. How wonderful for her to have it, all five floors of it, just a stroll away. She says it is heavenly. She could walk there but takes a hansom cab instead because of all the inevitable purchases she makes. I am going to send off for the catalogue, see if I can't order some bits and pieces.'

Violet scanned the letter, reading her aunt's gossipy snippets and humorous asides. Muriel sounded her usual maverick self. 'Surely *we* can't afford to buy things from such a fancy shop?'

'Oh, you know me, anything Muriel has, I want it too,' said her mother. 'She tells me they have the most incredible Indiennes fabrics.'

Violet bit down on her response for a second, then spoke her mind anyway. 'But we don't have the Penruth money any more, do we Mother, so how can we afford everything Aunt Muriel has? And I am not yet earning my keep.'

Her mother looked sharply at her, almost in admiration.

'We don't expect you to, dear. And that money all went on your school fees, as you know,' said her mother, her face animated with mystery. 'Please don't mention it to your father. He wants it all forgotten about. We are grateful to Mr Penruth, of course we are, but it has always been rather thorny. The least said on the matter the better, don't you think?'

Violet folded Muriel's letter away.

'I just hope Mr Penruth doesn't imagine he'll see a return for his money, and assume that I will become a scientist, or something.'

Her mother's laugh sounded like a tinkling bell.

'Oh, Violet, you are so amusing sometimes.'

'But, you're right, Mother. It is *thorny*. I do find it rather mortifying; I didn't even know that Claudia—'

Her mother stared past Violet's shoulder and out the window, her face fixed.

'Don't look now, but we have a visitor. The very man himself.'

'Oh heavens, this will be the second time this week,' said Violet. 'We saw him at the cove. Mother, you receive him, will you? I want to go and fetch Jess.'

'Don't you dare. He is obviously here to see you. Look what he is carrying.'

Weston Penruth paused under the sweet chestnut at the front gate to Old Trellick and shuffled at his necktie, before swapping a basket into his left hand and back again. A basket full of flowers.

'Put another log on that fire, get it going,' her mother said. 'Take the chill off. I will show him in.'

Suppressing discomfort and her urge to flee, Violet knelt on the hearthrug and concentrated on coaxing more flames. Why did that man give her family such attention? Why did he unnerve her so? Violet wondered, attacking a wad of ash with the poker. The door opened and she scrambled inelegantly to her feet while her mother showed Mr Penruth into the room, basket, and all.

They exchanged the usual good morning pleasantries.

'Please,' said Violet, 'take a seat.'

Weston placed the basket, overflowing with lilies, roses, and crimson peonies, their heads held at stiff, unnatural angles, on the side table, and sat down, planting his boots firmly on the carpet. He tucked a handkerchief deep into his top pocket and fixed a rather alarming smile on Violet.

Her mother sidled towards the door, nodding peculiarly at her before ducking out of the room.

'And what brings you this way this morning, Mr Penruth?' Violet said, unnecessarily, glancing at the basket.

'I hear how much you love flowers—'

'Doesn't everyone?' she interjected, with a broad smile.

'—and so, I have brought you some rather glamorous specimens,' Weston said, sounding thrilled with himself. 'I thought, I know a young lady who will love some fragrance and bright colour in all this chilly, wet weather we've been having. I didn't have what I needed in my hothouse for you, so this arrangement has come down all the way from Covent Garden on the night train.'

Violet inhaled in astonishment. 'That is so kind,' she said, hesitating over how pleased she should sound. 'They are beautiful. And yes, I do love flowers, so I thank you, very much. Although really, there was no need...' She reached a finger to touch the head of one of the scarlet rosebuds. It felt like a tight little roll of velvet. 'How incredible to see a rose, a lily and a peony at this time of year,' she said. 'Really, very incredible.'

And, how utterly wrong.

'I knew you'd like them, Violet,' he said.

She thanked him again and her voice drifted into silence, their exchange as uncomfortable and as clumsy as it had been at the cove. Weston looked at her expectantly beneath drawn-down brows, turning his hat over through his hands, crossing and uncrossing his legs. In the soft indoor light, his manner and his face appeared more tender, a little more appealing, and yet Violet still struggled for something to say.

She peered at the flowers. 'And how... how are they able to stand like that? You see, for me, lilies always flop, the ones I grow in the garden, that is, the ones that come out in June – ah, I see...' Violet stared at the mesh wound around the stems. 'They are held together with wires.'

'Now, you must remember not to overwater them,' Weston suggested. 'My man advised me.'

Violet flinched. What pleasure he seemed to take in having a second-hand understanding of flower arranging. For a gentleman of such standing, his lack of conversation seemed to cause him pain, and she, like Claudia had, felt a strange pang of sorrow for him.

'Mr Penruth, would you like some coffee, because I think that Mother might be making some?'

'Coffee? Yes, yes, indeed.' He brightened, allowing his gaze to alight on her face for a second as if he could not bear it.

'Excuse me while I go and get it. I have to do this myself, you see,' Violet found herself giggling, 'as our maid does not work on Wednesdays. And we don't have a "man".'

He stood courteously when she got up, as any gentleman might; his manners, Violet conceded, impeccable. But out in the kitchen, she begged her mother to come back through to the parlour with her.

'Don't you dare leave me alone with him. He professes to know me because he has brought me flowers,' she said, 'I need you for your conversation, Mother. You might be able to make him laugh.'

'I, for one, wouldn't turn my nose up at such flowers,' said her mother, lifting the tray. 'Now hold the door open for me, that's it, and I'll come back in. I won't abandon you, Violet. I need to know what's going on.'

Her mother, ever the perfect hostess, poured coffee and offered home-made saffron buns. Weston seemed to relax and appear not nearly as alarming as before. He even smiled.

'I bumped into Dr Prideaux just now on my way over. He seems very well,' he said.

'It would be no good for any of us,' said Violet's mother, 'if the doctor fell ill, now, would it?'

Weston allowed a small laugh. 'And, Miss Prideaux,' he said, looking around the room pointedly, 'I was wondering where the puppy could be?'

'He's safely biding his time in the garden,' said Violet.

'You were going to take him out before luncheon, weren't you, Violet?' prompted her mother.

Weston leant forward, his expression eager. 'I'd be happy to accompany you, Miss Prideaux. As you may realise, my experience with training dogs is second to none.'

'Oh, I don't want to bother you, Mr Penruth,' she offered, giving her mother a glance. 'And Jess is fine in the garden. I don't want to overtire him.'

'I thought that is exactly what you should do,' her mother said. 'Then at least he will sleep through the night.' She laughed. 'Listen to us, Mr Penruth, it's like we are talking about a child.'

Weston sank back in his chair. 'Well, if you ever need guidance, or a hand with training while you are out walking him, then don't hesitate to ask me,' he said, and, for a moment he kept eye contact with her, his gaze warming. 'It will be no trouble at all.'

'See, Violet,' said her mother, 'Mr Penruth knows his dogs.'

'In actual fact,' he continued, clearing his throat, 'there is something else I'd like to mention... to ask, you see, Miss Prideaux,' he said. Again, catching her eye seemed to pain him. 'Would you like to accompany me to the Spring Ball at Looe Assembly Rooms? On Saturday week? It would be a great honour for me.'

Violet caught the sudden solemn edge to his voice and her stomach flipped with alarm.

'Oh, Violet, isn't that wonderful,' her mother sounded triumphant.

'I assure you, Mrs Prideaux,' Weston said, 'that I will take great care of your Violet. My driver will see us there and back in absolute safety.'

Your Violet? How odd, how intrusive, Violet thought, for Mr Penruth from the Big House to ask her to the Looe Ball, and use her first name with such relish. Her skin prickled.

'You are free that evening, aren't you, my dear?' her mother went on, relentless.

'I am,' Violet admitted weakly, wanting to have an excuse but, seeing her mother's bubbling glee, felt herself give way. 'So, I think my answer is yes, Mr Penruth. Thank you.'

'And, of course, Claudia Ainsley will come with Violet,' said her mother, her eyes glistening. 'A chaperone, you understand Mr Penruth. Then that will be most satisfactory.'

Satisfactory seemed a definite underestimation of her mother's true feelings. She looked undeniably ecstatic.

'Very good,' said Weston. 'I will say goodbye to you both now, but, Violet, I will be in touch again nearer the date.'

He stood up to take his leave, and his frame seemed to suddenly darken the room. Violet, stunned and unable to muster a response, stayed stock-still in her seat, while her mother excitedly accompanied her guest out of the room, gesturing for Violet to follow.

'And I do hope that afterwards, at some point,' Weston said, pausing at the front door, 'in the near future, Violet, you will do me the honour of taking tea with me at Charlecote.' He tipped his hat. 'I shall introduce you to my mother.'

'Oh my.' This from Violet's mother.

Violet, her face aching with forced smiles, uttered that she'd look forward to it.

'My goodness,' her mother whispered beside her, as they stood together under the stone porch, and he strode away down the path. 'The lord of the manor has asked you to visit. To meet his mother, for goodness' sake. *And* he called you Violet.'

Weston turned and lifted his hand in farewell, and Violet found herself immobile once more as her mother waved delicately, saying, 'What a gentleman, Violet. *What* a gentleman.'

3
IN APRIL, RAIN AND SUNSHINE BOTH TOGETHER

At the little attic window under the eaves, her nature journal open before her, Violet watched the sky. Inland, over the moors, stacks of snowy cumulus set up camp, and south over the sea, beyond the garden and beyond the woods, a haze sparkled with tantalising light. A sweetness in the air came through the casement and Violet heard the chorus of birdsong. Straining to separate the voice of robin, of blackbird, and, heavens, the song thrush, she inhaled the tender air. But its usual promise, the joy, evaded her.

The first warm breath of spring today,

Violet wrote at the top of the blank page.

Will I hear the first cuckoo?

She added the date, then turned back several pages to her record of a much chillier day, when she and Claudia had walked to the cove and run shrieking down to the waves.

Violet's pressed sprig of gorse remained a golden-yolky yellow, the petals appearing plump even though now in two dimensions. The spines still sharp and perfectly vicious-looking. She used tweezers to hold it and carefully painted the back with gum. Placing the specimen in her *Flower Book*, she held her breath until it rested satisfactorily on the page, and wrote underneath:

The gorse that ripped Claudia's skirt.

She glanced at her pocket watch. Her friend was due any minute and the dress she was going to lend her, waiting for her – aired, and ironed and hanging on Violet's wardrobe door.

At her mother's insistence, Violet had tried on her own gown yesterday, a pearly shell-pink with a flattering square neckline. While her mother had dipped around her checking for loose threads and sagging seams, Violet had stared into the full-length mirror. The delicate colour had brought out the russet of her dark-brown hair, caught pleasingly at the green of her eyes.

'It's as if you are in candlelight, my dear. It makes you utterly glow,' her mother had said, fluffing at the sleeves. 'Oh, I'm so pleased. Mr Penruth will *adore* you.'

Violet's pulse had switched to an uncomfortable beat. She did not want him to adore her.

Up in the garret, she went over to the trestle table and heaved the *World Atlas* off the top of the stack of books. Opening the book below, she found the peony that she'd plucked from Weston's bouquet. It looked stricken and rather undignified pressed between pages stained with petal juice, its colour as flamboyant and as false as the day he'd given it to her. It certainly had no place in Violet's journal, but she gave it its own page and pasted it down, adding the date. She had no desire to elaborate.

* * *

From downstairs came Claudia's cheerful 'Hello.' Her father, out in the garden pruning, called to her friend to go straight up and she soon bumped the door open with the tea tray. Jess, close on her heels, scampered in and made a beeline for Violet, resting his paws on her knees.

'Tea, Violet! I've brought you tea. Your mother has just brewed it.' Claudia's cheeks were flushed. Laughter seemed to bubble out of her.

'And look who's followed you,' said Violet. 'Down, Jess. That's it. Go and chew a slipper.'

The little dog retreated to the corner to his stash of old shoes and set to gnawing one of her father's rejected slippers with a concentrated look.

'Oh, your hair is lovely, Claudia,' Violet took the tray from her. 'Whatever is the matter? You can't stop smiling, can you?'

'We're going to the Looe Spring Ball! I am beside myself. Look at my hands trembling.' Claudia could barely keep up with her own excitement. 'Mother spared me some time to do my hair this morning.' She twitched her shoulders and her silvery fair hair worn in smooth coils around her ears, making her look poised and grown-up, caught the sunlight. 'What are you going to do with your hair?'

'I haven't thought, I...' Violet swallowed the dryness in her throat. For weeks, the ball had squatted in her mind as something she must simply step past, to get over with. But that morning, the idea that she had to, indeed, *get ready* and *go* caused an oily sump of dread to ooze through her stomach. And now Claudia had arrived, there seemed to be no going back.

'Perhaps you'll help me later,' she said, weakly.

'Later? We'd better start soon, or I will rush and panic and mess it all up,' Claudia said. 'We can't have that, can we? You must look wonderful for Mr Penruth.'

Violet turned her back on her friend to hide the despair breaking out on her face, busying herself by sorting her flower-pressing paraphernalia.

'Before that, however, I need to pack all this away.'

'And what time is Mr Penruth expected?' Claudia chattered, restacking the heavy volumes on the table.

'Far too soon, I fear,' Violet said, concentrating on wiping her paintbrush on a piece of old rag.

Claudia gave her a sharp look. 'What do you mean?'

Violet sat down, suddenly, brutally, exhausted. She knew there was nothing wrong with her, except that her spirits lay in tatters.

'Claudia, I'm really not feeling very well.' She felt ashamed by the pathos in her voice.

'Oh no, no. You must rest, then, have some tea, come on, I'll pour.' Claudia's face widened in dismay. 'You'll perk up.'

Violet tentatively sipped her tea, pressed her hand to her stomach as it lurched with real nausea.

'Is it something you ate? What did you have for breakfast? Last night's supper? You didn't drink any of last week's milk, did you? Come, now, you can't let me down, not this evening. We have a party to go to,' Claudia trailed off sadly.

'I think I better go and have a lie down,' Violet said. 'I haven't dared tell Mother yet. She is more excited about tonight than I am.'

'I think I am too,' Claudia muttered, following Violet down the stairs to her bedroom. 'Oh,' she sighed, seeing Violet's gown hanging next to hers. 'And your dress is beautiful.'

'Perhaps you should wear it in my place.'

A shadow of delight moved over Claudia's face, but she took down the dress next to it, the one waiting for her and held it against her, touching the cream satin.

'Oh no, this is what I shall wear. I am so very grateful that you are lending it to me. And,' she said pointedly, 'you shall wear yours.'

Anxiety seemed to thin Violet's blood. 'I really don't think I can.'

'You do look very pale. I'll go and fetch your mother.'

'I don't want to bother her. She will be furious.'

But Claudia left her anyway and hurried downstairs.

Violet gave in and lay on the bed, breathing deeply, steadying herself, telling herself that it was simply a ball, an evening out. It didn't need to mean anything.

Ever since Weston Penruth had called in with the flowers and asked her to go, her mother had gossiped and supposed and surmised eventualities, including going as far as Violet being married to the lord of the manor and settled over at Charlecote. Her father had perked up enough from behind his newspaper to concede that Mr Penruth would be a fine catch for anyone, but his gaze had been sympathetic and a little more penetrating than her mother's, sensing Violet's unease.

She knew she should be flattered or at least sociable, but something about Weston left her sour. He stunted her, sapped her spirit, made her insides shift with a strange sort of sorrow.

Jess trotted into Violet's bedroom, wondering where she had got to. She reached down and rubbed his puzzled forehead and told him to be good.

'I just don't like him very much,' she whispered to Jess, who ignored her and settled his little russet body onto her hearthside rug. 'Is that such a bad thing?'

Violet heard her mother's cry of dismay all the way from the parlour, followed by inevitable and immediate footfalls across the stone hallway and up the stairs. In the pause while her mother caught her breath on the landing before launching herself at her bedroom door, the cheerfully double-beat piping of the cuckoo sounded in the wood.

* * *

The car, so grand, so large, so important, pulled up outside the gate and Mr Penruth's driver leapt out to open the door for him. The fenders gleamed, the lamps were polished, the engine hummed like a snoring beast.

Violet stayed upstairs, her curtains drawn at her bedroom window. She peered through a gap. Weston climbed out of the car, a bright eagerness about him. He tugged down his waistcoat and sniffed the fresh evening air. His driver handed him two corsages, which he held aloft awkwardly as he walked up the path.

Feeling foolish and oddly sad, her stomach a hard knot, Violet came away from the window and sat on the bed, pressing her hands over her ears. Even so, she could hear voices below, a polite murmuring of good evening, and then a mumbling drawn-out explanation from her mother. And no word from Weston.

Some excruciating moments later, Violet heard Claudia's excited voice ring out goodbye, and she went to the window. Her friend all but skipped up the path beside Weston, one of the corsages pinned to her dress. The driver opened the door and she hopped into the car, smilingly waving back towards the front door where, Violet presumed, her mother stood in fuming silence.

Weston closed the car door on Claudia and Violet watched as he walked around the back of the vehicle. He stopped, fishing in his pocket to draw out a flask, and took three sips. He threw a grimace of sadness back at Old Trellick, looking older in his disappointment than his twenty-eight years, before climbing into the car beside Claudia.

4

IN THE LANGUAGE OF FLOWERS: FOXGLOVE, INSINCERITY

Violet sat on the bottom stair and ran her fingers inside Jess's collar where his silky fur curled like a cavalier's ringlets.

'You've grown bigger, haven't you, these last few weeks?' she said. 'Let's loosen this up a bit. That's it. Give you a bit more breathing space. It'll be a three-mile walk today, so I hope you had a good breakfast.'

'He did, that's for sure,' said her father, coming out of the parlour with his pipe tucked in his mouth. 'I saw to that. Plenty of scraps in his bowl. Where are you taking him?'

'I thought I'd go to the cove, look for sea holly in the dunes. But it's so blustery out there, it might feel rather unpleasant. Especially for this little one.'

Her father agreed. 'It's certainly whipping up, we might even see a storm. Not good for May, is it?' He tapped the barometer on the wall and adjusted the needle. 'Says "wind and rain". But with any luck it should blow itself out over the sea.'

Violet clipped Jess's lead onto his collar and told him to sit while she buttoned up her coat. She rather hoped the feeling that shrouded Old Trellick, the stifling cloud of disappointment, would blow itself out too. Her mother been prickly with her since the evening of the ball, her father acting as a rather ineffectual go-between when Violet had tried to explain. But how could she tell her mother how she felt about the whole sorry mess, when she could barely articulate it to herself. Her mother simply didn't believe Violet had been unwell, which in all honesty had been nearer the truth, and that she'd snubbed an esteemed gentleman, lost out on a chance.

'Not my *only* chance, surely, Mother,' she'd said.

'With Weston Penruth, yes.'

'Say goodbye to Mother for me, won't you, Papa?' said Violet, with a weary catch in her voice. She put the strap of her canvas bag over her shoulder, checking inside for her scissors, notebook and paper bag for clippings. 'Tell her I should be back in time for lunch.'

Her father shifted his gaze to the open door of the parlour where his wife sat, in full earshot, noisily snapping the pages of *The Times*.

'I know how bedevilling she can be...' he said, his hushed voice trailing off. 'Anyway, keep your eye on the weather.'

Violet whistled for Jess and headed up the path, one hand holding the lead, the other clapped on her hat to keep it on. The breeze felt wild, flapping at the trees. Through a cleft in the hills the sea looked lively, the gulls bouncing on currents of air.

'Come, Jess, let's go to the pinewood,' she said.

* * *

As she walked along the sheltered track, overarched by a tunnel of trees, she thought about Claudia's evening at the Looe Ball. Her friend had visited her the next day, and once Violet had assured her that she was quite well, really, Claudia broke into a full stream of chattering and giggling at the memory of dancing with each of the Davey twins in turn. They were both in the rudest health, she reported, as their ruddy faces and strong fisherman arms affirmed, and had broken their mourning for little Benjamin to come to the dance.

'It seemed to be just what they needed after their poor little brother,' Claudia had said. 'The music, the laughter, all that shuffling round the floor. I had a wonderful time. I have trouble telling them apart at the best of times,' she laughed, 'and by the end of the evening, I was even more confused. Perhaps I should tell who is who, by the way each of them kisses.'

'Claudia!' Violet had laughingly chastised her, enjoying hearing about everyone else's amusement, deflecting attention from herself.

'And what a grumpy gentleman Weston Penruth is,' Claudia had confided.

'*This*, we already know, Claudia.'

'But he wouldn't dance one tune, and all those young ladies there trying to catch his eye. Of course, I don't count myself among them. Yes, so I arrived in splendour with him in his motor car, but he dropped me as soon as we went in and headed for the beer barrels. I was pleased, really. The looks people were giving me! As if to say, who does she think she is coming with Lordy? I was perfectly happy with Peter and Eddie, thank you very much.'

Claudia had suggested perhaps a night of dancing might have cured Violet's ills, just as it did for the twins. But Violet had dismissed the very idea with a forced laugh. Dancing with Weston Penruth would certainly not have helped. One little bit.

Violet came out of the bridleway and into the pinewood. Jess tugged to be let off the lead, so she unclipped him and he bounded ahead, his ears streaming. Drops of rain peppered the wind and the tops of the pines roared. And yet beneath, in the cloister of dark trunks and soft fern beds, with pink foxgloves curling upwards, all felt soft and silent, like the interior of a wide and scented cathedral. As Jess snuffled and pattered around her, she felt grateful to the wood, its solace helping her to see clearly.

Stopping at a fork in the path to cut an exquisite fern specimen to press for her book, Violet resolved to make more effort with her mother, to show how sorry she felt for disappointing her. She began to gather fern fronds and foxgloves into a posy to take home as a gift for her, while the little dog rustled in the undergrowth and scuffled up the high banks where white wood anemones faded. The wind eased and the rain-washed day felt more promising. Could that be a glimmer of sunlight, at last, in the top-most branches?

The wood fell silent, a strange enormous stillness, and Violet could no longer hear Jess. She scanned the fern mounds, calling for him, her voice a tiny echo. She peered down the footpath fork that hugged the side of the slope, plunging down to the stream in the crook of the valley, calling again, this time his name a hard *hiss*. But the empty pinewood threw her voice back at her. Jess had gone.

Violet hurried down the lower path, imagining Jess had smelt a rabbit and had darted after it. The path became steep, and she remembered why she avoided it as her boots slithered on the sodden ground. Breathless, she called again.

'He can't have simply vanished,' she muttered, peering to left and right.

Violet's foot slipped violently, and she lost her balance, landing on her bottom on the edge of the slope, teetering precariously. She laughed nervously as she began to topple down the bank in a bizarre, crouched position, unable to stop herself, her heels gouging earth. She reached for something that would break her fall, but ferns folded under her weight, and shoots snapped in her hand. She tumbled and stumbled and finally came to a soft rest near the stream at the bottom. The wood towered above her and in the dank shade, the trickling water smelt earthy, sluggish in the gloom.

She called for Jess again, sounding hopeless. Craning her neck, she uttered in surprised at how far down the bank she'd come. She cursed Jess and the mud all over her skirt and boots, and then swallowed hard in shock. A figure tramped along the top path where she'd toppled. Weston Penruth. Violet shrank beneath the green-black undergrowth, the dampness sinking through her coat, hoping he wouldn't spot her, thanking God that she hadn't bumped into him earlier. But where was that damn dog?

A sharp dreadful yelp split the ferns, and two lurchers emerged and came churning through the shallow stream. And in front, a whisker away from their snouts, Jess. The little dog paddled through the water towards Violet, his eyes black and fixed with instinctive terror.

'Leave him, leave him!' she cried and stepped into the stream but froze, calf-deep in water, terrified by the thrashing, the utter mayhem.

In one slow, dreadful motion, one of the dogs snapped its long head up, caught Jess in his jaws and flung him through the air. Violet leapt, sinking to her knees in the water her arms outstretched to pluck up the little dog and cradle him close to her face. The lurchers' shoulders barged her, their tails lashed, teeth snapping. She felt hot breath on her neck and her hands.

The water felt cold, shockingly so. She wanted to yell, to warn them off, but only managed a trailing moan of fear. Her bones locked, her sodden clothes weighing her down. Wiry fur, jaws and bright animal eyes filled her senses. Snarls so sharp they pinched the air around her ears. She cried out, helpless, believing this moment to be her – and Jess's – last.

The air behind her switched into an odd warm presence. Two hands gripped her under her armpits and tugged her upwards, bearing her out of the water. She sensed who it may be, this large figure behind her bellowing in her ears, splitting her head, carrying her and her limp furry bundle tucked under her chin over to the mossy bank. She recognised the boots kicking the dogs away, knew the voice ordering them, ordering her.

Violet sank to her knees as Weston's arms held her, keeping her upright. The dogs circled, cowered, and retreated into the ferns, their heads and tails low to the ground.

'My good God! Violet!' he cried, his voice hoarse and broken. 'Are you all right? Did they bite you? If they did, by God, I'll get my shotgun. Look at me, Violet. Let me see. Are you all right?'

'Never mind me,' she murmured, looking at the twitching form in her arms. 'What about Jess? What have they done to Jess? What have they done to him?'

Weston's fingers eased her grip and prised the little dog away from her.

Blood soiled the collar of her coat and Weston's palms; Jess's head tilted, his eyes closed.

'It's his shoulder.' Weston rummaged in his pocket and drew out a handkerchief. 'Thank God they didn't get his throat.'

He cradled Jess on his lap and spun the handkerchief around his body, tightening it. Speechless with terror, Violet stared at the concentration on Weston's face, his blank encompassing concern, the red flower of liquid that immediately stained the linen.

'Another one, another one,' he said.

She gave him her scarf and he used it, expertly binding the little dog's shoulder.

'He needs a veterinary,' said Weston.

'Please help him,' Violet whispered. She stared at him, at his sopping trousers, his blood-smeared hands. His eyes, dark and distressed, sent her arrows of his own pain. His guilt. 'Weston, please help him.'

'I will, I will, but are you all right? Give me your hand, are you hurt?'

'Not at all. Take him.' Impatiently, she shook her hand free of his. 'I am fine. Take him now.'

He placed Jess carefully on the ground and stood over her. He bent down, resting his hands on her shoulders, their weight conveying his will. 'You are still shaking, Violet. I cannot leave you here.'

'You must,' she spoke faintly. She snapped her head up to look him in the eye. 'I will find my own way. I need you to help Jess. He's hurt more than I am.'

'Come, do as I say.' Weston slipped his arm around her waist, and he pulled her up, helping her find her feet. She leant against him, as shock momentarily eased its grip on her and left her weak. His body, so fierce and masculine, felt surprisingly warm. He scooped Jess up and made her walk with him, moving her along the side of the stream, pushing aside the undergrowth, finding a way through. She did not want to fight him any more. If she did as he asked, she thought, then he will help Jess.

At the top of the slope, she sat down on a log, her breath hard and high in her chest, her clothes damp and clammy, her muscles burning. A film of sweat drenched Weston's face.

'Take him now,' she said. 'I insist. I can get myself home. I am not hurt. I will just slow you down.'

'Violet, really...'

She reached out to touch Jess's forehead. The dog, lying in Weston's arms, looked stunned, his eyes blank and far away. Whimpering bubbled from his mouth.

With all her strength, she said, 'Do this for me, please. He means everything to me.'

Weston looked down at the dog, back at her, nodded succinctly and turned to go.

'I will make the veterinary save him,' he called over his shoulder. 'I will do my best. I'll be at Old Trellick before sunset.'

* * *

Violet's father opened the front door as she walked unsteadily up the path.

'Good God, Violet! What on earth has happened? Have you had an accident?'

'I need a bath,' she mumbled, barely able to look at him. 'I fell in the stream.'

'You did what? Are you all right? Where is the dog? Is he wet and dirty, too? You know your mother won't have him in the house if he is covered in mud.'

Dazed and trembling, Violet stood in the hall and gingerly lifted her canvas bag off her shoulder. Slowly she began to unbutton her coat. Her hands were grimy, the bottom of her skirt tide-marked with dirty water. She had lost her hat.

'Jess is with Mr Penruth.'

Her father exclaimed with surprise and a clatter of a teacup and saucer sounded from the parlour. Her mother appeared swiftly at her side.

'What did you say? Weston Penruth has the dog?'

'There's been an accident, Eleanor,' her father said. 'Violet fell in the stream.'

'I need a bath,' Violet said again, longing for hot, steamy water to melt the deep chill from her bones. She peered inside her bag: the foxgloves and ferns were crushed and useless.

'I better fire the copper up,' said her father. 'It's not our usual day for bathing, is it?'

'Never mind that,' said her mother. 'Violet, did you say Mr Penruth was with you? Did you just happen to bump into him? Were you meeting him? And, why has he got the dog?'

Violet mused how easily her mother had come out of her sulk at the very mention of Mr Penruth's name.

'Jess is injured, Mother,' she said, her words cracking with exhaustion. 'Mr Penruth is taking him to the veterinary. If you'll excuse me, I'm going upstairs.'

'But *Mr Penruth* was walking with you?' Her mother seemed unable to contain herself.

'He wasn't. I was on my own. I didn't go to the cove, I went to the pinewood.' Oh, if only, she thought, I had gone to the cove. 'His dogs attacked Jess. They nearly killed him. He was nearly ripped to shreds. I think he is going to die.'

Her father stepped closer. 'Oh, Violet! How awful.'

'But *Mr Penruth* has taken him to the vet?' her mother insisted, as Violet wearily climbed the stairs. 'Well, isn't that wonderful.'

* * *

Violet's father pulled the best armchair closer to the fire and stacked the logs high, and Violet sat with a blanket around her, a hot-water bottle at her feet and a bowl of broth on her lap. And yet her shock still did battle with her, the shivering inside not letting up. Her father sat turning the pages of his newspaper at the card table by the French windows, commenting every so often on the activities of the Kaiser who, he thought, had a very worrying sense of importance.

'He's the old Queen's grandson for goodness' sake,' he said. 'And he's carving up Europe. Throwing his toys out of the pram. Does he have no sense of family loyalty?'

Her mother, meanwhile, sat in the chair opposite her, chatting and twitching with little glances at the clock. She read out Aunt Muriel's latest letter from London. Violet listened to tales of supper clubs and bridge games, haberdasheries on Bond Street and the new blossom over Regent's Park. Her mother said she would write to her sister that evening and tell her all about the day's events. In the hope, she added with a glance at Violet, for the happiest outcome.

The wind grew louder, rumbling over the chimney top, making its presence felt at the hearth. Violet watched through the French windows as the breeze curdled the lilac bushes, petals scattered like snowflakes, catching only snatches of Aunt Muriel's account of a visit to one Lady Welstead of Cumberland Terrace. The hard shock of the dog attack merged from nightmarish flashes into a much cooler reality. Inch by inch Violet's nerves became used to what had happened, her consciousness slowly playing over the horror, absorbing it, and accepting it.

The evening was drawing down and a lone blackbird still sang gamely against the breeze. Sunset, Violet thought, he said he'd be here before sunset. If he doesn't come, that means Jess is dead. She remembered the look in Weston's eyes. It came back to her then, as she sat in the safety of her own parlour with her parents' conversation in the background. His face had glazed with shame and sorrow as he walked away with her stricken Jess in his arms.

She heard then a sound, deeper than the grumbling wind in the chimney. Her father stood up abruptly, causing a sheet from the newspaper to drift to the floor.

'I hear the motor car,' he said.

Her mother snatched the soup bowl off her lap, muttering that she did not want Violet to look like an invalid and pulled the blanket from around her shoulders. She folded it and stuffed it behind the sofa.

'How pale you are,' she said, admiringly. She followed her husband out to the hallway.

Left alone, Violet heard an exchange of men's voices, quiet and deep. She gripped the arms of the chair, braced against an excruciating mixture of fear and hope. She shut her eyes to listen harder, to catch their inflections. Her mother's words were more discernible, so much more high-pitched. How very grateful and obliging she sounded.

'Not at all, Mrs Prideaux,' Weston said. 'Now, may I please see your daughter?'

He came into the room carrying a wrapped-up bundle, and Violet felt her body slump back against the armchair as if she had emptied, in that moment, of everything sensible. She saw a floppy, curly-haired ear, a wet-nosed snout, protruding from the blanket.

'Here he is,' said Weston.

He knelt down by the fire and settled Jess on the hearthrug. The dog remained still, but rested, snuggling deeper and gratefully into his blanket.

'Veterinary's given him a thorough check-up, and seen to his wounds.'

'Is he going to be all right?' Violet's voice seemed to disappear into the room.

Weston turned to her, his eyes wide with amazement, a smile breaking over his face.

'Of course he is.'

She blinked away stinging tears and she swallowed hard. At last, her voice returned. 'Thank you... so much. I can't tell you.'

Weston drew a chair to her side. 'Try.'

Violet dipped her head, shy at his sudden closeness. And, after a few moments, realised that he had taken her hands in his. Her surprise swept the chill and horror away but aware, suddenly, how pleasant it felt, she drew her hands back and went to kneel beside Jess. She stroked his forehead and spoke softly to him. He groaned, the noise she knew well when he was sleepy and happy.

'Give it two weeks,' Weston said, 'and that dog will be giving you trouble again.'

Violet glanced at him. He sat, poised on the edge of his seat, his whole stance appeared friendly enough, but she noticed troubled tension in the set of his jaw, the flick of his eyes. He seemed cautious of her, dancing around her, not sure of what she may say next. Violet wondered how a man who had the world at his feet could be so ill at ease with it.

'We will leave you both for now,' said her mother, urging her father to follow her to the door.

'Can I offer you a brandy, Mr Penruth?' asked her father. 'It's the least I can do.'

Weston looked at him, astonished. 'Dr Prideaux what I have done today for your daughter doesn't go even halfway to meet my gratitude towards you—'

'Well, really, Mr Penruth,' her mother butted in, 'there's no need to mention... that is all water under the bridge now, surely...'

Violet's father muttered about feeling much obliged in any case and they left the room, muttering between them, shutting the door behind them.

In the quietness, the clock on the mantel offered its familiar hollow tick, and the fire crackled. A log fell in the grate with a contented thud and the sparks made Jess lift his head briefly before he settled back with a deep, doggy sigh. And Violet felt the weight of Weston's hand, once again, in hers.

5

IN THE LANGUAGE OF FLOWERS: CLOVER, BE MINE

Within a week, Jess's shoulder had begun to heal, and his mischievous spirit reached new heights. By the stream, Weston had assured Violet that Jess would survive, but locked in crisis, her mind screaming with terror, she hadn't wanted to hear such reckless, sweeping promises. But Weston had been right, and his charismatic presence, when he came to check on Jess, brought her more flowers or walked with her to the cove, had tugged at her sleeve ever since. He had also been true to his word when he'd said he would invite her to Charlecote and, a month later, Violet sat on the lawn behind the grand manor house, watching her little dog chewing the guy ropes of the canvas gazebo set up for afternoon tea.

A fountain bubbled, the standard roses were ablaze with bees and the breeze scented with cut grass. The sun twinkled on the table of perfectly laid silverware and bone china, and over the faces of her parents in their Sunday best, and Claudia and Eddie Davey, with Mrs Penruth, broad-bosomed in all her finery, presiding.

'It's a wonderful day, isn't it?' said Violet's father to his formidable hostess, not daring to stray away from small talk. 'Such a change from the sopping awful month we've had. But all that rain was worth it, don't you think, Mrs Penruth? Just look at this garden. I must congratulate you.'

'I leave all that to Weston,' the elder woman said, stiff-backed, barely moving her head. How heavy her hat must be, Violet thought: a towering creation perched on her equally elaborate hairstyle. 'Weston and his gardener seem to be the best of friends these days. And don't get him started on his hothouse.'

Violet caught her mother's eye, remembering her saying that as she got old and stout and more old-fashioned, Violet must let her know if she ever began to resemble Queen Mary. Her mother glanced at Mrs Penruth and, knowing what Violet was also thinking, gave her a reproving look. Violet took a sip of tea to hide her smile.

'And I must say,' her father persisted, 'Charlecote is looking stupendous. I have never seen it from this angle before.'

Violet gazed past him at the gothic façade of Weston's home, with its mighty chimneys and palatial windows. Built a mere fifty years ago, the house did not sit as naturally in the Cornish landscape as Old Trellick, which had stood for more than five hundred. Weston's grandfather had made his fortune from Devon wool and bought the estate this side of the Tamar. He'd knocked down the old manor and built the new one, staking the Penruth claim to Charlecote. From the upper windows, apparently, you could see the sea.

Violet felt curious enough to wonder if you'd ever be able to hear it from there but knew it a far too fanciful question to ask Mrs Penruth. Instead, she called for Jess to stop worrying the guy ropes, behave himself and come and sit at her feet. The spaniel rested his face against her skirt, and she smoothed his forehead, thankful the lurchers were securely in their kennels at the farm.

'Do you have a house in town, Mrs Penruth?' Violet's mother asked.

'If by town you mean London then yes, we do. Cadogan Square.'

Her mother threw a happy look Violet's way.

Mrs Penruth turned to the butler, hovering efficient and docile nearby. 'Are we having buns, Willis? Bring a fresh pot of tea, will you. And find out where that son of mine is.'

Willis stalked back across the lawn with his tray, coat tails flapping.

'My sister Muriel lives not far from Selfridges,' Violet's mother went on eagerly, 'In Fitzrovia, you know. Well, on the borders of—'

'Yes, yes, quite,' Mrs Penruth said, clearly unimpressed.

As Mrs Penruth turned the conversation with Violet's parents to one of her own liking, Violet felt Claudia lean in close.

'Where *is* Weston?' her friend asked, her cheeks glowing with the momentous thrill of taking tea at Charlecote. She was as out of her depth as Violet, perhaps, but was coping admirably.

'Tending his hothouse plants?'

'Well, yes, he did talk a great deal about that in the car on our way to the ball,' Claudia said. 'On our way over here today, I told Eddie how I used to tag along with Mother when she came over from the farm to clean the Charlecote silver. And how cavernous the house is, how empty of voices. All those closed doors, rooms I was not allowed in. It scared me half to death.'

'Hardly surprising,' Eddie said, looking unaccustomed to his jacket and starched collar, his eyes large and watery, a shaving rash blooming on his neck. He lifted the delicate teacup to his lips, the china looking like it was about to snap in his robust grip. 'I'd imagine both our cottages would fit inside just one drawing room here.'

'Claudia, then you certainly have seen more of Charlecote than I have,' Violet said. 'This afternoon, I simply walked through the hall and straight out here.'

'I've only ever seen the inside of the scullery, really. Bent over the silverware and being told to give it some elbow grease. Anyway,' Claudia drew closer, her breath sweet with macarons, and said, 'Eddie and I are not quite sure why we are here but...' she giggled behind her hand, 'this all seems to be laid on for *you*, Violet.'

'Now, now, no whispering,' commanded Mrs Penruth across the cake stand. 'I know what you girls are like. You're not in school now. If it can't be said to all of us, it shouldn't be said at all.'

'Yes, of course. I'm so sorry, ma'am,' Claudia blushed furiously. 'I was only saying—'

'Oh, never mind, dear, and I was *only* joking.' Mrs Penruth bit into a raspberry pierced on her tiny fork. 'I'm hoping this one will be sweeter than the last. My son does insist on forcing his fruit in that stifling orangery of his. I don't believe in raspberries this early. What is it, late May? In my book, we should only be having the first strawberries.'

Violet's father chipped in, 'Raspberries are usually brought down from the Scottish glens in August. We rarely have them at home. Such a luxury. I can't remember the last time—'

'But how lovely, isn't it, George, that Mr Penruth has grown them himself?' Violet's mother interrupted, drenching her bowl from the sugar dredger.

Violet glanced at the house to see Weston emerge from the French windows and walk down the terrace steps, dark hair bouncing in the breeze as he strode across the lawn. Usually, he held himself as if he could not bear the cloth of his shirt to touch his skin, but his demeanour seemed a little easier, a little more relaxed today. How quickly Violet's thoughts of him had swooped from puzzled agitation to somewhere near admiration; although, she'd not had the chance to stop and ponder, to question them.

Weston dipped under the gazebo – looking pleased with himself – and sat down next to Violet. She immediately felt the momentum of his energy, raw and static in proximity.

'Well, here we all are, then, at last,' said Mrs Penruth. 'What on earth have you been doing, Weston?' She fixed her firm gaze on Violet. 'He does seem to plough his own furrow, Miss Prideaux.'

'I don't doubt it,' Violet said, hesitantly, wondering why Mrs Penruth should tell her this specifically.

'If you must know, Mother, I was going through the wine cellar,' Weston said. 'Checking on the champagne stock. The finest vintages. Dusted one or two off.'

Violet's mother made a little noise of surprise, and looked under the rim of her hat at Violet's father.

'A little early in the day for that perhaps, Weston,' said Mrs Penruth, indulgently. 'But then nothing you do surprises me these days. Actually, it never has done.' She looked around the table. 'So, I know all about you, Miss Ainsley. You grew up under my nose, up there at the farm. And I know a reasonable amount about Violet. Particularly her schooling. It looks like Exeter Priory did you a world of good, young lady. But what is your background, Mr Davey?'

Eddie spilt his tea into his saucer and set the cup down with a loud clink.

'Fishing, ma'am.' He fumbled with his collar. 'Our family have been fishing out of Lansallos for centuries.'

'As well you know, Mother,' Weston said. 'You surely don't need him to spell it out. Eddie is one of *the* Daveys.'

'Ah yes, of course... you are the fisherman. Ah yes. Davey... Davey. I did hear about your recent bereavement. A terrible to-do. May I offer you my condolences.'

Eddie graciously accepted them.

'And I was only making conversation with my guest, Weston,' Mrs Penruth said. 'Oh, how serious you always are. You'll have to watch that, Violet. In fact, Weston can never take a joke. But, of course, we must all laugh at his own.'

A prickling sensation inched through Violet's scalp. The sun grew hotter, her hat tighter and itchy around her forehead, her thoughts tumbling over Weston's mother's pointed comments.

'In the meantime,' said Weston, standing and offering his arm to Violet, 'Would you, Violet, and Miss Ainsley and Mr Davey, like a tour of the house?'

Violet's mother gleamed with pleasure, and her father looked mildly gratified, and Violet hoped they'd both stop. After all, they were simply having a pleasant afternoon tea with the Penruths at the Big House.

As the four of them walked across the lawn towards the terrace, Violet felt pleased with how courteous Weston had been towards Eddie. His reputation as a complete curmudgeon seemed unfounded and her old muddle about him had indeed melted away, to be replaced with another more bewildering tangle of feelings.

'Let the older generation chat among themselves. They'll go straight to the Kaiser, Germany, and impending war any moment. Not the most gracious of subjects for afternoon tea,' Weston said. 'Mr Davey, I do apologise if my mother sometimes appears rather overbearing. It's simply her way. You know what some elder ladies are like.' He stood aside to let the younger man walk through the French windows in front of him. 'I'm afraid I'm used to it, so I let it pass me by.'

'Please,' said Eddie. 'No need to mention it.'

Claudia linked Violet's arm and drew her back.

'Isn't he a lovely man?' she whispered.

'You mean...?'

'I made the right choice. The right twin.'

'Ah, I see.' Violet blushed with confusion. 'Eddie is coping very well with visiting Charlecote,' she said. 'But I don't think I am.'

Claudia laughed. 'Of course you are, Miss Violet Prideaux! And I think you like Mr Penruth,' she whispered. 'You have always hidden it, circled round it, that's all. It has taken you a while to realise. This often happens with love, my mother told me.'

In a daze, Violet followed her friend through the French windows into the cool drawing room, Claudia's words settling in her mind. The dark-oak panelling made the grand room feel cool and restful after the bright sunshine. And while Claudia admired the fine curtains, the woven rug, the tassels on the chairs, Violet looked around her with fresh alarm.

'And look how shiny the silverware is,' Claudia laughed. 'I am happy to say I had a hand in that somewhere along the way.'

Weston, waiting for them by the door out to the hallway, caught Violet's eye and she found herself smiling appreciatively at their mutual amusement. She felt a strange softening inside.

'Yes, it looks wonderful, Miss Ainsley, shining still after all this time,' Weston said. 'Come on, I will show you all the ballroom. You, too, Violet.' He held his arm out as if to pull her towards him across the room.

Violet and Claudia stood in the centre of the majestic ballroom while Weston and Eddie opened every shutter. And, little by little, shafts of sunlight shone in to illuminate the vast parquet floor, duck-egg blue walls, scrolling plasterwork and enormous chandeliers.

'Goodness me,' Violet breathed. 'How beautiful.'

'You could hold a ball here, Mr Penruth,' said Claudia, playfully. 'To rival the Looe one.'

'It would certainly do that,' Violet said.

'It would fair put them out of business,' Eddie laughed.

'I'm glad you mentioned that, Miss Ainsley,' Weston said. 'How about I host a ball in honour of Violet's birthday. September, isn't it?'

Claudia's patted her hands together, beaming with joy, but Violet winced in surprise. She had never told him when her birthday was.

'But it... it is not a special birthday,' she said.

'No matter. We will fill this room with lilies,' said Weston, 'we will fill it with roses. And orchids. Absolutely stupendous orchids.'

'Ah, but, Weston,' Violet offered, thinking of late-summer dahlias, and chrysanthemums and the hips of wild guelder rose that coloured her birthday month. 'Not all those plants will be at their best come September.'

'You and your flowers, Violet,' he said, a sharp edge to his laugh. 'I will see to it that they are all at their best. Even violets, if I must.' He turned to Eddie with a snap, another more-pressing thought igniting in his head. 'Next stop, Mr Davey, my orangery and hothouse. There you will see some, dare I say it, unseasonal wonders.'

'Thank you, sir,' Eddie said, 'but I'm not sure we have time for that.' He took Claudia's arm and she stepped effortlessly to his side. 'We had planned to leave soon unfortunately. I am going out on the night boat.'

'Another time, then, Mr Davey, another time. And you, too, Miss Ainsley. Now let me show you the way. We can go through here...'

Weston led them out to a stone-flagged corridor lined with perspiring windowpanes. Violet glimpsed giant ferns and monstrous palms, stuff of fantasy from the other side of the world, through the misted glass.

'It's been a pleasure.' Weston shook Eddie's hand, and grasped Claudia's fingertips in courteous *adieu*. 'I'm glad you could both come.'

'We'll pop out and pay our respects to your mother, Mr Penruth,' Claudia said. 'It's been such a charming afternoon.'

She hugged Violet goodbye and Violet watched them leave, their playful voices teasing each other, laughter receding down the corridor. As their footsteps faded to silence, she realised how badly she wanted to go with them.

'I better go back outside, too,' she said, 'and see if Jess is all right. He might be bothering your mother.'

'Never mind the dog,' Weston said, smiling persistently. He opened the door to the hothouse. 'Come on, Violet, I have a new orchid I want to show you. It is *exquisite*. And strawberries. Did I tell you about my strawberries? Every fruit and flower you will ever dream of, Violet, awaits you in here,' he said with a flourish. 'Now be quick, because I don't want to waste the heat.'

Violet hesitated. But, imagining her mother's delight when she confided that Weston had given her a personal tour, she walked through the door he impatiently held open for her. As soon as it closed behind her, she took two shallow breaths and coughed. The moist heat hit her, seemed to embed itself inside her, radiating outwards.

'Goodness, how stifling it is.'

'I had the furnace specially built. It's underneath us.' He stamped on the terracotta-tiled floor. 'You will get used to it, Violet, I promise you. Now the best thing to do is walk slowly and don't talk. I'll do all the talking,' he chuckled and placed a finger over his lips. 'There, that's it. Come this way.'

Weston ushered her along the terracotta-paved walkway, through the tangle of glossy foliage, Antipodean plants lit by merry English sunlight through the high glass roof. Rampant creepers reached curling tendrils to strangle other plants and, indeed, themselves. The heat churned and her skirt brushed dewy ferns bulging out of the beds. Not her delicate, beloved hart's-tongue from the pinewood but sturdy primitive specimens. Violet reached out a finger, daring herself to touch one.

'The seeds for that came all the way from New Zealand,' Weston said. 'Ferns are a tough one to propagate but well worth the effort, don't you think? Now here, over here... my orchid bed.'

Violet stared at the serene white flowers, impossibly curved and stiff, splashed with blood-red and a rather rude pink inside their throats.

'They don't look real,' she said. Moisture settled on her top lip, the humid air compressing her chest.

'Oh, they're real enough, and worth a fortune,' Weston said. 'I hope to start selling them soon to discerning county people. Send them up to Selfridges. That should please your aunt. Terribly delicate, though. One mistake with watering or feeding or heat or shade and they die. Have to treat them with great care.' He paused and gazed at her. 'Great care,' he repeated, a whisper to himself. 'Violet, look, see how your hair sticks to your neck. Allow me.'

Violet felt his fingertips brush over her collar, and then inside to touch her throat and she felt something swing inside her, like the clang of a bell, sounding a warning. She stepped back in dismay, but could only utter, 'Thank you, Weston. That feels better.'

She took out her handkerchief and dabbed it under her nose.

'It's rather too hot for me in here,' she said.

'I'm sorry, I do get carried away. You see, I do love my plants. And Violet, you are... have always been—'

'Can we go now, please?' she said, wishing more than anything to be breathing fresh air.

'Of course, this way.'

He led her through to the orangery, a separate cooler anteroom, much more comfortable and furnished with a wicker sofa, a small table and an Oriental cabinet. The sun sent shards of light flickering through more foliage, making dappled patterns on the floor and on Violet's hands.

'I don't know how you can spend so long in there, Weston,' she said, inhaling, feeling refreshed.

'This will suit you better, I feel. This is my temperate area and much more pleasant. I'm sorry that the hothouse is rather overwhelming. Take a seat, and I will mix you a drink.'

'Oh, that's lovely but shouldn't we be getting back outside? Your mother will be wondering.'

'Let her wonder,' he said. 'I have everything I need here.' He opened the cabinet and took out a bottle of gin. 'I imagine you would prefer lemonade. Why don't you pick your own lemon for your drink? I have a knife here, some cocktail sticks. Everything.'

She glanced past citrus trees heavy with fruit and through the arched windows. The benign summer's day seemed to call to her; she longed to be in the garden but an enduring sense of courtesy to her host, to be eternally polite, made her acquiesce. She perched politely on the sofa.

'This little room is more pleasant,' she agreed.

'Good old Willis,' Weston cried. 'He filled the ice bucket. Still got some cubes, not all turned to water. And look, lemonade for Violet. You are in luck.'

'Lemonade would be lovely,' she said, as patiently as she could muster.

Weston took out two tumblers and tinkled ice into them with a flourish. Violet felt she was indulging a little boy desperate to show her his latest toy, and her stomach twisted in sorrow. It was sadness, she realised, that she always felt for Weston. She rubbed her perspiring palms together.

'And here,' he said, presenting her first with the drink and then an orchid, 'is the *Phalaenopsis* I promised you. As beautiful as you.'

The orchid offended her. Stiff and rather vulgar, nothing like her, surely. It looked like a fake. She thanked him all the same, her heart dropping. Why was he always trying his best with her, and getting it so wrong?

'How well you know the Latin names,' she said, cheerfully, but sounding as false as the orchid looked.

He sat beside her, swirling his gin and tonic.

'I know how you love your flowers and plants, Violet,' he said. 'How about, one day, you start a logbook for me and record my plants here, all the correct names? The germination, the setting of seed. Flowering times, number of leaves...'

Violet uttered a half-laugh. Weston did not know her at all, suggesting the exact opposite of her real love: roaming the lanes and the fields, observing and gathering at her own pace. Discovering nature's peace and purpose and putting it all together in her *Flower Book*.

'That sounds like a life's work, Weston.'

'It will be.' He turned in his seat to gaze at her.

'I'm afraid I always have to look up the Latin names,' Violet said brightly, but with her energy draining and a fist of discomfort deep in her stomach. 'I like to use the common names. More memorable and so beautifully descriptive. They seem to have a story to tell, don't they? A little bit of country lore.'

'But this rare orchid isn't a plain old marshmallow, Violet.'

His remark tore her down. Any lingering admiration vanished. A strange dead sensation filled her chest. In all truth, she realised, she simply didn't like him.

'We don't have a lot of time to talk alone together, do we?' Weston ploughed on, not noticing her struggling to hide her outrage. 'Your parents always seem to be there or your friend, or your little dog...' He trailed off. 'My mother. You will get along with her, won't you?'

'And why should that be the case?' she muttered, weary and wanting to cut the conversation short, longing to be outside in the garden.

'Oh, Violet, stop pretending you don't know! I have loved you since you were a little girl.'

Violet recoiled, her insides flipping in alarm. He dropped to his knee in front of her, looking handsome and hopeful, but verging on pitiful.

'Don't you know that? You must know that. We're meant to be together.

That's why you're here.' His eagerness tripped up his words. 'You're here now... with me.' He grasped at her hands. 'Please marry me, Violet and we will be happy, so very happy.'

Violet exclaimed, pulling her hands away, staggered, unable to believe what she'd heard. She gaped at him, shock sending a plunging coldness over her skin. And yet Weston continued to smile at her, pinning her with his gaze, his mouth fixed and taut. He dipped into his waistcoat pocket.

'Here, I have the ring already for you.'

The humid air in the glass-walled room grew hotter, vibrated in Violet's ears. Sweat chilled her skin under her waistband and between her shoulder blades. Her mouth felt parched, her tongue heavy. Violet thought she'd forgotten how to speak.

Weston held the ring towards her pinched between his thumb and forefinger.

'It was my grandmother's. That's mother's mother. But a Penruth heirloom all the same.' He spoke with innocent pride, like a true fool might, either not noticing or not caring that she must look horror-struck at his proposal. 'There's three garnets and seven pearls, see? I had it reset. Sent it up to Bond Street. One of the stones was loose, and it had to be perfect. Perfect for Violet.'

She stared at the ring. She'd never been one for garnets, and weren't pearls meant to be unlucky? In any case, the ring looked hideous. But why even be thinking this? Was her mind trying to distract her, trying to help lighten this appalling situation?

'Violet, darling...' he said, peering at her.

She shivered, hauled herself together. She needed to say something, to tell him no, but the earnest set of his eyes spoke to her, and she struggled to pin her thoughts down. Pity rose inside her, churning in an odd soup of compassion.

She took a breath, a moment of clarity, reminded herself: Weston did not see her, did not see Violet. Only what he imagined her to be.

'Weston, I cannot marry you.'

He flinched, gave a minute shake of his head and continued to smile.

'I see, I see. Not yet. You are still so young and I must seem an old man to you.'

'No, Weston, really.'

He stood up, paced to the cabinet, back again, fighting whatever puzzled him. 'You can't mean that, Violet. Why don't you want all this?' His exasperation distorted into strange, suppressed resentment.

Violet kept her nerve.

'It's because of all of this...' she swept her hand around to take in the glass-walled room, the sweltering jungle beyond the glazed walls. 'Because of you. Because I don't love you.'

He leapt on this. 'You will. You will learn to. Just like you will learn the Latin names.'

'You are not paying for my education now, Weston.'

He froze and glared at her, his eyes brightening with anger, his mouth in a firm bitter line compressing whatever fury curdled inside him.

'Weston, I have to leave. I... I thank you... but I must go.'

She hoped he would not try to convince her and argue it out. She didn't have the strength.

His jaw moved as if fighting his own fury, but his face softened as he grasped at his upbringing, the sense of decorum that must have been drummed into him, striving to be ever the gentleman.

'Then, dear Violet, may I escort you back out to your parents...?'

'If you must.' Violet sighed, her voice breaking in weariness.

Weston offered her his arm, and she took it cautiously. Hadn't her mother also taught her to be courteous in any situation? They went outside the orangery and stepped onto the side terrace where pots of ragged tropical specimens struggled to thrive and walked off around to the lawn.

* * *

Outside in the balmy Cornish afternoon, Violet felt within inches of freedom. If only she could get back to Old Trellick, back home with her *Flower Book*, with Jess at her feet, chatting with Claudia, then everything would be normal and settled again. But Weston's presence spoiled her optimism. In the silence between them as they walked, his energy, now soiled by anger, suggested something more violent.

As they stepped down to the lawn, he uttered, 'Damn the gardener. I shall be having a word with him. He is supposed to get all this out.'

Violet looked to where he pointed, at delicate pale flowers scattered among the grass.

'But clover feeds the bees, Weston. It is not doing you any harm tucked away around the edges.'

'It's a bloody mess.'

'But this is *why*, Weston,' she cried. 'This is why I can't marry you!'

He dropped her arm as if flinging her away.

'You spoilt girl. After everything I have done for you. If you don't want this, you don't know what you want,' he said, the menace in his voice altering the air around them.

Violet felt floored with confusion, her mind veering off to the conflicting notion of why Weston had paid her school fees in the first place. And why had Weston assured her father – when he'd brought Jess home to Old Trellick – that he himself, after everything that had happened, was still in debt to *him*.

'You'll live to regret this, Violet.'

For one perplexing moment, she thought she'd misheard. But the rage festering in his eyes left her in no doubt that she had not.

Weston turned and stalked back into the house, his fury lingering as a huge dark cloud to blight the perfect summer's day.

* * *

Numb and shaking, Violet made her way alone back across the lawn towards the little soirée under the gazebo. They spotted her in one excruciating moment and made restless gestures, shifting in their chairs. Her mother twitched her head to peer past her, looking for Weston. Her father seemed more guarded, tucking his chin into his collar in the way he did when thinking. And Mrs Penruth, as rigid and forbidding as ever, kept her firmly in her sights.

'Well? Well?' she asked, her beady gaze latching on to Violet's left hand as she walked under the canopy.

'So where is your happy gentleman, Violet?' her mother beamed an expectant smile. 'Where have you left him?'

The eager silence and the static expectation of the small gathering dipped to confusion. And Violet's instinct to be well-mannered and dignified in company, eclipsed the fear Weston's last words instilled in her. But that exchange must only ever exist between them. For how would anyone understand?

Jess darted forward, his tail thrashing with devotion, only to be snapped back smartly by his lead tethered to a chair. Willis stood at Mrs Penruth's shoulder poised with a perspiring champagne bottle, doubtless one that Weston had organised earlier to be put on ice. The butler waited, his thumb expertly primed to pop the cork.

'Well?' Mrs Penruth asked again, glancing once more across the lawn for her son.

Violet could not answer. Her parents traded worried glances, and Mrs Penruth, something dawning on her, looked incensed.

'Did you not like the ring, Miss Prideaux?' she asked.

'I apologise, Mrs Penruth,' Violet said, her mouth tasting as dry and as bitter as the lemon Weston had put in her drink. 'I assume you were all expecting something else to have happened just now...'

She used the back of a chair for support. She needed to hold herself up, brace against the storm radiating around the table, to do all she could to alleviate the appallingly embarrassing situation.

'I was indeed, young lady,' Mrs Penruth said, the ribbons on her tall hat trembling. 'We all were. And where is Weston? Where is my son? What has happened?'

'I really don't know. He left, went back into the house... I assume back into the orangery.' She felt she might choke. She turned to her parents who stared at her aghast. 'Mother, Papa, I should like to leave now,' her words thin and faint in the summer air.

'Are you saying,' Mrs Penruth probed, 'that you have refused my son?'

Violet's clothes, damp from when she'd perspired in the orangery, turned cold and encased her body like a dead woman's shroud. She nodded. Within the outraged silence, from the trees at the back of the lawn, she heard a cuckoo. But this time, sounding different. *Cuc-cuckoo*. The weeks had rolled on since she'd heard her first cuckoo of spring from the attic room, since the first time she snubbed Weston Penruth. And now, so much had altered, now it was so much worse. The cuckoo had changed its tune. The summer visitor will soon fly away.

'Like to leave now?' Mrs Penruth echoed her. 'Yes, I would leave now if I were you, young lady. I cannot believe that you saw fit to do such a thing. That the name of Penruth has ever been insulted so.'

'But we can't know what has transpired between the two young people...' Violet's father tried for diplomacy, his neck bulging over his collar with the effort. 'It is between them both, not for us to speculate...'

Weston's mother cut him down. 'I would like to think, Dr Prideaux, that such an expensive education provided for your daughter would have taught her better manners.'

'Well, really, Mrs Penruth, I must protest...' her father began.

Violet's mother winced, her eyes watery with embarrassment as she stood up, bashing her knee clumsily on the table. She gathered her handbag and shawl, fumbling for her parasol, uttering apologies to her hostess. Violet dipped to untie Jess, longing to rescue him and herself from the agonising situation. She offered Mrs Penruth a firm nod, could not trust herself to speak. Neither, it seemed could Mrs Penruth.

They walked off across the lawn, an undignified trio with Jess trotting around them blithely. Out of earshot of Mrs Penruth, her mother, breathless with trying to keep up as they circled around to the front of the house, began to mutter, 'Oh, the scandal, Violet, oh, the utter shame. How are we going to live with this? So humiliating. Such shame. It'll be the talk of Lansallos and Looe, and—'

'Eleanor, best we leave talking about this until we get home,' reasoned Violet's father, opening car doors for them. He looked ruddy and winded. 'Let's just get home.'

He bent over the fender and began to crank the starter handle and Violet, climbing into the back seat with Jess, willed the vehicle to prove itself reliable, this one time.

Weston appeared at the front door as the engine fired, standing motionless, watching from the top step. Violet caught his eye and turned away, unable to tell if she'd seen agony or anger blistering over his face.

The car eased out of the gates and her mother twisted around in the passenger seat, her glare from beneath her hat piercing Violet.

'Oh, you have done it now, haven't you,' she said. 'You have turned down Weston Penruth well and truly. Never mind the ball nonsense. Think about what you have done this afternoon for a moment, Violet, will you? What it has done to us. Our family. You could have been Mrs Penruth, living at Charlecote. What do you think you were doing? How could you do this to us? How will we ever live this down?'

Violet had no will left inside to answer and in silence, her father drove them back to Old Trellick along lanes ripe with cow parsley where scarlet poppy and dusky cranesbill would soon show their fragile faces. The view through her window no longer gave Violet pleasure. She no longer felt safe, no longer at home. Weston had taken it away from her, taken peace from everything.

6

IN JUNE, ALL DAY AND NO NIGHT

The train laboured over the tracks on its approach to Paddington and Violet peered through the carriage window, shifting where she'd been sitting for so long, wanting to stretch her legs and ease the tenderness in her back. She glimpsed the backs of terraced houses along the side of the tracks, their blank grim windows, and wondered how many souls lived within such mean confines. Above the chimney pots, the evening sky appeared a dense blue, just this side of dark.

Violet's journey had passed in an endless blur of trees and farmhouses and wheat fields, and her confidence had flourished in fits and starts the further the train took her from home. But now, as the brakes strained, the engine groaned, and steam billowed and the train pulled into the station, the reason she'd left Old Trellick and Jess behind, returned to sting her. Her mother's anger, her disappointment, her convincing herself that Weston will throw them out of the house, and it would be all Violet's fault. Violet's shame, Violet's absurdity. The family were disgraced, to be laughed at. And her father's passive inept responses. Him trying to reason, to keep the peace, but shot down by her mother.

But when Muriel's telegram arrived for Violet in response to her own desperate letter, stating *Come whenever you wish*, Violet fell into a bright moment of relief.

Grabbing her suitcase, and adjusting her hat in the mirror over the seat, she willed that feeling to continue. She opened the carriage door before the train had entirely stopped and stepped off onto the chaotic, crowded platform and the reality of a new life.

Porters bellowed 'mind your backs', wheeling carts stacked with trunks. Passengers knocked past Violet, bent on getting on their way, while she walked along, drawing her shoulders up, holding her suitcase in one hand, her ticket in the other. But, already, she felt battered, parched, and hungry, and ready to drop.

Outside, taxis waited with headlamps gleaming and engines rumbling, and through the din, Violet heard a driver call out to her through his open window. It was her turn, and she didn't know what to do. She stepped forward and felt a man nearby make a grab for her suitcase. Startled, she shrank from him, a cry of shock breaking in her throat. He felt far too close to her, and she flinched, remembering Weston's proximity in the orangery, his bottled-up anger.

'It's all right, miss. Just helping you with your luggage. And this one's kosher.' The porter's voice sounded high-pitched and cheery as he launched her suitcase into the back of the cab. 'He's done the Knowledge. Just tell him where you're going and remember the tip.'

Violet ducked into the taxi, and the door slammed unceremoniously behind her. She asked for Montagu Square.

'Just off the Plymouth train, are you, miss?' the driver threw back over his shoulder as the taxi chugged forward.

Too tired to say much more, she muttered, 'Yes... yes indeed.'

The cab smelt fuggy with pipe smoke, and the air through the open window was thick with diesel and manure. She tried not to breathe deeply, remembering in a painful flash the purity and sweetness of the pinewood. She wondered when she would ever see it again.

Horse-drawn carriages hustled for space on the street ahead and a bus rattled past, brutally close. On either side towered dark terraces illuminated by gas streetlamps. The gloomy sky had been lost to the night, Violet a tiny speck in the city. She held onto the seat with both hands as the driver overtook a coal cart, smothering her desire to squeal in fear.

'Won't take long, miss,' he said. 'Won't touch the Marylebone Road. Just down the Edgware Road and left onto George Street.'

This meant nothing to Violet, but she felt obliged to say, 'Its sounds like you know all the streets, sir?'

'Bless you, darling. 'Course I do. And you know what else I know? All the clubs, hotels, railways, tube stations, theatres, music halls, hospitals, police stations... let me think, what else... prisons, docks, wharves, banks, museums, mortuaries, cemeteries. Everything in this blessed town. Everything.'

Violet glanced out at the teeming city in which every part of a person's life was tended to and taken care of, one way or another. The cab turned sharp left and abruptly, the racket from the traffic fell away. She was taken through a grid of silent Georgian streets lined with ghostly white flat-faced mansions four storeys high. The tyres trundled blithely over cobbles instead of sticky asphalt and they entered a square, all elegance and serenity, pulling up by railings around the central garden.

Aunt Muriel's house stood pale in the darkness with a lamp burning at the first-floor window. All seemed peaceful in night shadow, canopied by plane trees dropping their flowers over the pavement.

'Very nice too,' the driver said.

She paid him and tipped him royally, heedless of her meagre allowance, and the taxi chugged cheerfully away.

* * *

Two columns guarded Muriel's front door, and steps lead down into darkness to the tradesman's entrance. She rang the bell and waited. As it sounded somewhere deep inside the house, she realised how far she had travelled. How far she was from home.

A housemaid, in white apron over dark uniform, opened the door and Violet stepped into a cool dim hallway. The corridor, paved with black and white tiles, faded into the gloom of closed doorways, while the staircase rose into the yellow lantern glow of the landing above. She followed the maid mutely up the stairs, her tired footsteps muffled by deep maroon carpet. Climbing, she glanced at oil paintings, framed watercolours, the fine scrolled wallpaper, noting the hollow knock of a long-case clock. The delectable peace inside the house worked to make the long stretching ordeal of her journey trickle away.

The maid opened the door onto the first-floor drawing room and Violet walked into a room she had not been in since she was a child. The delicate elegance of the Georgian interior was stuffed with bookcases, with knick-knacks, pot plants, statuary and endless books gleaming in lamplight, each window muffled with velvet drapes. The grandeur and glory seemed as familiar and as frightening as before. Even so, Violet felt she had been released. She could breathe. At last, here inside Aunt Muriel's home.

'Madam is in bed with her ankle,' announced the maid, who had clearly been expecting her. 'Would you like some refreshment?'

Violet, painfully aware of her train-crumpled coat, of the smuts of dirt on her cheeks and how late in the evening it was, suddenly felt like an interloper and stupidly shy. She simply told her she'd like some tea.

The housemaid took her hat and coat. 'When you are ready, Madam would like you to go straight up to see her.'

In the water closet near the backstairs, Violet peered at her reflection in her aunt's bathroom mirror. She patted down her hair and washed away the grime of her journey. Her face looked pale, and her eyes flickered with exhaustion, but she gave herself an encouraging smile.

She found Muriel sitting up in bed in her boudoir on the second floor. Her salt-and-pepper hair in pins and covered in a queenly nightcap. A scarlet eiderdown shrouded her leg, propped up on pillows, and the salmon-pink ruffles of her bed jacket shimmered in lamplight as she beamed at her, gestured for her to come in.

'My, my, what a journey you've had. You look all in, my dear. Sit, sit here, and let me look at you.'

Violet pulled the dressing chair close to the bed as Muriel's sharp gaze scrutinised her.

'Nothing that a hot bath and a good night's rest can't put right. And soup. Cook made some mulligatawny this morning.' Muriel leant over and rang her handbell. 'I will get Smithson to bring you soup.'

Thanking her, Violet still found it an effort to speak. She hoped she could go straight to bed without too much conversation or explanation but knew Muriel would most certainly want to talk.

While her aunt ordered her food for her, Violet thought about the life she led, up here on the edges of Fitzrovia's fashionable quarter. Muriel had married well, to Mr Jeff Strachen, and as she might often quip herself, had been widowed well too. Uncle Jeff, who had made it big in the City, had died when Violet was young. She did not remember him. Muriel – childless, supremely confident, and forthright – shook off her widow's weeds quickly and carved a life of sociability and amusement, determined to seek out people and things to enjoy within the tight confines of her blessed, polite world. Her life, in vast contrast to Violet's mother's, as well as being the subject of entertainment at Old Trellick, Violet guessed engendered sibling envy, too.

'Your mother will be worried and not happy that you travelled without a chaperone,' Muriel said gravely. 'I frankly didn't see the need for such a rush. When I got your letter, I wondered if you were desperate to come up to town to shop for your trousseau. I thought, what fun! But from that look on your face... ah, Smithson.'

The maid came back in with the soup and tea on a tray, set it down on the bedside table, and Muriel dismissed her for the night.

Violet's shoulders sagged with the effort of eating, but she took the napkin and spread it over her lap.

'Your silence speaks volumes, my dear.'

'So, Mother hasn't written to tell you?'

'I've had nothing from your mother this past week, highly unusual, apart from your rather mysterious letter,' Muriel said, peering at her. 'This *is* something desperate, I'll wager. Something far more serious than a bride's empty bottom drawer. But you don't have to tell me now, my dear. You look shattered. Maybe tomorrow. Have some soup. Sip your tea and ask me how I am.'

Violet gazed at her aunt's kind, expectant face and felt a stinging tremor around her nostrils. The events of the Charlecote afternoon soirée slapping into her. Tears pooled in her eyes.

'Auntie, you didn't think I'd marry him, did you?'

'Ah, so there's the rub. It was exactly what your mother thought, my dear. Her letters have been filled with assumptions and excitement. She has been, frankly, unable to contain herself. Talk of you becoming mistress of

Charlecote. I think she even moved herself in! She said it was on the cards. Meant to be.'

'Oh, Auntie,' Violet blurted, surrendering to tears.

'You've bolted!'

Violet didn't know how or whether to agree. She had no idea, really, what she had done.

Muriel's face paled and then reddened. Delight sparked at the corner of her eye, and Violet wondered if her aunt didn't look a little excited.

'I assure you, my dear Violet,' she reached forward to pat her knee. 'I am excellent in a crisis.'

Violet spooned her soup, relishing the warmth spooling inside her, and the comfort of her aunt's assurances.

'I just feel...' Violet began, struggling to pin it down. 'I feel pressure... *such* obligation...'

Her aunt waited.

'He unsettled me. I never felt safe with him.'

'Well, then, Big House or not, that is not to be tolerated...'

The doorbell rang two floors below.

'Oh heavens, what now?' Muriel muttered and cocked her ear to listen for Smithson, who surely had not gone to bed yet.

The bell sounded again, and Violet's heart dilated in fear. Had he followed her here?

They waited. The front door below opened, and an exchange made. The front door closed. Footsteps approached up the stairs and someone knocked on the bedroom door.

'Goodness, Violet, dear, you look *terrified*...'

Smithson came in, apologising, carrying a telegram on a tray. 'For Miss Prideaux,' she said and left.

Violet's fingers trembled as she fumbled with the envelope, her aunt sighing with impatience.

'Well, my dear. Well? Tell me. Is it from your mother? Has he extended an olive branch? Are you to be friends? What is to happen?'

Violet scanned her parents' telegram, confusion switching to horror, palpitating through her mind. She handed it to her aunt, who took it and read aloud, her voice as flat and neutral as the post office clerk at Looe who would have taken it down and then repeated the instruction to Violet's mother, just to make sure.

'Very disappointed at your departure. Weston enraged. Shot his dogs.'

* * *

Through the half-dark watches of that summer night, Violet lay sleepless on the bed in Muriel's guest room, staring at the light rising beyond the half-open curtains. He crept around the fatigue inside her head, sparking unanswerable questions, leaving traces of his perplexing behaviour, his inhumanity. She imagined the lurchers running eagerly and blissfully, obediently to their master's whistle. And the shotgun exploding, once, twice, again and again.

7

IN THE LANGUAGE OF FLOWERS: BURGUNDY ROSE, UNCONSCIOUS BEAUTY

A slice of sunshine found its way around Muriel's immemorial morning room drapes, which worked to trap everything in a strange twilight. Nibbling the corner of her toast and sipping Earl Grey tea, Violet drooped with exhaustion. However, lack of sleep had left her mind feeling fortunately numb.

Muriel peered at her over the top of her newspaper.

'It's joy to have you here, Violet,' she said. 'A break for you and for me. You can help me get about a bit more, with my blessed ankle. And, if you don't mind, to and from the commode. I don't like to bother Smithson too much. She can be rather brusque at the best of times.'

'I'm sure that would be no trouble, Auntie. I'm grateful to be here.'

'And you can stay with me as long as you like,' Muriel added, her sentence ended on a high note, as if in question. 'As long as you feel is necessary?'

Violet did not have an answer.

'Don't think about him,' her aunt declared. 'He is a madman for slaughtering his dogs. And that's all I wish to say on the matter. Unless, of course, you'd like to talk about it.'

Violet shook her head. What happened to the dogs felt too appalling to put into any more words. But, also, her parents' disappointment in her, their not understanding her, and Violet's inability to do anything about it floored her. 'Not really, auntie...'

'My dear, I won't press you. Listen, you need to get yourself outside. You don't want to be stuck in here around a middle-aged lady all day. It's a short stroll to the park, and it looks like a lovely day out there. Get some colour in those cheeks.'

'Yes,' Violet agreed. 'I think I must go out, or I feel I might break in two.'

'I've never seen you look so pale.'

Muriel pressed on her a parasol; Violet had arrived at Montagu Square ill-prepared for most things, including bright June sunshine.

'If you go directly across Gloucester Place and Baker Street, you'll reach Marylebone High Street,' Muriel said. 'On the corner is my little grocer's. Could you pick up some Robinson's lemonade for me? They missed it out of my delivery last week and I could do with some to go in my gin. Turn left there and you'll eventually get to the park. Now, go quickly. The sunshine will dry your eyes.'

* * *

Violet walked across shady, quiet Montagu Square. Smartly upholstered nannies pushed prams along the pavement. The bread man came and went, doffing his cap and telling her good morning. She passed a block of new red-brick mansion flats with pristine net curtains and geraniums spilling from window boxes. But, reaching Baker Street, the hot chaos of taxis, horses and buses snuffed out the tranquillity. She stopped, frozen at the kerb, breathing fumes and steaming dung, and squinting against the hard sunshine. But this was all part of London life, she told herself, and if she was going to stay with Muriel, then she must get used to this madly endearing city. She put up her parasol and carried on.

Posters for Bourneville and Pear's soap invited her to stop at the grocer's, but she decided to drop in on the way back for the lemonade, and treat her aunt to a little confection for she had some shillings left from her allowance. Perhaps some glacé fruits or ginger in syrup, or a bit of chocolate?

Further ahead, the dense hedges of Regent's Park bulged through iron railings along its sweeping boundary – a verdant glimmer beyond the grey asphalt. Violet crossed the road and walked over a little bridge. Ducks paddled and shook themselves among lily pads in the water below, and as she inhaled the balmy, green-scented air, the menacing feeling squatting inside her head seemed to ease.

Around a shady corner of tall willows, appeared a rose garden bathing in the sunshine, clouds of colour under dazzling light. Enticed by flowers of lemon-yellow and dusky lilac, the profoundest red and the snowiest white, she walked over and strolled among Bourbon, damask, and tea roses. She soaked in their tranquil company, and every now and then, stopped to press her nose to a bloom, drinking in perfume. The scents were light and spicy, hypnotic and distracting. Violet thought of Claudia and how she would love them, how she would bury her face in their beauty. How Violet missed her company.

She wondered what, if anything, her friend knew about her sudden departure from Old Trellick, and her thoughts tightened again. Claudia would be worried and confused, but surely reassured by Eddie Davey. The days after the disastrous soirée had been fraught and wearying at home. And Violet had felt it would be unfair to involve Claudia. But that night, Violet decided, or at least tomorrow, she would write to her friend and try her best to explain.

Violet spotted a bench beneath a canopy of trailing roses, and climbed the three shallow steps to claim it for herself. Sitting with the light dappling her cheeks, she shielded her face with Muriel's parasol, seeking a private moment, alone with herself. The perfect June day seemed to blow kisses around her, and she turned her face to catch the breeze, allowing it to blow unpleasant thoughts away and scatter them in the air.

She amused herself watching the world go by. Gentlemen strolled with their ladies, the couples behaving kindly and courteously towards each other. Female silhouettes were slender with the new fashions, topped by hats of stupendously wide concoction. One man ask his companion to smell a deep-burgundy rose as he cradled it delicately in his hand for her. The tenderness in their exchange brought a thickness to Violet's throat as she remembered Weston forcing her to admire the orchid.

She shook him off, cursed him, and gazed around to fill herself again with the day's beauty, to haul back happiness. At the corner of her eye, she spotted a man sitting on a stool, sketching. Dressed in working-man's blue, with a soft hat to shade his eyes and his artist's board perched on his lap, his hand moving rapidly over the paper. Violet idly watched him, enjoying the rhythm of his creativity, the confidence and peace in his attitude. He appeared to be a little older than her; his fair-reddish hair clipped short, his shirt open at the neck. His collar flapped in the breeze, but he seemed unaware, such was his rapture with whatever he drew, his pencil, a mere stub in his fingers, carving shapes and swirls in front of him. He looked up at her, straight at her, and his gaze held on to her, as if, in that moment, he owned her.

Violet stood up and, in a flash, moved away through the mass of roses, feeling exposed, and spied on, and that she didn't belong there. She took a long circuit of the park, keeping her head down behind the parasol, not wishing to catch anyone's eye. She wanted to hide, and felt ridiculous for it, and scooted through the gates she'd come in earlier.

Walking past the mansions of York Terrace, the park behind her, she broke into a laugh. How silly and how vain! The artist had been capturing the roses, the sunlight, and the dappled shade. He could not have been less interested in Violet, and she'd only caught his eye because of her fidgeting.

Feeling the fool now she'd broken the magic of the day, she hurried down bustling Baker Street, wanting to be safely behind her aunt's front door. She felt weary and longed for sleep. Surely, now at last, she would sleep. Abruptly, she stopped. She'd walked straight past the grocer's by mistake. She turned to go back, to cross the side street and he was there again. Right there.

He stood some hundred yards away outside the grocer's, clutching his canvas bag, his artist's board under his arm, his gaze open and expectant. Passing pedestrians hid him from Violet and then revealed him again. Had he spotted her? With courteous instinct, she lifted her hand to acknowledge him, as she might any acquaintance she'd chance upon in Looe, Lansallos or at the cove. But a bus lumbered past, slowing at the junction, blocking her view. And when at last it pulled away with a plume of exhaust, the artist had gone.

***

A week later, Violet sat at the desk in the guest bedroom overlooking Montagu Square. Gas lamps burned in the twilight, and lights glowed in the houses opposite but, in her head, she was at Old Trellick watching the gathering dusk alive with birds singing, melodious and indistinct, honey around her ears. She imagined the long evening stretching over the south Cornish coast, the half-light hours in which farmers brought in their hay and herded their stock; in which cows would plod out to pasture through lingering haze. She remembered how she'd listen for the sea, longing to hear it from her bedroom at Old Trellick. Fleetingly, she hungered for home, until she remembered her mother's telegram.

She took out a sheet of her aunt's headed paper and the comforting London twilight wrapped itself around her as she, at last, wrote to Claudia.

> *How are you, my dearest friend?*

She stopped, her mind blank, wondering what had prevented her writing in the last few days. Was it that she had half expected to receive a letter from Claudia anyway, and would have responded by return of post? The days since her trip to the park had passed quickly with outings to Fortnums and shopping sprees along Bond Street, her aunt waiting for her in the gig with her ankle, enjoying herself vicariously, and boosting Violet at the same time with lively chatter and humorous asides.

> *So sorry not to have been in touch until now. As you can imagine, something went horribly wrong between Weston and me after you and Eddie left Charlecote, but I am fine...*

Violet wrote, but had to stop. Claudia would know all too well.

The thought of what Weston had done to the dogs reared again. Had it been to make a point, to show how much he despised her, the girl so spoilt that she did not know what she wanted? Her skin prickled. She shuddered and laid down the pen. She longed for Claudia to be here with her, and so they could speak about it, carefully and slowly, explain it to each other.

Violet jolted. Smithson knocked at the door and came in to tell her that her aunt would like her company downstairs.

The drawing room drapes muffled the evening light and oil lamps glowed yellow. Muriel looked happily settled with her ankle propped on a stool, a glass of sherry at her elbow and, on the little table, a china plate of the candied fruits that Violet had bought her, her first day here, the day of the roses; the day she saw the artist. Muriel's playing cards gleamed as she sifted them, flicked them over, toyed with them.

'Would you like me to read for you, my dear? I'm in the mood. I'm feeling rather lucid tonight.'

Violet sat down and forced out a laugh. 'Really, Aunt Muriel? Then you are doing far better than I am.' She humoured her, feeling an odd mixture of fascination and disbelief. 'But I don't think I have a choice, do I?'

Smithson brought Violet a sherry and she settled back, relishing the distraction of her aunt's parlour game, watching her shuffle, cut, and lay the cards. She sipped at the heady liqueur as Muriel ruminated over the spread on the table, sighing as she turned over each card.

'Goodness, Violet, the Hearts are all over the place.' Muriel tapped the cards with her fingernail. 'This indicates love, emotion, your inner life... you know that, don't you. Goodness me, my dear... Look where this one has landed. The King of Hearts. This tells me you will certainly marry this year.'

Violet laughed. 'Impossible, Auntie. Really!'

'Well, I agree,' huffed Muriel. 'The way things have been going on for you lately, this is ridiculous. Unless we have a complete turn of fortune. I must be losing my touch. We'll do it again later, another day.'

'Later, next month, next year! Can we not talk about marriage, please?'

Muriel gave her a glance of admiration as she tidied away the cards.

'Understood,' said Muriel. 'I'm sorry. Rather insensitive of me, isn't it. I'm just so damn bored today.' She flinched, moving her bandaged foot, and asked Violet to slip another cushion under it. 'Doctor's visiting tomorrow to have another look at it. I wonder if it's broken? Should have been healed by now, don't you think?'

'I am wondering if you'd be in a lot more pain if it was worse than a sprain,' Violet said.

'Yes, yes. We will have a jaunt around the park in the gig together as soon as I feel able. Haven't been calling for many a week, and I am missing out,' Muriel said. 'I'm sure the doctor will have a prod about and dismiss me as a fussy lady of a certain age, and prescribe some tonic or other to perk me up. Well, that's what I pay him for, isn't it? I'll tell him I have all the tonic I need in this little glass of sherry.' Muriel focused on Violet. 'How are you, anyway, dear? No more telegrams from your mother? You'll be getting a letter soon, no doubt. She'll still be incensed, if I know her. All tied up in knots so far that she cannot pick up a pen and put it to paper.'

Violet sighed. 'I can only guess at what such a letter might say, going by the telegram that very nearly beat me here. But,' she said. 'I've just started a letter to Claudia.'

'There we are! She will be happy to hear from you.'

'But I miss simply *talking* with her, Auntie,' Violet said. 'We'd walk for hours, down to the cove, along by the sea, through the pinewoods and scarcely draw breath!'

Muriel nodded and sipped her sherry, while Violet recalled their chattering, their blunt exchanges, laughing about everything from Claudia's wine-making skills and insubstantial wardrobe to Violet's spoiling of Jess and her precious *Flower Book*.

'She's missing you, of course she is,' Muriel assured her. 'Sometimes a turn of events like this, this rather embarrassing sticky spot between you and Mr Penruth, stifles people, makes them hesitate to make contact. But she will.'

'She *knows* me, do you understand?'

'Violet, I do.'

Violet smiled at the thought of her friend happy with Eddie. Who knows, perhaps her aunt's card reading was for Claudia, and she would become Mrs Davey before the year was out?

'She's the only person I will allow to tease me about my nature journal,' Violet said. 'She always laughed about the fact that the one lesson I was interested in at school was simple old nature studies, even though I was enjoying an expensive education...' she trailed off, not wishing to remind herself of the man who had provided it.

When Muriel's head nodded, her eyes drooping closed, Violet went back upstairs. She sat back at the desk, lit the lamp but left Claudia's letter for the time being and pulled out her *Flower Book*. Opening it, she caught the comforting scent of the paper, ran her fingers over the pages and the deep-green jacket, the colour of pinewood shadows. She browsed, turning pages slowly, revisiting her pressed flowers, the weather lore and field notes, feeling herself surface into her own world, the private spaces in her mind. Her observations over months and years past spoke to her, soothed her. But they stopped abruptly the day of the Charlecote soirée as if her life then, too, had ended.

With a flash of anger, Violet turned back to where Weston's peony sat flattened and pasted alone to its blank page. She filled her pen with ink, lined up her thoughts into a pristine row, and wrote underneath:

Today is not the day I pressed and pasted this flower, but today is the day I wish to record how I have found a new meaning to myself, to my life... A week ago, I walked for the first time in Regent's Park among the roses... a week ago, I saw beyond sorrow and constraint – the only things offered to me by a person from my past...

A week ago, among the roses of Regent's Park, I glimpsed beyond the sorrow, I glimpsed a new beginning. I discovered a new day. A new self.

Violet Prideaux
Montagu Square, London, 15th June, 1914

8

IN THE LANGUAGE OF FLOWERS: RED PIMPERNEL, CHANGE

'Shall I not order the gig around for you, miss?' Smithson asked Violet as she pulled out a large umbrella from the stand in the hallway and handed it to her. 'William is always ready around the back with the carriage. It shouldn't take many minutes and it is such filthy weather. It's meant to be midsummer.'

'Thank you,' Violet said. 'But I really don't mind the rain.'

Her aunt had already berated her over the breakfast table on her plan to leave the house that morning.

'You will catch your death and then what will I tell your mother and father? They are already not speaking to me.'

'But think about how much time I spend outdoors back at home,' Violet had reminded Muriel. 'I am hardly going to shrink away from getting a little wet.'

Her aunt had sighed. 'I suppose I shall have to adjust to your ways, Violet dear. I don't know. Is it the same with all you girls these days? Travelling all the way on the Plymouth train on your own like that. Unthinkable in my day.'

'I will take care,' Violet assured her. 'I won't be more than two hours or so.'

Aunt Muriel offered her cheek for her to kiss. 'I will be keeping time.'

'Nice weather for ducks,' said the grocery man, coming up the outside steps from the basement as Violet left the house. 'Typical weather, isn't it? I suppose it's all we deserve.'

Violet said good morning, lifted the brolly over her head, and crossed the square. Trees dripped and pavements sparkled. The air smelt fresh and earthy, and downpipes rushed with rainwater. She loved the rain, truth be told, but something was missing from her side. Her walks at home would be accompanied by Jess, or Claudia, or both. Now under the saturated grey city sky, their absence cut her keenly.

She decided to avoid the park that morning, and kept to the road that led north to Hampstead, skirting the park on its western side. Through the mesh of her veil, the hectic streets and the parades of buildings looked murky and subdued. The houses remained reasonably grand, if a little shabbier than Montagu Square. But, the further on she went they became smaller, windows dirtier, steps unscrubbed and, in Muriel's world, undesirable. Her aunt would certainly wonder why on earth Violet would choose to take herself off to such a place, as she went down steep steps at the side of the bridge over Regent's Canal.

'I'm curious, that is all,' Violet said to herself, finding herself on the towpath.

Below the level of the road, the waterway eased its quiet way through the city. Backs of sheds, and small factories and coal yards, their brick walls either mended or crumbling hopelessly, shadowed the dark, oily water pitted with raindrops. Two or three barges exhaled smoke from chugging engine stacks, the bargemen at the helm. Behind her she heard the shriek of a Midland Railway train as it crossed the bridge and slowed down for Marylebone Station.

The humid, gritty air smelt of industry, of tar. Unsurprisingly, the towpath was empty, as most sensible and respectable people who didn't have to go out – again, in Muriel's opinion – were cosy in their parlours.

Perhaps Violet wasn't sensible, she chuckled to herself as she walked along, scanning the verge where the plants that many would call weeds were tangled among long grass bent under the weight of the rain. In her head, she named them all, enjoying the chant she struck up as she went: nettles, dandelions, creeping buttercup, woundwort, and red pimpernel like little drops of blood; the Latin names lost to her, meaningless. She had no need for them.

A narrow boat chugged closer, wafting exhaust fumes Violet's way. The bargeman at the wheel wore a heavy cape of sackcloth over his shoulders to protect him from the rain and against his knee leaned a young boy, his jacket tied on to him with a piece of rope around his middle. Resting against the rail, the bargeman's wife held a baby wrapped in a mess of shawls. She looked pale, her eyes deep-set and haunted by fatigue, and yet she had adorned her sopping hat with a ruby-red flower as a defiant badge in the grey urban landscape. The baby in her arms squawked and a little white fist found the drizzly air. The woman tenderly tucked the hand away and dipped her mouth to kiss the hidden forehead. Mesmerised, Violet stopped to watch them go past, a mysterious emotion stirring in her chest. None of the family glanced her way and yet she gave them a wave anyway.

She must be missing Jess, she thought. She longed for Jess like she might a child. If Claudia had been walking by her side, she would have confessed how seeing the family on the barge had made her feel. And Claudia would have understood. They'd talk it over, get to the root of it. And the silence, now, bothered her.

It had been a week since she'd written to Claudia, and she still had not heard from her. Something didn't feel right, she thought, walking on along the towpath. Perhaps Claudia had fallen ill. Perhaps the postman was ill, or a letter lost along the way. Her friend would always respond, whenever Violet wrote to her from school, by return of post. Even a quick postcard promising to write a longer letter later. She pictured the last time she'd seen Claudia, saying goodbye outside Weston's orangery, and she'd looked so well, so happy, walking off with Eddie Davey.

Something caught Violet's eye. Bright-yellow tansy flowers blazing from an ivy-encrusted pile of bricks, like a beacon in the mizzling rain. Violet folded away her umbrella, opened her canvas bag and snipped some flower heads, keen to tell Claudia where she stumbled across that elusive little weed, the yellow buttons, that Claudia's mother swore by.

Violet left the canal before she reached the Zoo to walk back through the, predictably, deserted park. She passed soggy gardeners hoeing an herbaceous border and spotted a handful of horse-drawn hansom carriages trundling around the outer circle, all battened down to the rain, conveying neatly dressed passengers to afternoons of *Bezique* or bridge at the mansions of Cumberland Terrace on the eastern side. By the time she reached the rose garden, the rain had stopped but the bench looked far too wet to sit on. Water dripped from leaves, in an ongoing little rain shower, and roses hung their heads. Crumpled petals littered the grass, their colour diluted.

The dank air and the soaked feeling from her wet coat crept into Violet's bones, and she felt her spirits dip. She shook herself, reminding herself what Claudia would have to say on the matter. That the sun will shine again tomorrow. That tomorrow was a lovely day.

Mindful of Muriel's clock-watching, Violet knew she should be getting back to Montagu Square, and spend the afternoon writing another letter to Claudia, hoping this one might prompt a response. But she took one more stroll around the empty, bedraggled rose garden, battling with foolish disappointment. For the artist was not there. Of course he wouldn't be. For who in their right mind, as Aunt Muriel would say, would come out on a day like today?

9

IN JULY, DOG DAYS BRIGHT AND CLEAR INDICATE A HAPPY YEAR

Aunt Muriel's single-pony gig pulled up outside Lady Welstead's town house on Cumberland Terrace at around four o'clock in the afternoon. The proper and perfect time to call, Muriel advised Violet, squeezed in next to her in the stifling confines of the little carriage.

'The visiting card should be left between the hours of three and six,' Muriel said. 'Any other time and we'd be well and truly denounced as socially inept.'

The leather seat sweated against Violet's back. She pulled her window down to peer up at the precise, gleaming white façade of the Welstead mansion looming imperiously over the park in the airless, sultry afternoon.

'It's all rather magnificent, isn't it?' she said, craning her neck to take in its, all things considered, discreet Regency splendour. She counted the floors.

'Ah, yes, she runs a very smart household. Sir Giles and Lady Welstead moved up here from Fitzrovia – they were my neighbours, you know – soon after he was knighted for his services to banking,' Muriel said. 'I often wonder where I would be now if Jeffrey had lived.' She drifted into a reverie for a good number of seconds before she snapped back with, 'But don't be intimidated by their titles, my dear. He's only a life peer. We're all *nouveau*, you know. I'd heard your uncle Jeffrey speak of him when he was simply Mr Welstead, the foreign exchange clerk.'

Muriel opened her handbag and drew out her little tortoiseshell card case. Violet admired the modest style of her visiting cards: plain cream, no decoration, just: '*Mrs Jeffrey Strachen*' printed in deep-brown ink in the centre and her address neatly on the bottom right.

'We must have some of these printed for you,' Muriel commented as she took two cards out.

Violet did not relish the idea. Whatever would Claudia say? She'd laugh, most certainly, wondering how well they would go down in the polite society of Looe and Lansallos. Violet touched her forehead with her finger to trap a drop of sweat. How close it felt, the long afternoon hours stretching and smouldering, the clouds thick and milky.

A footman from the Welstead household walked down the steps between columns that would dwarf Aunt Muriel's and offered a silver tray on which Muriel placed her cards: one for Lady Welstead, the other for Sir Giles. The footman informed that her ladyship was not at home.

Muriel reached back for the cards and pinched down the top-left corner of each one.

'That's to let Lady Welstead know I've called in person,' she whispered to Violet as the footman retreated. 'My, he's a fellow, isn't he? Lady Welstead insists her footmen are all six foot two. We'll keep our fingers crossed that her own card will be delivered to us tomorrow or the day after. And then, perhaps we shall have a morning call. Just imagine, after that, an invitation to dinner, or to the box at the opera. We went when Jeffrey was alive. The Royal Opera. Such a spectacle. I don't want you to miss out on any of this, Violet. If Lady Welstead doesn't invite us, I shall take you. My ankle seems to be holding up, so we can keep our fingers crossed... well I never, don't look now.'

Violet suspected that she should do just that.

The footman held the front door wide as a young man exited the house and strode down the sunny white steps with a cane and an energetic pace.

'It's their son, Sebastian. Just down from Oxford for the summer. Ha, who said I'd lost my touch. The playing cards may yet be right. Thank goodness you are with me, Violet, looking beautiful, and not at home pressing flowers.' Muriel laughed teasingly.

Violet cringed, leaning back into the seat as if to hide behind her aunt, perspiration tingled down her spine.

Muriel slammed the window down and called, 'Good afternoon, sir.'

'Ah, madam. How do you do? Blasting hot, isn't it?' Sebastian Welstead stopped and lifted his hat, revealing a large nose set in a kind, bland face with not much of a chin. It seemed obvious to Violet that he had forgotten Muriel's name.

'May I introduce my niece, Miss Violet Prideaux?' she ventured.

'So pleased to meet you.' Sebastian Welstead bowed, squinting through the glass in the glare of the sun. He did not meet Violet's eye. 'What stinking weather this is. Dog days they call it, don't they?' He switched back to Muriel. 'My mother is not at home, I'm afraid.'

'Not to worry, I've left my card.'

Sebastian said 'good day' and on he marched in the direction of the Euston Road.

'I saw him a week ago, you know,' Muriel said, slipping her card case back into her handbag, 'When I was here for his mother's At-Home and you had gone for one of your walks. All he could talk about was the assassination. Earnest, he was, and sad. Terribly worried about the state of Europe. But he seems a lot more chipper today. Perhaps, like me, he has decided that there isn't going to be a war.'

'But the newspapers are full of it,' Violet said.

'Oh, I think it's all a lot of hot air being blown over from Germany like this blessed weather. The Kaiser's the King's cousin, for goodness' sake. Anyway, enough of all that. Mr Sebastian Welstead. What do you think, Violet? You can do no better.' She snared Violet with one of her outrageous glances, laughed and tapped the side of the carriage and called, 'Right, William, on we go.'

The driver snapped his whip and the pony's hooves began to ring brightly over the cobbles. Muriel chattered about Sebastian, and how pleased she was that Violet could accompany her these days on her little diversions around town. But Violet only half listened, sinking under the heat. Through the towering horse chestnuts, she glimpsed the park, blushing in the sunlight. How she longed to be out of the stuffy carriage and somewhere in the shade. The great stretches of grass looked like they'd quench her thirst.

'I'd like a walk, Auntie,' she said.

'Oh, for goodness' sake, now you're playing truant. We can't possibly stop here. Whatever will Mr Welstead think – we've nearly caught up with him – that I've turfed you out of the gig? You girls these days. Next thing I know, Violet, you'll be marching on Downing Street with a placard, or chaining yourself to railings. You know you're going to miss the At-Home at Mrs Emsworthy's on Dorset Street?'

'I just need some air, Auntie,' Violet said.

Muriel relented: 'We'll drop you further along, where no one will see you.'

Violet stepped down from the gig and folded her veil over her face. 'I will be home for supper.'

'Take this.' Muriel handed out her parasol. 'That sun is a demon.'

Violet watched the little carriage bowl off down the street, smiling at her aunt's taste for the old-fashioned. Muriel would not be persuaded to exchange her gig and pony for a motor car 'even though the Queen has one'.

* * *

Keeping to the shade under the chestnuts, where filtered sunlight turned the air to powdered gold, Violet relished the moments to herself. The rolling grass ushered in breezes, the heat did not feel as molten, and the rose garden gleamed like a fallen rainbow. As she drew nearer, she saw roses emerging in a second flush and the two gardeners meticulously dead-heading. And between them, watching them, and making them both chuckle while they worked, stood the artist.

Surprise made Violet hesitate and want to veer off in another direction. But, then again, she also felt curiously drawn.

The artist had rolled up his shirt sleeves, and one shirt tail had come loose from his trousers. His frame was slender, Violet noted, and his shoulders had the mesmerising combination of being both broad and lean. His hair looked fairer and sandier than she'd remembered, caught by the dazzling sunlight.

He'd left his hat on his canvas, stool by his easel, where his artist's paraphernalia lay scattered, his work-in-progress sheltered by a large umbrella.

Violet swung her parasol down to cover her face as she approached. Twisted tubes of paint littered the glittering grass. A rag and a flask of water had found a patch of shade, while brushes dried off in an old jam jar. Violet paused, trying to appear casual, and stopped at arm's length away from the painting. She stared, her eyes rounding in astonishment. Her cheeks singed with a furious blush. For there, in the painting, was Violet, walking through the rose garden. A parasol – the very parasol she carried – reflected an unearthly green light, like water, over her face and her hands and her throat. Her mouth a ruddy smudge, her eyes pools of an uncertain shade. Her hair a smudge of darkness under her hat, her expression ponderous and sad. The curve of her shoulder and the lightness of her hand looked exactly as she saw them each morning in her mirror. Violet stood still, trembling.

His shadow fell across the grass, and yet she did not dare look at him.

'Madam,' he said in a mellow tone lacking all trace of surprise, as if he had been expecting her. 'I'm Jack Fairling.'

Violet saw his hand move towards her, an offer to shake hers, and her mind crashed in protest: *I cannot shake your hand. We have not been formally introduced. I do not have a chaperone. We have not exchanged visiting cards.* She kept her own hands clasped to her parasol and purse, and looked at his face as another slurry of phrases thickened inside her mouth. *How dare you paint me. How dare you do this!*

And yet, still, she could not speak.

Jack Fairling beamed at her, thoughtfully celebrating her. His eyes charming and crinkling in the brightness. She thought him presumptuous, but then wanted to laugh, for it struck her suddenly, ridiculously: *How could we possibly exchange visiting cards? I do not have any.*

'I'm sorry, madam,' he offered when it proved evident how lost for words she was. 'This is not how this was meant to happen. I have been working on the painting for weeks in my studio and have brought it out today to finish it. *En plein air*, you know? I had meant to warn you—'

'Warn?' Violet exclaimed in a flash of fury.

'I mean... I do apologise, ask your permission, but, you see, I lost you that day. The day I saw you, here in the rose garden. You left so quickly. I did not stand a chance.'

She placed one finger just below her collarbone, where her heart shuddered. She stared at him, at his eyes that looked like dancing periwinkles, and his stubbly trimmed beard which seemed to be formed into a permanent smiling shape.

'Why didn't you ask me... before you even started... I was only there for a few moments... I sat just for a minute... how could you have painted all of this?'

She gestured towards the painting, too alarmed to look at it again.

The artist laughed lightly and tapped the side of his temple. 'I keep it all up in here. You see, as Degas says, "imagination collaborates with memory".'

'Degas can say what he likes. This is preposterous.' Violet lifted her chin. 'I refuse to give permission.'

'I'm very sorry to hear that.' He bowed and stepped away, moving as if to take down the painting. 'I have been experimenting,' he continued in quiet explanation, 'taking my idea of Impressionism a little further. When I spotted you the other week, walking there among the roses, and then you sat, briefly, and it was all so fleeting, and spellbinding, I had to capture it. The light was incredible. It was a moment I could not let go of. Your face—'

'But you've made me look sad.' Violet felt outraged. 'It's...' She wanted to insult him, tell him it wasn't very good. But she would be lying. How could he have got her so precisely in those moments she had lingered in Queen Mary's Rose Garden? She remembered, she had been thinking of Weston and what had transpired between them, and missing Claudia, missing her home. And it had blighted her – the shape of her face – momentarily. And Jack Fairling had captured it – and the blaze of light around her – like a butterfly in amber. The painting was good. She looked back at the easel. It was incredible.

Jack busied himself with the clips that held his canvas in place.

'I will destroy it, of course. I had no right. But then I did not expect to see you again.' He laughed at himself in a radiant outburst. 'You were my evanescent, mysterious stranger. But here you are. You have caught me out.

And who wouldn't be drawn back to such a place. It's an oasis here, isn't it? It's heaven.'

Violet watched him squat down to collect up his tubes of paint, quickly scooping his possessions together. He opened a large bag and began to throw in his equipment, winding his brushes in rags and stuffing them in a pocket.

'You will destroy it?'

'Of course, madam, you have my word. In fact, let me do it now, right here.'

Her hand whipped out and tugged at his sleeve.

He stopped and looked down at her fingertips as they plucked at the fabric and then back into her face.

'I think you have surprised yourself, madam.'

Violet whispered reluctantly, 'I can't see something so beautiful destroyed.'

The heat seemed to crack the air. Beneath her parasol she noticed the skin on her forearms saturated in the same watery light as in the painting.

'I will give it to you,' Jack said.

'It's not finished,' she replied, trying not to smile. 'You must finish it.'

His face grew round as he chuckled. 'I will, then. Most certainly. By your command.'

He took down the painting and rested it carefully on the grass, and folded up his easel.

Violet knew she must leave now, for wouldn't that be the right and proper thing to do? What would Aunt Muriel say, what would her *mother* say, if they knew she had been talking to a complete stranger, a *man*, in the middle of the park, for everyone to see? She felt fresh anger growing. It did not matter any more whether he finished the painting or not. That he seemed to have snatched a part of her, without permission, mattered. But she struggled to find fault, to pinpoint exactly why it bothered her so. For hadn't he, truly, *seen* her. She turned to go.

'Would you like to get out of the heat, madam?' he asked, his voice so modest and agreeable it made her pause. 'Would you like some tea?'

'I think I would,' she said with a refreshing reckless feeling. 'What can I carry?'

He handed her his sketch book, gathered the rest of his things, and they walked side by side to the Pavilion.

Sitting at a table by the open window, shaded by a weeping willow, Violet removed her hat and welcomed the blissful fresh air coming off the boating lake. The waiter handed them menus and conscious of their sudden unprecedented nearness they both quickly ordered, brandishing the cards like shields. Violet, not wishing to gaze directly into Jack Fairling's face, glanced around. Other couples and groups of ladies were taking tea and enjoying the languid, discreet service. She heard a gentle tinkling of silver spoon against teacup, soft conversation. *Other* couples? she corrected herself. *We* are not a *couple*.

'Everybody's melting,' she said.

'It looks that way,' he answered, and they waited in a companionable silence for the tray to be brought over.

The tea tasted good and strong, and Violet drank a great draught of it, quenching her thirst. Jack thoughtfully stirred his own cup three times, lifted the spoon and tapped it twice on the rim. A funny little habit, thought Violet, smiling to herself. His presence felt like a cooling breath on her throat.

He watched her for some moments, tilting back a little as if to get her in focus. And she wondered if he might lift the teaspoon and use it to check the size and perspective of her head.

'Didn't Mr Gladstone say,' Jack said, '"if you are cold, tea will warm you; if you are too heated, it will cool you"?'

'I believe he did,' Violet said, enjoying his aside. Her earlier outrage had vanished like a forgotten snatch of a song. 'How right Mr Gladstone was. I'm afraid I don't have any quotes up my sleeve to throw back at you.'

'Do you realise you have yet to tell me your name?'

'I'm Violet Prideaux. Very pleased to meet you.'

They exchanged a brief and comical handshake across the crockery and she explained about staying with her Aunt Muriel in Montagu Square, and that her home was in Cornwall, near Looe. But went no further. Talking about herself gave her the same uncomfortable feeling as seeing herself in the painting.

'Ah, I once went to St Ives to paint,' Jack said. 'The light there, right on the tip of the peninsula is beyond belief.'

'It's a long way to go,' she said. 'And it takes forever, even to where we are, not far from the Tamar.'

'Something tells me you are missing home. Are you going back soon?'

His question sounded breezy enough but it stung Violet as if she'd brushed past a nettle.

'I haven't really thought... I don't think so,' she said, her voice faltering.

Violet poured more tea for them both and he gave her the courtesy of not asking why. She took a breath. 'Are you from London, Mr Jack Fairling?'

'I was brought up in Kent, went to school in Canterbury. My father still lives there in a little place to the east of the city.'

Jack told her about the village of red-tiled houses, and beyond, where hop gardens patchworked the countryside and the land flattened out to marshes. Where the standing water on the flood plain looked like a hundred mirrors reflecting the sky.

'Which you've painted, of course,' Violet said.

'I studied art, much to my father's disappointment. He wanted me to be an engineer. And I came to London to make my fortune. Some fortune.' He shrugged, his eyes glittering with humour, and Violet joined in with his laughter. 'Now I live in Camden Town, just a short stroll that way.' He hooked his thumb over his left shoulder. 'I rent rooms over a pharmacy. And I have had the honour of sitting in with a local group of artists. And what venerable men they are. I'm learning a great deal from them.'

'I can see that, your painting, it is...' Violet wanted to say *sublime*, but worried it might sound insincere, '...lovely.'

'They've let me in to their salon, that's enough for me,' he said. 'They're doing what I want to do, taking urban scenes and making them beautiful, but always with an edge of realism. It could be St James's Park, the Holloway Road, inside the Café Royal.'

'My that sounds so inspired,' Violet said, wanting to tell him a little more about herself, to tell him what she loved to do, about Jess and her *Flower Book*. And yet it all sounded so simplistic and unambitious. Instead, she asked, if he had been to art school in Canterbury.

'Yes, I had a scholarship, lucky me. Yourself? Where did you go?'

'Boarding school in Exeter.' She warmed her story with the ludicrous incidence of her climbing out of the window and running away.

His laughter rang out delighted and cheerful. But the memory of school grew dark, and Weston returned to her. The question of why he'd paid for her education had been skirted round by her parents, and never up for discussion. But now it hammered for attention.

'My goodness,' she glanced at her pocket watch. 'I really should go. Aunt Muriel will be wondering.'

She spoke in complete opposition to what she desired: sitting there, drinking tea, and discovering more about Jack Fairling. His growing up in the countryside sounded not dissimilar to her own young life, and yet how free and motivated he seemed now. It drew a hard comparison. Being a man made all the difference, granted, and yet a few minutes with him seemed to open a doorway for Violet. She could break away from the world where her aunt wanted to convey her to the drawing rooms of people of a different class; where money was exchanged in clandestine fashion between Weston Penruth and her parents; in which her mother seemed eternally livid with her for not complying with her wishes; where her closest friend had chosen to ignore her letter; where a man could shoot his dogs because she'd snubbed him.

'There's that look again,' said Jack, 'the one I saw when you sat on the bench, when I dreamt up the painting. You look troubled, Miss Prideaux. Oh, I'm sorry, are you quite all right?'

Violet put down her cup, slipped on her gloves and set her hat firmly on her head.

'I must go.'

He stood as she did, and hurried round to move her chair away for her.

With another glance at his face, she shuddered with the realisation that she trusted him, absolutely. She trusted this stranger who somehow seemed more familiar to her than anyone she had ever known.

'It has been a pleasure.' Jack plucked a card out of his top pocket and handed it to her. 'This is my lodgings and my studio. If you ever want to buy a painting...'

'*Buy* a painting...?' she asked, she giggled as she pulled her veil down to cover her face.

'You know I don't mean that,' he said, his expression indistinct through the netting. 'When this painting is finished, Miss Violet Prideaux, I shall present it to you, most certainly. My gift to you.'

10

IN THE LANGUAGE OF FLOWERS: WILD TANSY, I DECLARE AGAINST YOU

The sun slipped behind the chimneys, yet the white façades remained luminous, glowing with remembered daylight. It had been another glorious day in London, but Violet had felt compelled to stay at home with Aunt Muriel, who felt under the weather, her ankle giving her gyp again. Violet commiserated with her, agreeing that perhaps she had been out one too many times to At-Homes and afternoon teas. Perhaps it had all proved too wearing for her.

Keeping her encounter with Jack Fairling to herself, Violet realised how daring she'd been to agree to take tea with him. Her parents would be horrified, and this, she admitted to herself, gave her such a thrill. She closed her *Flower Book*, shutting the newly pasted pages where the yellow tansy found by the canal lay flattened into two dimensions, and gazed out of her bedroom window. The lamplighter had set a flame in the far corner of Montagu Square and would steadily make his way round. Violet glanced at her watch: ten minutes to nine. Perhaps some warm milk to go to bed with; she better ring for Smithson. A taxicab puttered up to a halt outside her aunt's house, and Violet idly watched the driver leap out to open a rear door, recalling how she had not had such personal service when she'd arrived some six weeks before. She reeled with blistering surprise as her mother stepped onto the dusty pavement.

The doorbell rang and hurried footfalls came up the kitchen steps. Violet heard a sharp call of surprise from Aunt Muriel below and she waited, her breathing shallow, trying to compose herself behind her bedroom door.

Her mother said a good evening to Smithson and complained of tiredness. Then silence as hat and wrap were removed, broken by a call from Aunt Muriel to Violet's mother for her to hurry up and come up the stairs to the drawing room, for she could not move because of her ankle. Violet waited some minutes, struggling to hold on to pitching emotions of surprise and dread, before she took a deep breath and made her way downstairs.

'Oh, my poor love.' Her mother turned at the sound of the door and rose from her seat, travel-worn and a little dishevelled.

Violet stopped in shock as her mother went to her, her arms outstretched for an embrace, concern fixing her face.

'Hello, Mother. What a surprise,' Violet muttered as her mother kissed the air by her cheek.

'Oh, my poor dear child, come and sit with me. Come on.'

Violet glanced in question at her aunt, whose expression remained nonplussed.

'Eleanor, it's not like you to travel so far, on your own, and spring this sort of visit on me. You usually spend months planning,' Muriel said. 'What on earth has happened?'

Violet's mother sat on the sofa, shuffling in agitation. She patted the seat next to her, meaning Violet should join her.

'I simply came to see how my incapacitated sister was,' she announced, 'and I've also come to take poor Violet home.'

'Mother, I'm perfectly happy here...'

Smithson came in with a tray of tea and spent some moments arranging the small walnut table, during which time Violet caught Muriel's eye with a searching look. At last, the housemaid shut the door behind her.

Muriel leant forward. 'Why *poor* Violet?' she asked her sister.

'Ah, now, let me drink some tea. I'm parched.' Violet's mother sipped at the steaming cup while Violet twisted her fingers together.

'What's happened?' she blurted. 'Is Papa ill?'

Her mother shook her head and set her cup back in its saucer.

'It's Claudia.'

Violet gasped.

'Oh no, nothing like that,' her mother said, almost enjoying Violet's reaction. 'She's well, I believe. Perfectly well. In clover, I should say.'

Muriel, from her throne-like armchair, her leg propped on a stool, said, 'Do get on with it, Eleanor, we are on tenterhooks.'

'Claudia has thrown over Eddie Davey,' Violet's mother said, relishing her snippet of news, 'and, you'll never guess, Violet. You will never guess what. She is now being courted by one Mr Weston Penruth.'

Both women turned to Violet. She swallowed hard, trying to disguise her shock and utter dismay. Claudia. Her dearest friend. What on earth had happened in the short time she'd been away? How wrong this seemed, how unsettling. And yet Violet did not want to appear churlish, or jealous. Far from it. Violet did not care about Weston. She would be happy for Claudia if she'd made the best decision for herself. But Weston Penruth was not the best for anyone.

No wonder, she thought, Claudia had not replied to her letter.

'Poor Eddie,' she uttered.

'I was thinking more of you, my dear,' her mother said. 'That's why I rushed up here to tell you so I would be able to comfort you. Whatever happened between you and Weston, your father and I thought that, eventually, you would make amends. See it as a first hurdle. But you can't mend anything when you are hundreds of miles apart. And that, Violet, is why we were so disappointed – apart from the terrible gossip we have had to endure – that you came away to London. But it looks like you are too late, and your chance has gone. And what sort of friend pulls such a trick? Steps into your shoes like that? You were about to be engaged! It's not acceptable.'

'There must be more to it.' Violet tried to swallow her shock. 'There must be some explanation. Oh, good God.' She smiled, for she did not wish her mother or aunt to know the full extent of her confusion. Claudia had been timid, almost frightened, of Weston Penruth, had not shown a jot of interest, had made fun of him even, as Violet had done, behind his back. She'd teased Violet that he liked her. Weston cannot be the man for her.

'I think this calls for something stronger,' said Muriel. 'Violet, please pour us some sherry.'

The bottle shook in her hands as she poured three glasses, spilling a little. She handed them round.

'From the look on your face, my dear,' said her mother, sipping greedily, 'I think you cared for Weston Penruth more than you are happy to admit.'

Violet shook her head. 'It's Claudia. I thought she was so happy with Eddie. What can have happened?'

Muriel shifted in her chair, holding her glass aloft so that the lamplight turned the sherry to the colour of embers.

'I think this young lady should stay here. You can't make her go back to Old Trellick with all this going on. The humiliation, Eleanor. It will be unbearable.'

Her mother bristled. 'We've gone beyond the humiliation, Muriel. I think she should face it, hold her head up. Show them all how she can rise above it, like we have done. Give them all something to think about. Show little Miss Ainsley and that Penruth fellow that this is not the done thing.'

'He's the squire, Mother,' Violet said bitterly, still unable to fathom the news, 'and he does exactly what he likes.'

11

IN THE LANGUAGE OF FLOWERS: SUNFLOWER, ADMIRATION

The next day over lunch, Violet's mother and aunt talked excitedly of a trip to Selfridges.

'We'll take a hansom. I will sit while you shop,' Muriel said. 'They have lovely waiting areas in the ladies' department. They'll bring me plenty of tea.'

'You too, Violet,' said her mother. 'Perhaps a new gown will cheer you up.'

'No, thank you, Mother,' Violet felt calm, her thoughts surprisingly clear, 'It's too nice a day to be shopping. I'm heading off to search for specimens. I've seen some lovely wildflowers growing along walls and pavements. Lots of them will be at their best right now.'

'Weeds, you mean.'

Violet ignored her. 'I have rather neglected my journal this last month or so.'

Muriel chipped in, 'It's what makes Violet happy, Eleanor. She can get that Weston fellow – and this whole debacle with her friend – out of her mind doing what she likes. We're better off just the two of us, anyway. We can really go to town and behave like respectable ladies of a certain age replenishing our wardrobes and drinking tea in the finest salons.'

'And I need to have some time alone,' Violet said, as evenly as she could manage. 'I need to get over the shock.'

Her mother gave her a dull look, scrutinising her face and settled back in her chair.

'Of course, my dear. Make the most of your time here, for I've already booked our train tickets home,' she said, triumphant. 'We leave next week.'

* * *

Beyond Cumberland Terrace, and the white mansions of the Outer Circle, the street turned a sharp corner to the right and narrowed abruptly. Towering chestnuts thinned out to be replaced by scrubby bushes behind railings and unkempt verges. The peace of the park fell away as the road took Violet over the Euston railway lines. The change in the air felt immediate.

Busy Parkway was crowded with pulsing noise: chattering in shop doorways, the clang of light industry from somewhere near the tracks and a low buzz of languid poverty. Men pushed carts of coal and scrap. Women swept steps or gossiped. Children scattered themselves among the crowd, running errands or playing on the cobbles, their faces pinched and grubby. Violet caught the whiff of straw and dung, raw meat and tobacco and the sewer. She had walked into a distinct enclave and, even though her instinct was to clutch her purse tightly, a peculiar exhilaration coursed down her spine. How far away she felt from the niceties of tea and shopping with her aunt and mother, calling cards and letters on the hall table. How far away she was from the great forbidding mansions belonging to the likes of Lady Welstead, and she had only walked a few hundred yards.

People turned to look, eyes peering at her under brims of hats. A self-conscious prickling crept over Violet's scalp. But she beamed and nodded good afternoon. Some faces ducked away while others cracked opened with a surprised and wide smile.

She found the pharmacy on the corner of Albert Street. A tinkling of a bell announced her as she walked in to scents of soap, camphor and charcoal, all calm and serene. Cabinets, stacked with row upon row of bottles neatly labelled and corked, reached to the ceiling. The counter looked pristine, the scales polished. The pharmacist, with apron and large spectacles, said, 'Good afternoon.' She asked for directions, and he courteously set her straight.

The door sat in a niche around the corner from the pharmacy. It needed a good coat of paint, but the entrance way looked clean and swept. Violet stood for a moment, composed and quiet, there on the steps of a stranger's home. Clutching his card, as if this would give her licence, she rapped on the door.

It opened and a woman peered at her, a pile of dark hair pinned around her head and sharp eyes in a smooth handsome face. She wore a rather worse-for-wear apron, and she'd rolled up the sleeves of her cotton dress. She did not speak, but stared at Violet, her cheeks reddening. She wiped her hands on her apron, and then across her forehead to smooth her hair.

Violet wanted to step back, suddenly doubtful, her resolve caving.

'It's you,' the woman said with astonishment, and she held the door wide open. 'The girl in the painting.'

Violet walked into a narrow, panelled hallway, catching the faint aroma of chemicals and cooked bacon. The door closed behind her, shutting out the light; the walls and floor now indistinct as if in a dream. She turned to the woman, holding out her hand.

'Good afternoon, I'm Miss Prideaux,' she said. 'I've come to buy a painting.'

* * *

Jack Fairling had his back to the door, his easel set up in front of the huge window overlooking the back garden. Daylight bathed him and his work, and his paints emitted their mineral scent. The same accoutrements of his art that Violet had seen in the park – brushes, rags, palettes and jars, balled-up newspaper and blunt pencils – lay around in ordered chaos. He remained still, his palm hooked over his chin, concentrating on the painting before him. His feet were planted firmly apart, and his slender back was steady and poised. The light through the window played over the hairs on his arms, sending out colours of bronze and gold.

The woman beside her coughed. 'Mr Fairling, you have a visitor.'

He turned, startled. His eyes grew large, and his head jerked back for a split second. He seemed unable to move and Violet knew she must walk towards him, extending her hand.

'Sorry for the intrusion—' she began.

'How are you? What a surprise. Are you well?' he asked, shaking her hand vigorously.

'I'm very well. I just had to get out... take a walk. I had to...' She wasn't at all sure now what she had meant to do by coming here.

Jack went through to the other end of the room where a chaise sat in front of the window overlooking the street. He gathered up the mess of folded shirts, books and newspapers, hid an odd sock in his pocket, kicked a pair of boots under the chaise and then plumped the large, brocaded cushion.

'Here, sit here, please,' he said.

Jack's landlady slipped away and quietly shut the door.

Violet perched on the edge of the chaise, her hands folded in her lap, and absorbed the apartment's deep warmth and charm. She took in the patchwork of worn Turkish rugs covering the floor, the scrolled wallpaper faded to soft gold and two scuffed Louis-style armchairs facing the earthy hearth. The folding doors halfway along were pushed back to increase the full glory of the room. On a table, a vase of long-spent big-faced sunflowers, their heads bowed, and petals wrinkled, littered the dusty woodwork with gold and ruddy flakes.

'What a lovely studio, Mr Fairling,' she said, noticing a sketch of the sunflowers pinned to another easel. It must have been completed days ago for in it the blooms were smiling and upright. Next to it, another, possibly dashed off that morning, of the now desiccated flowers.

'I like the dead sunflowers, Mr Fairling,' she said. 'Goodness, what a profound thing to say, but they seem much more fascinating than when alive.'

Jack looked at her, clearly delighted. 'I thought we'd got past such formalities in the park, Miss Prideaux. First names?'

Violet laughed and dipped her head, blushing, her thoughts thundering. Here she was, sitting on a man's sofa, alone with him, in his own home, and her mother had no idea.

'So... Violet...' Jack said, teasingly. 'Would you like tea or coffee?' He stooped by the grate to shuffle at the embers. 'I don't have gas here. Have to boil the kettle the old-fashioned way.'

'That's nice,' Violet said. 'I like the smell of the fire. But, Jack, I do feel I have intruded. You are obviously working.'

He turned, beaming, charmed by her use of his name.

'Oh no, this is the sort of intrusion I like.' Jack chuckled, opening his tea caddy.

An easy silence followed. Through the open sash Violet heard the street below: a tuneful whistle from a delivery man, the sudden bursting of a woman's light and happy laugh. She settled back into the chaise.

'So, you met Mrs Ellis, then,' said Jack. 'She is a fine landlady. Firm and fair. She certainly looks after me, sees me as a project, I think. She loves us artists, always has us as lodgers. Often leaves a plate of food outside my door if she knows I'll be painting all night. Sometimes a carafe of wine.'

'She sounds adorable,' said Violet.

Jack paused, gesturing with the teapot. 'It's a warm day, so seems unnatural to have a fire going, but I need my tea,' he said. 'Or, perhaps, something stronger?'

Violet looked at him with a tremor of rebellion. 'Only if you are...'

He brought over two glasses of wine the colour of rubies.

She took a delicate sip. 'Thank you. That's good.'

As he sat at the other end of the chaise, she caught the scent of fresh linen. He wore a baggy shirt, his elbow easing a hole in the right sleeve, and a waistcoat of peacock-blue. His eyes, as he smiled at her, reflected the colour.

'Well,' he said, 'it's lucky you called in today for I finished the painting last week and it should be thoroughly dry now.'

He placed his wine glass on the floor and crossed to the opposite corner of the room to pick up the canvas that had been facing the wall.

'I've called it *Violet in the Daytime*,' he said, approaching. 'If that's not too preposterous. I think that was one of the words you threw at me in the park.'

He stopped five paces away from her, looking nervous as he presented the painting like an offering.

Violet gazed at Jack's work capturing a fleeting moment of light and shadow and colour and tone. She, the subject, looked radiant despite her inner turmoil. He had captured her mood, had looked into her eyes – although briefly – and she saw within the brushstrokes and the dabbed detail, that at that moment, she'd felt a blinding burst of anger. She'd felt powerful and potent; her true self, the real Violet.

She glanced at Jack, a comforting tingle coursing in her blood. 'It is truly beautiful. Thank you for what you've done. Thank you so very, very...'

The trust she felt in him, her admiration, switched into strangely pleasant agony. She felt confused and frustrated, and pressed a hand to her chest to stop her impulse to explain, to blurt everything out. Tears sprung from her eyes, hot on her cheeks.

Jack placed the painting down, rummaging in his pocket for a handkerchief. She grasped it and covered her face. It smelt of astringent lavender. She inhaled and felt him take her hand, not in polite greeting, but tenderly cradling her fingers, his thumb moving over her palm in a circling motion.

Violet pulled her hand away.

'Are you all right now? Can I fetch you something? You better stay sitting down. Shall I call for Mrs Ellis?'

Violet shook her head. 'No, no, it's a shock, to see... to see myself like that.'

'At least sip a little wine,' he said, and held her glass to her with a soft, generous smile.

'That is a very good idea,' she said, wiping her face with his handkerchief.

The wine comforted her, as did Jack's presence. He waited, didn't press her to explain anything, but kept a careful eye on her all the same. How different she felt, here with Jack, compared to times spent with Weston. The extraordinary feeling opened inside her like a spring finding its way out of the earth.

'I feel that I have done a rather unconventional – and brave – thing to come here like this,' she said, eventually. 'I barely know you. In a way, it is terribly rude of me, to visit unannounced. Against everything I have ever been taught. If my mother and aunt knew where I was...' She laughed briefly. 'But I don't think it was a foolish thing to do, Jack, because despite being upset just now, I feel so *rested*, so *right*.'

Jack watched her, a little mystified. But delight flickered over his face.

'You are most welcome,' he said. 'So very welcome.'

'Can I just sit here? Would it be such an odd thing to ask you if I could just sit here and watch you? It's so peaceful. I love the sound of the streets outside, all of Camden out there. And in here, it feels like—'

He completed her sentence, 'home'.

* * *

Curled up in the corner of the chaise, Violet watched Jack work on his painting of Camden Lock. The still, fathomless Regent's Canal filled the foreground, while ramshackle stables, red chimney pots and tiled roofs formed a backdrop against a stormy battleship-grey sky. He had pinned sketches all around the easel to guide him. His strokes came in quick surges, applying oil paint in blobs and daubs. He stood back, suddenly, contemplating with tense stillness before beginning again.

The afternoon grew cloudy, and the light Jack needed faded. He stopped, methodically cleaned his brushes and tidied his paints away. And Violet, feeling assured and contented, drifted to sleep, waking with a start to see the lamps lit, the room in shadow, although the ceiling remained highlighted by subdued daylight.

'That was a lovely afternoon nap, Violet,' Jack said.

'Oh, good God.' She sat up and rubbed her face. 'What on earth is the time? They'll have the police looking for me.'

'It's only six, but it's grown cloudy. I think we're in for thunder,' said Jack from his armchair by the hearth. On his knee lay a sketchbook and on the table next to him, a scattering of pencils. 'Would you like some supper? Some tea? I was going to smoke my pipe but thought the smell might wake you.'

'Please, smoke your pipe if you want. I have to go.'

'Mrs Ellis can get you a hansom, if you like.' Jack closed his sketchbook and placed it down beside his chair. 'I really must introduce you properly to her. Earlier, I'm afraid, I was a little lost for words. She is a gem, as I said before. She will find you the best cab in Camden to speed you home.'

Barely listening, Violet felt panic and the need to please her mother filling her head. She stood up, found her hat, gathered her purse.

'I really must go,' she said. She glanced at Jack, his peaceful face stirring again a sureness inside her, making her want to linger. She noticed the sketchbook on the floor. 'What's that you have there?'

He picked it up, releasing along with it a rogue ball of dust, and smiled broadly.

'I don't know why I feel coy about this, felt the need to hide it. After all, you have invaded my home and spent the last hour snoring on my sofa.'

Violet laughed. 'I do apologise. I'm so sorry. And I drank a glass of your wine. But what have you been drawing?'

'It's *Violet in the Evening*.' He handed her the sketchbook.

There, in charcoal on thick textured paper, he'd drawn a sublimely accurate sketch of Violet slumbering on the chaise. The crook of her elbow looked divine, the tilt of her chin exquisite. She gazed at, incredulous and speechless.

Jack stood up and took the sketchbook from her and tossed it to the floor. Taking her hand, he raised it swiftly to his lips. She inhaled, letting the moment flood over her, feeling utterly safe. Trusting him with her life. She felt a sudden pulsing, a heaviness in her belly. Her lips trembled into a glorious smile.

Jack beamed at her, confident and supremely happy.

'Wait a moment while I wrap *Violet in the Daytime*... your painting,' he said.

'Oh, of course,' she said, struggling to break out of the spell they had both cast, wanting it to continue. 'And you must tell me the price. How much do I owe you?'

He glanced at her, laughing. 'Oh, Violet, you know you don't have to keep pretending. I told you before, in the park. It is my gift to you.'

Violet watched, fascinated by him, even as he wrapped the canvas in brown paper, tying it securely with string to make a little handle for her.

'Perfect,' he said.

She accepted the painting, intensely aware of him, of the bond linking the space between them, in that sharp, decisive instant. It felt like a promise made physical and Violet did not want to leave his side. She saw a look of recognition, an understanding, flash over his features.

'Yes,' she said. 'It's perfect.'

* * *

Violet arrived back at Montagu Square within half an hour. The hansom Mrs Ellis efficiently hailed for her had squeezed itself over the railway bridge next to a coal cart before bowling speedily around the park and down to Fitzrovia. And she hadn't long been upstairs in her room when her mother knocked on her door.

'Where on earth have you been 'til this time? It's getting dark. And it is going to pour down. I said to Muriel, "thank goodness she had the sense to take a cab".'

'I have been to Camden. I have been buying art,' Violet said, feeling brave and rather proud.

'Buying art? Have you indeed? *Camden?*'

'Yes, Mother, and I know you will say that it is the wrong side of the tracks.'

'I don't know where Camden is and it sounds like I shouldn't want to.' Violet's mother gave an indifferent glance at the brown-paper wrapped painting, propped against the bed. 'You will have to hide it away in your room when we get back home. You know how particular your father is about this sort of thing. In any case, how is it you had the money to buy this painting? We must be giving you far too much allowance.'

'It was a gift, Mother.'

'A gift! You said that you were *buying* art. I thought these artist types needed all the money they could get their hands on.'

Annoyed, Violet turned to her mirror and began to unpin her hair, noticing in her reflection a secret confident glimmer around her eyes.

'You're all flushed and in a daydream, Violet,' her mother pressed on. 'Who is this artist, anyway?'

Downstairs, the first gong sounded for dinner.

'You better tell us over dinner. Hurry up, dear. You need to change, you have the dust of the streets on your cheeks. And we can't keep Cook waiting.'

Violet felt her spirits plummet. Another evening of course after course of extravagant dishes, *amuse-bouches*, palate cleansers, and other culinary experiments lay ahead of her. Last night, they'd had a medley of wobbling blancmanges for pudding, and she felt sure Muriel's cook simply liked to show off and the thought of it made her weary. In so many ways, this world of Muriel's, and marginally of her mother's, had no place for her.

Violet's mother squinted through the lamplight at her face.

'I must say, dear, you're looking very vexed,' she said. 'Have you seen the evening paper too?'

'No, Mother, I haven't,' Violet exhaled in exasperation.

How could she have done? She had been too busy enjoying Jack's company, the soothing freedom of being immersed in his space, his life, even for a snatched afternoon, to have bought herself the *Evening Mail*.

'Well, it is grave news, I'm afraid,' she said. 'Your father predicted it, so he will be pleased with himself when he gets *The Times* tomorrow morning. But I know what he will say – let the French slug it out.'

'What on earth do you mean, Mother?' Violet asked.

'The Germans are mobilising their troops along the Belgian border. It looks like war.' She sounded exultant. 'Just as your father said they would.'

12

IN THE LANGUAGE OF FLOWERS: BLUSH ROSE, IF YOU LOVE ME, YOU WILL FIND IT OUT

Next morning, amid a flurry of worrying news and rumour and much turning of newspaper pages, Violet's mother remembered the painting.

'I want, Violet, to see exactly what this presumptuous... *person* has seen fit to give you.'

Violet fetched the painting. As she began to untie Jack's complicated knots in the string, and fold away the brown paper, she felt as if she peeled away a layer of her own skin. She propped the canvas on the table and her mother and aunt stood side by side, cocking their heads in unison, taking a step back to view it. Violet busied herself with balling up the string, the brown paper crackled loudly as she folded it, waiting for one of them to speak.

'My goodness,' cried Muriel. 'Violet, how lovely!'

Violet's mother, with guarded eyes, said, 'Well, it's a good likeness, I suppose in that he has got the colour of your hair, but why aren't you standing still? Why is it all blurred?'

Violet began to explain about Jack's technique, how he wanted to develop Impressionism with more realism, but her mother interrupted. 'You weren't posing in his studio were you? I have heard about ladies like that!'

Muriel laughed mischievously. 'Eleanor, no, she wasn't in his studio.

She's in Queen Mary's Garden. Look at all the roses. A very respectable public place. Nothing untoward could possibly have happened.'

Her mother peered at the corner of the painting at Jack's signature. 'Who is this artist, then – anyone I would know?'

Violet wanted to say, *Of course not, Mother, because like Papa, you don't know anything about art.*

'Jack Fairling,' she said, hearing the pride in her voice. 'He hopes to be accepted into the Camden Group soon.'

'Is that so,' her mother muttered, not about to admit that she didn't know the Camden Group.

'And, what's more,' Violet braced herself and took a daring leap, 'I'd very much like to invite him here for tea.'

Her mother bristled, 'Well, really...'

But Muriel beamed, delighted. 'Any excuse for a social occasion,' she said. 'I've never met a proper artist before. We can praise him on his enchanting work, can't we, Eleanor?'

Violet's mother forced a smile.

'I say, Violet,' said Muriel, 'do you have his card?'

'Of course I do,' Violet beamed back, feeling her confidence surge. For hadn't her friendship with Jack so far had been built on a little cheekiness and a lot of bravery?

'Then I will send Smithson over with mine straight away.'

* * *

Two days later, as the clock struck three, Violet followed Smithson along the gloomy hallway, with its black and white floor and pots of ferns, as she went to answer the door. She knew that she ought to be sitting upstairs in the drawing room ready to receive him like a proper lady would, but simply could not help herself.

She waited, bubbling with excitement, convinced she would laugh out loud with pleasure as the housemaid took Jack's hat in silence and set it on the coat hook. She gave Violet one of her old-fashioned looks and slipped away down the backstairs.

Jack stepped forward, his hand offered in greeting. Violet clutched it with both her own, feeling greedy and childish, and Jack raised her hands to his mouth, a jubilant flash in his eyes as he kissed them. A moment of understanding, exquisite and unspoken.

'Come with me,' Violet said.

A tremor of shyness caught at her as she led him up the stairs, across Muriel's back drawing room and out through the French windows. Tea had been laid on the little ironwork table on the patch of lawn surrounded by high, sun-warmed brick walls. Her mother and aunt sat pretending to chat, with their eyes slanting towards the house. Behind them grew a bank of roses, the colour of Violet's blushing cheeks and giving off a spicy scent and the vibrating sound of bees. How alike her mother and aunt looked, Violet thought, sitting there in their high-necked blouses with leg o' mutton sleeves and large hats suitable for afternoon tea. Both had the same bearing, hands folded on laps, a tilt of the chin. Each of them tapping a finger or two as they spoke. Physically alike, yes, but perplexingly different in many other ways.

Muriel stood up and gave a wide smile. She exclaimed, 'So this is the famous Jack Fairling.'

'Hardly, madam,' Jack laughed and shook her hand as Violet introduced her aunt and her mother.

'Lovely day,' her mother said, tilting her head to look at Jack and cast her eyes up and down. 'How did you get here, Mr Fairling?'

'Oh, I walked,' he said, sitting at the table. His smiled curved his newly clipped beard. His shirt looked crisp, and he wore his usual peacock-blue waistcoat. 'Fought my way through the crowds in Regent's Park and along by Baker Street. All the Union Jacks are out, brass bands, the lot. The Royal Fusiliers were causing all the mayhem, marching along from St Pancras.'

'They've all gone a bit mad, a bit too jubilant in the face of such disturbing news,' said Violet lifting the teapot. 'It's become a celebration.'

'A chance for the Empire to flex its muscles again,' Jack said. 'It's been a good few years since the last African war.'

'Are the King and Queen going to appear on the balcony, I wonder?' mused Muriel. 'Sugar, Mr Fairling?'

Violet helped her aunt with the tea, grateful to be busy with something while the conversation span around in search of a comfortable level.

'And what will you do, Mr Fairling?' Violet's mother asked.

'You mean in reference to taking the King's shilling, madam? I'm not sure yet. They are sending the BEF to France. They're the professional soldiers. I think we should leave it to them.'

'Is that what you think? Oh, of course you're an artist. And what can an artist do?'

Violet gave a horrified gasp. Tried to disguise it as a cough. But Jack's face appeared as open and peaceful as ever. He smiled warmly as he stirred his tea, tapped his teaspoon on the rim.

'I read an article in the *Daily Mirror* this morning, saying that the army needed medics, tradesmen and motorcyclists and I thought, why not artists too?'

Violet looked at him in alarm. Jack joining up had not crossed her mind.

Her mother asked, 'You read the *Daily Mirror*, Mr Fairling?'

'Actually, it is my landlady's copy. My expenses don't always run to the newspaper.'

'It's all talk,' Muriel broke in. 'Something and nothing. I'll read the cards later, see what they have in store for us. But I must say, I did them last week and I didn't see this coming.' Everyone laughed then and sat back in their chairs, pursing their lips over steaming cups, while Violet handed out saffron buns.

Muriel said, 'Violet spent her morning down in the kitchen, bothering Cook and baking for you. A little taste of Cornwall. I expect there was flour everywhere.'

'This one's perfect,' Jack said, biting into it and licking the end of his finger. Violet felt sure she'd seen him give her a ghost of a wink. 'Your own recipe?'

Violet shook her head, her joy simmering again. 'Mrs Beeton's, of course.' She struggled to look away from him, but she must engage with her mother and aunt.

'Perhaps, Mr Fairling,' her mother persisted, putting her cup down, 'you'll go back to your home in Kent? Join a local regiment? Of course, Violet's father will probably make noises about joining up.'

'Oh, Mother,' Violet said. 'Papa is far too old, surely?'

'But they may well need his services. He's a doctor, you know, Violet's father,' her mother said to Jack.

He nodded. 'So, Violet tells me. She has told me a great deal about her home in Cornwall. In a way, our upbringings have not been dissimilar.'

Her mother leant forward. 'You also went to private school?'

'Indeed, I did, madam. In Canterbury.'

This seemed to satisfy her, and she stopped looking like she had a nasty taste in her mouth. Conversation tinkled around schooling and the comparative joys of the Kent and the Cornish countryside and those counties' boundaries with the sea.

'Well, Violet, my dear,' her mother said. 'I can tell that you are missing the cove and the pinewoods. Lovely Old Trellick. We live a stone's throw from the sea, Mr Fairling. And we can hear the waves from our house.'

'No, we can't, Mother,' Violet said.

'Really, dear...? Well, isn't that extraordinary? I thought we could.' She fished out her pocket watch. 'In any case, we should really start packing our trunks this evening, for the train leaves quite early tomorrow.'

Jack's surprised gaze darted around the table, ending with Violet. She saw the blunt question in his eyes, and she nodded.

'Mother, I have decided to stay here, if Aunt Muriel doesn't mind. I do miss home but—'

Muriel clapped her hands. 'Oh, joy! Violet, you are most welcome.' She looked cheekily towards Jack. 'Most welcome indeed. You are a delight to have around. If you can spare her, Eleanor, I'd love her to stay, even for a short while.'

Violet's mother glanced from her to Muriel and back again. 'What your father will say is another matter.'

'Papa won't mind,' she said breezily, already knowing that her aunt will present her case to him most effectively. 'If you'll excuse me a moment...'

On her way upstairs to the water closet, she paused at the landing window and glanced out to see Muriel pouring more tea for Jack. She looked thoroughly delighted with him, insisting he have another bun. Her mother, meanwhile, settled herself back with a scrutinising stare. And yet, in that instance, Jack engaged both women, and they laughed.

Violet folded her arms around her middle to contain her elation. 'Well done, Jack Fairling,' she whispered to herself. 'Well done.'

She went back down to the garden feeling refreshed and joyous but, as she drew nearer, heard her mother say, '...broken love affair with Mr Penruth. An important local landowner, you know. All very shocking. All very sad.'

Jack stirred his tea, his face impassive and civil.

Violet inhaled in fury, and her aunt threw a warning look at her.

'Really, Eleanor. That's all water under the bridge now.' Muriel forced a laugh. 'What young lady doesn't have a frisson like that at an early age? I must say, I can barely remember my first flush.'

'I'm sure Mr Fairling appreciates knowing a little more about Violet,' her mother said.

Jack cleared his throat, 'Indeed. I look forward to learning more of what Violet wishes to tell me.'

Violet gazed at him, capturing his smile, returning his. She knew, in that bright moment, while the rest of the world around them did battle with itself or faded away, that she didn't want to go anywhere without him.

Muriel, seeing the look between them, said, 'Goodness, Eleanor, can you hear the band? The wind must be coming in this direction. Must be in the park bandstand.'

Segments of a bass *oom-pah* reached them like distant retorts as the band played on.

'Sounds like the regimental brass are in full swing again,' said her mother.

'I am finding it hard to accept that they sound so *festive*,' Violet said, shuddering, 'when it's war.'

'How everything can change in the space of a few weeks,' Jack said, planting his cup back on its saucer. He caught Violet's eye, his smile quenching her fear.

'The music is to fire them all up,' said her mother. 'They'll be joining up in droves.'

'Well, it will be quite a spectacle,' said Muriel. 'Why don't you two young people walk over to the park, pay your respects to our fighting men? After all, Mr Fairling, it is on your way home.'

* * *

The good folk of Marylebone, St Pancras and Camden picnicked on blankets, drank beer from bottles, and brandished Union Jacks, while the City of London Regiment Band played an upbeat 'Land of Hope and Glory', uniforms, buttons and colours brilliant in the sunshine. Couples waved from horse-drawn carriages trotting by and cheers and applause rose up as the music finished.

'Here we are,' said Jack, as they walked around the boating lake to avoid the crowds. 'Feeling the full effect of imperialist propaganda.'

'Thank you for coming to tea, Jack, and enduring the ordeal. I'm sorry my mother was so—'

'Forthright?' Jack laughed. 'She cares, that's what it is. She wants the best for you, like any mother would. She wants to make sure that I...' he paused, adjusting his smile '...that I possibly – dare I say it, Violet? – am the best for you.'

Violet linked her arm through his, a sign of her consent. He closed his hand over hers, pressing it to his sleeve, and they continued to stroll, falling naturally in step. The busy park became a blur while she savoured the contentment of walking with Jack. But, it felt that as soon as she forgot, she remembered, and the difficult situation with Weston, and her mother's revelation, returned to darken the moment.

'Jack, I want to say that I would have told you about Mr Penruth,' she said. 'I wanted to tell you myself. It was a mistake. A relationship I did not want. We were wholly unsuitable. I didn't like him very much, in all honesty. It really was not suitable at all. But you can see what my mother is like...'

'Again,' he said, and pulled her to a stop in the middle of the path, 'your mother.'

He looked at her, his eyes flicking over her features as if following a familiar map.

'I felt surprised when she blurted it out,' he said. 'I may not be as brilliantly educated as she might have expected or from the right background, but I know how to have polite conversation around a tea table. Thank God for Aunt Muriel.'

'Yes, thank God,' Violet uttered.

'But you do look awfully sad,' Jack said.

Violet sighed, feeling the complications of the past few months chafing in her mind.

'I think it's the news today. War declared and all this jubilation.' She gestured to the people, the picnickers, the band having a well-earned cup of tea. 'It's very unsettling. Come, let's walk.'

They reached the newspaper boy who'd come into the park to take advantage of the crowds. The headline on his sandwich board read:

Reservists & Territorials Galvanised for Action!

And the second:

German Advance on Paris

Jack bought a copy, rolled it up, tucked it under his arm and they strolled on. They reached the rose garden, filled with overblown August roses, and Violet stopped to smell a fading flower.

'Here I am again,' she smiled, her mood lifting. *'Violet in the Daytime.'*

'And this time, you have a different expression on your face.' Jack plucked the rose and handed it to her. 'That's better.' He touched her cheek, his expression hopeful and trusting. 'Not angry, like the first time with your gorgeous, trapped inferno as you sprang up from the seat and blazed off through the roses. Or when you caught me, later, having painted you. You're smiling now, Violet, but you still look troubled. I want you to know that I never want to see that look on your face again. I want to paint it out...'

He grasped both of her hands, and Violet knew this gesture would be the one that would always knock at her heart. She whispered his name and gasped in shock as he sank before her onto his knee.

'Miss Violet Prideaux, I have known you such a short time, but I think we both know, don't we? I think we do.'

Joy rose through her, and her mouth felt full of all the heavenly words that she wanted to say, if only she could contain herself.

'Violet, will you do me the greatest honour... will you?' Jack's face looked open, serious and determined. He reached to touch his fingertips to her chin and her cheek, her elbow, her shoulder, caressing her gently, thoughtfully. 'Will you marry me?'

* * *

When she got back to Montagu Square, her mother's trunk waited in the hall, packed and labelled. Violet glided straight past it and up the stairs, clasping the rose that Jack had plucked for her. But, as she cradled it in her palm, the petals began to loosen and fall from its overripe heart. No matter, she decided. She would keep it safe between the pages of the heaviest book she could find in her room. And nothing could stop her. This moment, her life was beginning.

She hurried past the drawing room on the first landing, but heard her mother's shrill call from inside.

'Is that you, Violet?'

She stopped, wondering who else her mother thought it might be, and poked her head around the doorway. The two ladies sat either side of the fireplace sipping their inevitable sherries.

'You were a long time,' her mother said.

'We got caught up in the crowds. There's lots of people about. Quite an atmosphere.'

'Well, that settles it for me,' her mother said, 'With this talk of war, and soldiers filling the streets and the parks, and who knows where else, you really should come home with me. You know your Papa would not like to waste your train ticket. And I didn't appreciate you saying you wouldn't come back with me like that, in front of a guest I've only just met.'

'Jack understood,' Violet said.

'Jack did, did he?'

Violet gave her aunt a look of appeal.

Muriel set down her sherry glass. 'I think, Eleanor, the way things are going, these soldiers will disappear across the Channel in a matter of days. London will be perfectly safe. In any case, Violet and I will use the gig.'

Her mother shuffled in her chair, flexing her shoulders. She lifted the decanter and added a splash of sherry to her half-full glass.

Violet stood in the centre of her aunt's fine Turkish rug, feeling exposed but firm with the new courage that meeting Jack had ignited in her. And, spurred on by her aunt's support, she said, 'Mother, Aunt Muriel, I have something I have to tell you.'

Her mother eyed her warily, taking tiny sips, her mouth not leaving the rim of the glass, while Muriel seemed to find it difficult to keep a straight face.

Violet sat on the fireside stool like a child might, her head suitably lower than her mother's, holding the bruised rose on her lap. 'The truth of the matter is that Jack and I wish to be married.'

Her mother cried out, patting a handkerchief to her chin to catch a dribble of sherry.

'What in heaven's name—?' she uttered. 'You hardly know him!'

'Mother, I hardly knew Weston Penruth but that didn't seem to bother you.'

'That is an entirely different matter. We know the *family*. They are the Penruths for goodness' sake. Your father's family, the Prideauxs of old, certainly have known them since time immemorial. That match had pretty much been ordained for years, ever since you were eight years old.'

'You mean when Weston Penruth took it on himself to pay my school fees?'

'Really, Violet, that is an entirely different matter!' Her mother's eyes widened. She gave a quick embarrassed glance at her sister.

'In all truth, Mother,' Violet said carefully, 'I don't think it is.'

'But this man – this Jack Fairling, this *artist* – is a stranger.'

'But Jack is so very different.' Having to compare Jack to Weston turned Violet's stomach. She did not wish to mention them together in the same breath ever again. 'Mother, I know, it has all been very quick, yes, I understand that, but we have reached the stage where—'

'*Quick?* I'd say.' Her mother's sarcasm seemed to make her increase in size. 'You've been flattered and seduced by him painting your portrait. He is a nice enough man, I'm sure, but he is totally unsuitable for you. He hasn't a bean. Your father will be furious. As am I. Now cut out all this nonsense, throw that dead flower away and go upstairs and pack.'

'Oh, Eleanor, really.' Muriel's calm tone tempered the shrill exchange. 'Look at the girl. Look how happy she is... well, how happy she was when she walked into the room, holding that lovely flower. Are you all right, dear? Did he propose in the park? Oh, how wonderful.'

'Not wonderful,' her mother snapped. 'Not wonderful in any shape or form. I give up. Is this just a ruse, Violet, to get back at Weston now that he's with your best friend?'

Violet swallowed hard, anger snapping inside her head. 'That has nothing to do with it. I don't wish to speak of that man ever again. As for Claudia, I will make amends with her, even if there are no amends to be made.' Her mouth twisted with sorrow.

'Have you not heard from her, dear?' Aunt Muriel asked.

Violet shook her head. 'I've written twice now...'

'Some friends, however dear, do slip away sometimes,' her aunt said, kindly.

'A fact of life,' said her mother, 'as is your need to do as your parents request, my girl.'

Violet ignored her mother's imperious comment.

'I miss her,' she said. 'I wish I could see her. Find out from her what has been going on.'

'You can, as soon as you come home with me,' said her mother, verging a little more on the kind side. 'Just put all this silliness aside, Violet. What this is with Jack Fairling is simply a romance, a passing fancy. Coming to the city has turned your head, as well it might. Come back home with me and all will be well. Think how long it's been since you saw Papa and Jess.'

Violet wrung her hands together. Of *course* Jess – she'd have to make arrangements for him to travel up to London. Or she could go back and fetch him herself. How he would love the park. She could see him settled by the hearth in Jack's studio. She looked her mother full in the face.

'I wish to stay here and marry Jack. We don't see the point in waiting.'

'What, and live in *Camden*?'

'We haven't decided on that yet,' Violet uttered, her head pounding. 'One thing at a time.'

'Well, I am going home tomorrow, whether you come with me or not. And, if there is to be a wedding, your father and I won't be there. Don't expect a telegram.'

Muriel turned on her sister. 'Eleanor, you don't mean that. You will regret saying that, and feel bad later, so stop it now.'

Violet's fingertips shook as she wiped her eyes.

'Please listen to me, Mother. I love him.' Her tears scalded her cheeks. 'That is the easiest, truest thing I have ever said in my life.'

Her mother's lip curled, her features drooped.

'What about Weston? We never did get to the bottom of it.'

'Come now, Eleanor,' Muriel sighed.

'I didn't love him,' Violet glanced at her aunt and back to her mother. 'What made you think I did? He clearly did not love me.'

'Well, if it wasn't for Claudia...'

'She has nothing to do with it.'

'But you had such a *chance*,' said her mother. 'Such a chance that any girl would dream of.'

'You mean *you* had a chance,' Violet said.

Her mother recoiled, pressed her handkerchief to her lips. 'I am your mother and I want the best for you. I want you, Violet, to have the chance of a *life*.'

Violet's sob sounded like a scream. 'But the only life I want, Mother, is my own.'

13

'...the bee has quit the clover,
   And your English summer's done.'

— RUDYARD KIPLING

St Marylebone Parish Church looked nothing like the stocky granite churches tucked away in Cornish villages. It resembled a classical temple, imposing and grand, presiding over the Marylebone Road and the mansion-lined avenue that led up to the park.

Violet stepped down from Muriel's gig, driven through traffic and parked with expertise by William, and took her aunt's arm. The air felt glorious – bright and breezy and sparkling with gold: perfect weather for a September wedding. And, indeed, for her birthday. Violet remembered the tenuous plans Weston had made in the ballroom at Charlecote. Such postering and insincerity; his shadow reached her, even now, as she stood beneath the London plane tree at the bottom of the church steps.

She heard a taxi draw up. A well-dressed couple emerged, and in that moment, Violet believed her parents had arrived, fresh from Paddington, to join her and Jack on their wedding day. But the people were strangers, arriving early for another ceremony. As Muriel had commented only the other day: 'Weddings are becoming more frequent and hastier these days, Violet, like yours. War does that to people. I had wanted to invite the Welsteads,' she'd said, 'among many of my other friends, but it was such short notice. They're at sixes and sevens anyway. Their son Sebastian – remember him? – has just enlisted.'

Violet glanced at the doorway where the vicar waited. He gestured, encouraging her. So, with one last backward glance, she took Muriel's arm.

'Not the society wedding I would have dreamt for you,' her aunt said in her ear as they walked up the steps.

Violet whispered, 'I can't tell you how relieved I am that it is not.'

Muriel squeezed her arm. 'I know, dear, I know.'

She felt very small inside the church, sensed an intense, waiting hush, as if the departed in the vaults beneath were listening. The organist struck up and she walked with Muriel, the space around her too immense to absorb, her eyes hooked on the end of the aisle where Jack waited. The scent of her bouquet, a motley assortment gathered from Muriel's garden that morning, intensified in the cool interior. Tight cream roses, a tangle of honeysuckle and a snatch of leggy poppies. Poor things, thought Violet, they'll be dead before the day is over.

Sunlight gleamed through windows behind the altar, illuminating the small congregation: some friends of Muriel's, including the Emsworthys of Dorset Street, plus Smithson and Mrs Ellis as witnesses. And there Jack stood waiting for her, an almost-silhouette in the beams of light and beside him an older man, his father she assumed, who'd travelled up from Canterbury the night before. Jack's father smiled at Violet, the spark in his eye matching Jack's, giving her a hint of how Jack would look in later years. And Jack took a step towards her, as if he could not wait for her to arrive. She quickened her pace, feeling her life opening up like a great road she longed to travel. But no Mother and Papa, and no Claudia here to witness it.

Violet's tears fell unchecked as she took her place next to Jack, slipped her hand into his. The organ music subsided. Briefly and solemnly, amid the perfume of the roses and honeysuckle clutched in Violet's trembling hands, the vicar married them.

* * *

The chamber music from the lobby followed Violet and Jack up the staircase of the St Pancras Midland Grand Hotel. Delicate notes drifted around them as they walked on deep carpet between terracotta-brick pillars colonised with flowers and leaves rising to the ecclesiastical ceiling. Every inch of the panelled walls was papered with ordered and gilded patterns, the corridors wide enough, as Muriel had mentioned, to allow ladies in crinolines to walk side by side in the old days.

Shutting their bedroom door muffled the music, but fragments lingered in Violet's mind.

'Do you think Aunt Muriel laid on the quartet especially for us?' laughed Jack, as he loosened his tie and snapped the catches on his suitcase.

'I wouldn't put it past her,' Violet said.

She turned up the lamp near the window, relishing the moment now that they were alone, at last. Pulling aside the tapestry curtains she saw the St Pancras platforms stretching away in a haze of gaslight. Beyond the station canopy, the evening darkness looked velvety.

'Isn't the hotel beautiful? So generous of Aunt Muriel to treat us to our wedding breakfast here, and to the room too,' she said. 'What a lovely surprise.'

'She thinks the world of you, Violet,' Jack said. He came over to gather her in his arms. 'As indeed do I.' He peered out of the window. 'Ah, we're on the railway side. It's late and the last trains will be leaving soon. Should be quieter during the night than if we were facing the main road.' He glanced at Violet. 'You're quite overwhelmed, aren't you?'

'I think I'm entitled to be,' she smiled.

They sat together on the cushioned window seat, and she felt filled to the brim with a solid sense of calm.

'I expect you'd like to sketch the staircase,' she said. 'I've never seen anything like it.'

'Certainly, if there is time,' he said, leaning to kiss her. 'But admittedly there are other things on my mind.'

Desire shot through her body but, by strange instinct, she pulled away. Jack smiled kindly, held her gently, whispering that it was all right.

'Let's have champagne,' he said and went over to the dressing table where a bottle perspired in a deep bucket of ice. 'Now, this treat is from my father.'

'What a pleasure it was to meet him,' Violet said, wondering why she'd withdrawn from Jack like that, hoping it had been subtle enough for him not to mull over.

Jack twisted the cork out of the bottle and poured two coupes. 'He's staying at my studio tonight. I do hope he's comfortable there. Perhaps we can have lunch with him tomorrow? Would you mind?'

'Of course not. I hope Mrs Ellis takes care of him and gives him some breakfast.'

'I'm sure she will.' Jack laughed, handing her a glass. 'I think she was giving him the glad eye over the table downstairs. Poor Father. He won't know what's hit him.'

'Funny you should say that, but I thought Aunt Muriel took quite a shine to him,' Violet giggled.

'Perhaps that's part of the peril of being an eligible widower.'

They laughed, chinked glasses and sipped.

The champagne tasted delicious, but Violet's strange, unsettled feeling returned. She felt distracted, as if she could not wholly concentrate on Jack.

'Ah, my bouquet,' she said. 'I wonder if I should have it put in water.'

She went over to the dressing table, picked it up and as crinkled petals scattered over the surface, she understood what still lay on her mind. Her parents' absence and Claudia's silence.

'I must choose the best flower heads for pressing,' she said, dropping the petals into the waste-paper bin. 'I think today of all days must command a double page in the *Flower Book*. Or even more...'

'Are you quite all right?' Jack asked, sensing a change in her voice. He gazed at her. 'I think I know... you're thinking of your parents, Violet. Try not to dwell on it. Don't let it spoil the day for you.'

'I'm sorry, I will shake it off. Everything else has been so wonderful. Everyone... you...' She hesitated. 'But is it simple spite on my mother's part? I just don't understand.'

Jack sighed and refilled his glass. She hated to see the troubled look on his face.

'I wonder,' he said, 'if I have simply not come up to their expectations.'

'Oh no, surely...'

'You heard her, Violet. I did wonder at her championing Mr Penruth in the way she did when I met her. It seemed so pointed.'

'But *you* mean the world to me. Everything.' Tears singed her eyes. 'Oh, dash it. I don't want to cry.'

'You may cry, my darling,' he said gently, 'if you wish to.'

Jack came over to her and held her like he might a child. To comfort and support. He placed a light kiss on her forehead.

She squeezed her eyes shut, wondering how it could be that Weston and all the bad feelings he invoked still squatted in her mind. She willed the long shadow he cast to vanish like the bubbles in her champagne. But how could she forget that he now courted Claudia? And she knew it could not be jealousy, simply bewilderment. And it remained, like a nasty taste in her mouth. Staying in the safety of Jack's arms, she reached for her champagne, sipped to wash the feeling away, passed Jack's glass to him. She rested her head on his shoulder.

'Some might say we have swept each other off our feet. You're still in shock, I suppose. I know I am.' Jack gently rocked her, speaking softly into her hair. 'But I will keep us both standing upright. We will not fall at this or any hurdle. This could not feel more real and right to me. Being here with you. Mrs Violet Fairling.'

They chinked glasses again.

'I will work out a way to have your parents like me and accept me. At least we have Aunt Muriel on our side. We should arrange a visit soon. You want to collect Jess, don't you?'

'Yes, yes,' she said, with renewed conviction. 'We've not had a chance to make proper plans yet, about where we might settle, in all this whirlwind.'

'I must say, living in Cornwall is very appealing to me... But in the meantime...' Jack took her hand and led her back to the window seat. 'Sketching that staircase is the last thing on my mind.' He gently brushed her cheek with his thumb. 'Because now I want to sketch you.'

Violet nodded with pleasure and settled back on the window seat with the luxurious cushions and the curtain forming a fantastical backdrop behind her. The lamplight and the tickle of champagne, the beauty of the room and Jack at work sitting cross-legged on the bed, his face transformed with concentration, unravelled her confusion, and allowed her sadness to float away.

'When have I ever known you not to have your sketchbook and pencil with you?' she mused playfully. 'Even on our wedding night.'

'It's like you and your *Flower Book*. Hush now, I'm doing your mouth.'

'Just let me get even more comfy,' she said.

She lifted her feet out of her soft shoes and curled her knees under, rearranging her wedding dress around her. The delicate grey crêpe, pleated over the bodice and neat at her waist, looked sublime and she inwardly thanked Aunt Muriel and her seamstress again. She turned her hand so that her ring – once belonging to Jack's mother – shone in the light.

'Jack Fairling,' she said, 'I don't think I have ever felt this happy.'

'If you are going to keep talking, Mrs Fairling...'

Jack put his sketchbook down and came over to her, admiring her, his gaze opaque with devotion. He lay a sweet kiss on her lips and touched the shoulder of her dress, his fingertips tracing up to her throat. Brushing her hairline, he grasped the tiny buttons under the collar and undid them. Longing to touch him, Violet ran her hands up his arms. She wanted him to kiss her again, to hold her and let her show him how she loved him. That all the hesitation and bad feeling sat firmly in the past. Jack eased her dress over her shoulders so that the fine fabric pooled in her lap.

'Stay still,' he murmured.

'How can I?' she whispered.

He went back to the bed, picked up his pencil and began to dash it lightly over the page.

Violet felt tiny shocks of yearning throughout her body.

'Jack...' she pleaded.

He put his pencil away and knelt in front of her. He tugged her chemise straps down and pressed his face into her naked shoulder.

'I will finish the sketch in the morning.'

14

IN THE LANGUAGE OF FLOWERS: CHRYSANTHEMUM, CHEERFULNESS UNDER ADVERSITY

The first trains woke her, steaming and sighing below on the platforms, and she turned in the luxurious warmth of the bed, marvelling that Jack lay beside her in such unfamiliar and miraculous intimacy. How effortlessly they had made love with each other and fallen asleep together. How easy, and right, it felt to share his bed.

Violet slipped out of the covers and went to the window seat, peered around the curtain. The expanse of St Pancras Station lay before her, gradually waking as the daylight grew. Trains pulled in, and passengers spilled out. A tide of soldiers, all khaki and kitbags, disgorging from every carriage and mustering under the barking orders of sergeant majors holding handfuls of lists. She lost count of them, these fresh-faced, bleary eyed, eager young men.

'It's a lot of effort to go into for a skirmish in Belgium,' Jack's father had said at dinner the night before, spotting a group of soldiers through the hotel restaurant windows being commandeered by an officer. 'It seems hardly worth it. This lot will go and come back before we can say Jack Robinson.'

Smiling as she remembered her father-in-law's turn of phrase, she glanced back at her sleeping husband. She saw the likeness to his father, and how gracefully Jack will age. And yet, there, sleeping still on their first morning together, he looked boyish and serene. He smiled, even in sleep. Last night, it seemed, had transformed them both.

Violet noticed on each bedside table the flowers left by the maid who'd made up their room before their arrival – two little vases of dahlias, zinnias and golden chrysanthemums. Next to her fading bouquet, the end-of-summer flowers had a simplicity, and a confidence that she found growing inside her. One for the *Flower Book*, she decided and went over to cut a perfect chrysanthemum head. Jack stirred in the bed, reached a warm hand out to her.

'Good morning,' she said, returning the squeeze of his fingers.

He kept hold of her hand thoughtfully running his thumb over her palm, tugged her down to sit with him on the bed, snug in the curve of his body.

'I have thought of the way to make your parents accept me and be proud of me,' he said, sounding gravelly with sleep.

'You're still thinking about that?' she said.

'But of course. I can't bear that things are frosty between you. And it is purely down to me.'

Violet turned to him. 'Oh really, Jack, you can't take all of that on yourself. There are reasons, *many* reasons – my mother, she can be difficult. I think sometimes, deep down she does not feel good enough and so tries to elevate herself by... frankly, misbehaving. She is envious of Muriel's life, even though Muriel lost Uncle Jeff. And Papa does not put his foot down with her. Plus, she is a bit of an awful snob.'

'A bit?'

They laughed.

'Well, Jack,' she said, toying with the cut flower head. 'We shall make a plan. For the time being, we can stay with Aunt Muriel, she is more than happy to have us, while we decide. Either Camden, or we find a place to live in Cornwall. Somewhere on the south coast, near enough to my parents so we can start mending everything that has happened. We can make our own home. And with Jess of course. I need him with me, whether it's London or Cornwall.'

'Yes, my darling, but—'

'And you can set up your studio down there. Remember the light, Jack? The beautiful Cornish light.'

He waited, and Violet heard the clamour from the station below increasing by the second.

'We will do all of those things, Violet,' he said, 'but there is something more that I can, and must, do myself to build your parents' trust and approval of me.'

He turned his head towards the window, and she understood immediately. Her realisation like a cold stone inside her.

'Jack, you shouldn't have to prove yourself...' she uttered. 'Not, not like that.'

'I do, because you are worth it. What your mother said to me, when we had tea at Muriel's, the way she looked at me has stayed with me. Has really bothered me. I should elevate myself to your level, I should—'

Violet began, 'Jack, really, I—'

'I am going to volunteer,' he said, bluntly. 'I'm going to head to the London Regiment barracks this morning and enlist. I want to do it for us, for you.'

A snap of terror jolted Violet's stomach. He can't go, she won't let him. He simply can't go.

'For me?' she cried, hauling herself up from the bed. 'Don't do it for me!'

He caught her, drew her gently back down encircling her in his arms.

'Stop shaking, darling, stop now. Oh God, you're trembling.' He pressed his lips into her hair. 'A few months across the Channel, that's all,' he said, quietly, cautiously, 'and then we can start our life. Move back to Cornwall. Find our perfect home. Our life can begin.'

In dismayed rebellious silence, she shook her head.

'You're leaving me already? We've not been married five minutes.' She let out a dry laugh. 'And haven't you heard, army boots have a dreadful reputation.'

'Violet, look at me.' Jack's eyes darkened with sorrow. 'Just think, for us, Christmas in Cornwall. It's something and nothing. That's what they're saying. Will be all over by then. You ask your Aunt Muriel.'

With a slow-burning surge of anger, Violet slowly and deliberately extracted herself from his embrace.

'What does she know?' she muttered. 'She gets it wrong more often than not.'

* * *

The might of the British Army, the efficiency of the London Regiment, had proved far too impressive, enveloping Jack in a straitjacket of procedures and checks, grasping him with open arms. Within days, Jack had received his orders and a fortnight later, they travelled together at dawn by hansom cab from Montagu Square to Paddington Station, Violet curling herself into Jack's scratchy uniform as they jolted over cobbles. The first time she'd seen him in it, she'd cried. He seemed smaller, vulnerable and so very honourable. Quietly, one evening by herself, Violet had tested the rigid army-issue boots with her own hands and felt repulsed.

'Plan our Christmas at Old Trellick,' he said as the cab approached the station. 'Send my regards to your parents and thank them for my telegram wishing me well. And don't forget that my pay will come to you. Think of the difference that will make. I am a poor artist, remember. This will be a windfall like no other.'

'War is a windfall? I had not thought of that.' She hated the sad, bitter trace in her voice. She dipped her head to kiss his fingers, hiding her tears. 'Do you have your sketchbook? And pencils? And the pressed rose from my bouquet?'

He affirmed that he did, patting one of his vast pockets.

But as the cab began to pull up in front of the station, Jack's smile broke with fear.

'Not sure I can bear this.'

'But look at them all. It must be half the London Regiment,' Violet cried, trying to sound encouraging as she stared out the cab window at the concourse heaving with vehicles, people, a strange jubilant noise. 'Good God, there's Sebastian Welstead.'

Jack peered around her. 'He, from the family Aunt Muriel calls on? Very nice too. Looks like he's joined as an officer. Good for him. Leapfrogged all us other fellows.'

He sounded weary as if he did not want to waste their precious time talking about a stranger.

The cab came to a standstill and they both got out, Jack throwing his kitbag with a slam onto the pavement.

'A quick goodbye, it has to be. I can't stand it,' Jack muttered.

They embraced. He ran his hands over her back, pressing her to his body. His epaulettes dug into her face. She clung on as hard as she could.

'Violet, you know I am not heading off straight into battle? I shall be on Salisbury Plain for training. They're not going to send me off completely green.'

Stop trying to fool me and coat it with sugar, she thought, a sob blossoming in her chest. *You are going to war*. The mob of soldiers moved around them, buffeting them; the chaos and whistling, the hearty singing heightening Violet's misery.

The cabbie shouted, 'I can't hold the horses here much longer in this crowd. Madam will have to jump back in, or I will have to go.'

Jack grasped her by the waist and propelled her back into the cab.

She leant out of the door, precariously, stretching as far as she could to keep hold of his hand.

'Come home safe,' she whispered. 'And keep your feet dry.'

He gripped her fingertips, his expression filled with honesty and pain. He did not, could not speak, and she looked at him, recognising misery. Jack shut the door firmly, the cabby brandished his whip, and the cab rolled on, tearing Violet away from him as he disappeared into the mass of khaki bodies.

15

IF THERE'S ICE IN NOVEMBER THAT WILL BEAR A DUCK, THERE'LL BE NOTHING AFTER BUT SLUDGE AND MUCK

Auntie Muriel, of course, always travelled first class on velvet seats in the reserved carriage, a far cry from how Violet arrived in London five months before, rattling along in third class.

They sipped wine and nibbled smoked salmon sandwiches from Muriel's hamper, and by the time they pulled out of Reading, Muriel dozed with *The Times* on her lap. Violet sat back to watch the sodden countryside slip by; saturated fields slumped under a hazy mist, and sheep huddled for shelter. The green of summer had been diluted by rain and wind, turning a dirty brown, but she willed the dull landscape not to dampen her spirits. For they were heading to Cornwall. And Cornwall, even within the dull embrace of November, was home.

Soon after Jack left for Salisbury Plain and the moment Muriel had heard rumours that the enemy would launch Zeppelin air raids, she'd grabbed her Meissen plates and cups and made Smithson box them up in the cellar. Reports came in from the front, a steady trickle of retreat and stalemate. Smithson answered the call for women to work in munitions and handed in her notice. William wanted to do war work too, and asked to be let go. The pony, Muriel decided, would be sold to the milkman. And the daily news turned from frustrating to harsh and depressing, an endless stream of calamity. How different, Violet thought, to the flag-waving and brass bands and the optimism of the summer.

When she plucked up the courage to write to her parents with *her* news – 'must be a wedding-night baby, how wonderful,' Muriel had said – a telegram arrived from her father, with the simple plea:

DEAREST VIOLET. PLEASE COME HOME WHERE YOU BELONG. PAPA.

'He's right. It's time to build bridges,' Muriel had said. 'Sounds like he has put his foot down with your mother, which will be a first.'

'Will you come too?'

'I thought you'd never ask. Something tells me,' Muriel had said, securing the last of her treasures in the cellar, 'it's time to abandon ship and shut up the house for the duration. Let us both leave London, and bury ourselves at Old Trellick, Violet. Get away from all this dull war talk.'

And at least at Old Trellick, Violet thought as she sat in the swaying railway carriage, leaving the city behind, she won't be much further away from Jack in Wiltshire than she had been in London. She allowed a glimmer of a smile, for hope to surface, for the time being at least.

Violet had packed up Jack's sketches and his artist's paraphernalia in a crate to be forwarded to Old Trellick for when he returned home. But *Violet in the Daytime* and *Violet in the Evening*, remained behind wrapped up in Muriel's cellar. And she'd hidden his last painting in the darkest, furthest corner. *Violet in the Night-time* had been sketched on their wedding night while she sat on the window seat at the St Pancras Hotel. She loved it, but could not risk anyone, *anyone* chancing upon it. Their own private joy.

Noting Muriel's sleeping face, Violet reached over for the newspaper. A first-page report told her that the trenches now stretched from the sea to the Swiss border. A dispatch had come in from the town of Ypres by a correspondent who could only pussy-foot around the matter with the meaningless empty headline:

British Repulse Fierce Attack: a brilliant charge by two battalions.

How does he know? Violet thought angrily. How does any of us *know*? As she read, places began to burn with alarming significance into her imagination: Menin Road and Sanctuary Hill. At least, she thought, glancing across the columns, the Germans never made it to Paris.

For her last few weeks in London, Lord Kitchener's piercing eyes had followed her wherever she went. What man could ignore the posters pasted in the grocer's shop window and on the noticeboard in the park. What man could pass it by? They answered the call-up in their thousands. Muriel had heard rumours of a massive backlog of recruits, with Jack, they both surmised, also part of this 'Kitchener's Army'. Ordinary men with soldier-ship thrust upon them. Jack had been promoted to corporal already.

As the train rolled on, Violet turned the page as she knew she must, to the casualty lists. She cast her eyes down lines of type. This dreadful routine had become a habit, Muriel said, as if they were reading the weather report. As weeks passed, hundreds became thousands, the type smaller and smaller to accommodate them all. How the cheering has quietened now, Violet thought bitterly.

And then she saw him:

Pte E.A. Davey, 1st Cornish Yeomen, dead.

She cried out.

Muriel stirred, and woke, blinking.

'Dash it,' she murmured, glancing at the window, 'I thought we might have at least made it to Exeter. Whatever is the matter, dear?'

'It's Claudia's fiancé...'

'Weston Penruth is in the columns?'

'No, no. Eddie.'

Muriel's shoulders slumped. 'Oh my dear...'

'Poor, poor Claudia. And Mrs Davey, and his twin brother and all of them... As if the loss of little Benjamin wasn't bad enough.'

'We're helpless, Violet. What can we do, but be strong for them. Take care of those he's left behind. I must say, when you look at the lists, and imagine what each one of them leaves behind... Let's have a tot more wine to fortify us,' she suggested, rallying, 'and have a look at the births, or the marriages, at least. Come on. Pass me the paper. We must keep our spirits up.'

Violet took her refilled glass from her aunt and set it on the table in front of her where it juddered and shook. She could not face it. And while Muriel scanned the columns, announcing every so often engagements and christenings of people who Violet did not know, she stopped listening.

Eddie. His modest smile came to her. Such a polite and innocent gentleman.

She clenched her fists on her lap. She simply did not understand. Had he joined up in a fit of heartbreak over losing Claudia to Weston Penruth? And what of Claudia? Had she heard? How she must be feeling seemed unfathomable.

'Well, I'll be blowed,' Muriel exhaled, snapping the newspaper wider. She glanced at Violet over the top of it with darkened eyes. 'Oh, my dear.'

'What, Aunt Muriel... what?'

'They're married.'

'Who?'

Violet's mind swung between all the socialites she'd met that summer in the salons of Regent's Park and Fitzrovia.

'Claudia and Weston. It's here. In black and white... pleased to announce... marriage of... solemnised at the Chapel at Charlecote.'

Violet slumped back against her seat.

'Dear God,' she uttered. 'What has she done?'

'Violet dear, this is difficult,' Muriel coaxed gently. 'But you can't possibly be pining for Weston Penruth? He sounded such a rotter.'

'He is. And no, I am not,' Violet struggled to speak, unable to articulate the reason for the shock spiralling through her bones. 'I'm not in the least thinking of myself. It's Claudia. This does not feel right to me, Aunt Muriel. This does not *feel* like Claudia at all.'

* * *

The taxi took them past her friend's old school, through the town, over the Looe estuary, and then back up the hill and into the dark wintry evening.

The wooded valleys around Old Trellick slept under the deepening chill, their secret dips and hollows trailed by ghostly plumes of mist.

Violet's father stood under the lighted porch to greet them.

'Oh, you've brought the damp in with you,' he said. 'Come on, both of you, get to the fire.'

Violet's mother stood in the hallway, very still, her face inscrutable.

'Are you well?' she asked, giving her a cold little hug and unable to resist glancing down at her stomach.

'A rather long journey,' Violet said. 'Caught the earliest train we could. It was dark when we left, dark when we arrived...' She trailed off. 'But in first class with Aunt Muriel... very pleasant, really.'

Jess flashed out from the kitchen with a yap and a scurrying of paws, jumping up to pummel Violet's knees. She knelt to grab him, bring him to her, his nose wet on her neck, joy washing over her. 'You scamp. Look how you've grown.'

'Naughty dog, always jumping up,' said her mother.

'*He* must have missed you, Violet,' commented Muriel so only Violet could hear, heading for the parlour. 'I do hope the kettle's on, Eleanor.'

Violet and her aunt exchanged a private smile.

With its thick curtains pulled against the night and glowing chunks of wood in the grate, the room felt cosy and familiar, but Violet had expected to feel more comforted. She sat back into an armchair, numb with fatigue, with Jess resting his chin on her knee. The journey had taken it out of her. She and her baby needed to rest. The dog's velvet eyes searched her face. His eyebrows lifting first one side, and then the other.

'We've just seen Eddie Davey's name in the paper,' Muriel said as Violet's mother poured tea.

'A terrible, terrible shame,' said her father. 'So many are leaving. The trains are full, coming up from Truro and Penzance, sending them on to Bodmin Moor or Salisbury Plain for medicals, training, and then on up to London. Of course, Violet, I don't need to spell it all out to you.'

'Jack's on Salisbury Plain,' she said, her voice a shadow.

Muriel reached out to pat her hand. 'Drink your tea, my dear.'

'And the horses,' said her father. 'Sending them off without a "by your leave". No sentiment, no explanation. Good old carthorses and farm mares, all gone. Army comes into town and within a few hours the stables are empty. But, what can we expect now it's war?'

'All the men, and all the horses,' muttered Muriel.

'I heard even Penruth gave up his stallion for a guinea...' her father stopped abruptly and glanced at Violet. 'I'm sorry. Perhaps I shouldn't have mentioned...'

'We can't skirt around this forever, George,' Violet's mother leapt in. 'They're married now, Violet. Did you know that?' The words fell out of her mouth, cutting through the quiet room.

'Mother, I am as surprised as you are, I—' She felt crushed, so very tired.

'And they've quit Charlecote, moved up to Cadogan Square. Mrs Penruth and all.'

Violet shrank with shock. 'My goodness...' she uttered. She could not see how Claudia would cope in London, how she would fit into that world, the girl who loved the simplicity of her life here. But she did not know Claudia any more. So many questions spun through her head, but she could only muster, 'When...?'

'Never mind that. Just tell us why. Why you refused him. I can hardly hold my head up around the county.'

Muriel butted in. 'Does any of this really matter, Eleanor? Violet has a new life now with Jack. She is here with us. And with the baby on the way...'

Violet felt utterly beaten. Her longing for Jack, her need for him, and the reality of their separation, cut through her. She said, 'I just want Jack here with me.'

Her mother clamped her mouth shut and bristled in her armchair. Even though she sensed she should not press any further, her resentment emitted from her like fumes. Violet glanced at her father in appeal, craving his support, to say something to settle the situation once and for all, but he concentrated on refilling his pipe and began to talk about the heavy weather expected that night. She made her excuses and made her weary way upstairs.

Lying in bed, with Jess heavy on her feet, Violet heard the storm rising, coming in from the west, and wondered how soon Jack, all those miles away, would hear it too. The wind surged in the trees, throwing rain against her window and any other time, being tucked up in bed at Old Trellick, on a night such as this, she'd feel safe and comforted. But tonight, all sense of security escaped her.

She turned over, cradling her stomach with her arms and began to whisper in hope – senseless with fatigue – that Jack's smile would keep him safe.

16

WHEN WIND TAKES FLAIL, LET NO SHIP SAIL

Violet waited while her father lifted the basket from the boot of his car, and they walked together to the huddled row of fishermen's cottages. The storm had lasted two full days and a night, and the aftermath, the soaking mizzle harried by a surging wind, blew straight through Violet's coat and wrenched dangerously at her hat. She shivered as damp seeped up from the rutted path leading to the Davey cottage. Moisture dribbled off the slate roof and glistened on the scrubby bushes around the porch.

Her father hesitated, let out a grainy sigh and rapped the knocker.

'Are you all right, Violet?' he asked, and she managed a quick nod, fibbing to cover her discomfort.

At breakfast that morning, she had assured him she wanted to come with him, to show support for the family of one of the first casualties of the neighbourhood. To pay respects to dear Eddie. To visit, in all honesty, for Claudia.

The door swung open, and her father slipped his hat off his head. Mrs Davey, emerging from the shadows within, gestured wordlessly, vacantly, for them to come in. Violet followed her father into the dank, whitewashed room where a black range smoked under the mantel, the wind moaned in the chimney and the air hung with the smell of old fish. Mrs Davey muttered that they should please mind the mess, her eyes blank and bewildered, her hair roughly tied behind her head. Her cheeks looked like they'd been slapped. She gestured to a wooden settle, where a young girl and boy, two of Eddie's siblings, sat playing quietly.

'Go on, you two, make space for the lady and gentleman. Get yourselves outside. Go on.' The children sloped off out into the wind and rain, coatless and hatless. 'Peter's out on the boat with his Da,' Mrs Davey said. 'Though shouldn't be. Not in this weather. It's still pitching high out there. But it's what keeps them going. Lord knows, I try to but—' She rolled her hands in and out of her apron. 'I need to fill the kettle as you will be wanting tea, doctor,' she said. 'The boys, you see, they always took it in turn to help me out as its blasted heavy. Peter forgot this morning. A lot of things seem to have been knocked out of his head, you see, now there's only one of him. Please, Miss Prideaux, do please sit.'

Fearful of catching Mrs Davey's eye, Violet perched on the settle and gazed around the room. On the deep stone windowsill sat a framed photograph of two identical boys. Peter and Eddie, a few years ago, on the quay at Looe, standing proudly by a great pile of fishing nets. Two peas in a pod, Claudia had said once. She'd also told Violet that she had kissed them both at the ball, to decide who she liked best. Had Claudia been so very fickle in love, in her charming and spirited way, as to have her head turned again so quickly by Weston?

'Sorry to intrude, Mrs Davey,' said Violet's father. 'And there is no need for tea. We simply thought we'd stop by to see how you all are.'

'And,' Violet piped up, wanting to sound hopeful. 'We have brought a few things for you, Mrs Davey. Some groceries, saffron buns, and a bottle of my aunt's wine.'

'Very nice, I'm sure,' uttered Mrs Davey, clearly not interested. 'I'd show you both through to the parlour to sit in a little more comfort,' she said, 'but we've just had him back this morning and I don't rightly know what to do with him.'

Violet glanced at her father, not understanding, a mess of wondering horror surging in her head.

'Do you... do you know when Eddie passed away, Mrs Davey?' her father asked gently.

'We got a telegram a week ago,' she said, her voice brittle with fatigue. 'And the notice went in the local paper a few days ago. You probably saw. But we don't know for sure. No one has told us. We don't know which day, or night, or when it was. I could have been doing my laundry, gutting fish, bathing my children when they got him. And I was just carrying on, oblivious. I didn't know. And I wanted to know. A mother needs to know.'

Violet's father made the best comforting, assuring noise he could.

'Come and have a look,' Mrs Davey said, opening the door at the rear of the room and standing aside. 'Parlour's through here.'

Violet's father nodded and slipped past Mrs Davey, and Violet felt compelled, as any well-mannered guest might, to follow.

Mrs Davey had lit a lamp and let the precious oil burn on in the small unused room. Its yellow glow sent arcs of soft light over the walls and the decent-looking chairs either side of the cold hearth. And there, on the rug, Eddie's uniform arranged as if clothing an invisible corpse. A cold fist pressed against the back of Violet's neck. She stared. She knew it to be a uniform by the stuff it was made of, by its lapels, buttons, front pockets. But not by its colour, nor its condition. The viscous, foul mud that soiled it did not seem to be of the earth, did not resemble the sweet freshly ploughed soil Eddie would have known come spring in the surrounding fields. The cloth excreted a story of violence, of despair and of chaos. And the smell. A sudden burst of rain rattled against the window. Violet took a step back and placed her hand over her mouth.

'They sent it back to us, with bits of his kit and all,' Mrs Davey said, as if unable to believe herself. 'And it's all we will have of him. They say there's no body. But there must be. How can he not have a body?'

Violet looked again in dismay at the uniform laid out on the floor like a hellish shroud, the shredded collar, half of the shoulder missing. She looked at her father's ashen face.

'We must do something, Mrs Davey,' he said, sounding clipped and decisive. 'We must speak with the vicar and have a proper service. Give Eddie... this... Some sort of a funeral. Have the children seen it? Good God, they shouldn't.'

Mrs Davey shook her head, pressed her hand to her side and dipped out of the room. Her father followed uttering his concern, and Violet, feeling clumsy and useless, waited a moment alone, before leaving Eddie's shrine and closing the door.

'I hope our hamper will be welcome, Mrs Davey,' she said, as her father prompted Mrs Davey to sit by her hearthside, found her shawl. 'You must all keep your strength up.'

Mrs Davey squinted at her, as if noticing her presence for the first time.

'You've heard about Claudia Ainsley as was, I take it, Miss Prideaux?' She dashed at her tears with the corner of her shawl.

'Yes, Mrs Davey.'

'High-tailed it up to London with Lordy. Married and everything.'

'Yes, indeed, quite the shock...'

'I heard you went to London, too, back in the summer. Married, and in the family way, aren't you? I take it you are happy now, Miss er Mrs... I am pleased for you.'

'It's Mrs Fairling now. Thank you, Mrs Davey, I—'

'But if you hadn't refused Penruth,' Mrs Davey became very still and hooked her with her gaze, 'then your friend wouldn't have stepped into your shoes and thrown over Eddie for him. God knows he was devastated by the little bitch. Couldn't understand. None of us could. Signed up to get away. Got swept up in it all.' Her words fired at Violet, tight and bitter. 'And then this, and then this...'

'Mrs Davey,' Violet started, 'Really, I—'

Her father broke in, 'We are both very sorry for your loss, madam. We will certainly call again.'

She folded her arms up inside her shawl as if to comfort herself.

'Thank you, doctor,' she muttered, unearthing her ingrained respect for him.

Violet said, 'Good afternoon, Mrs Davey.'

But all Eddie's mother could offer in return was a look of exhausted despair.

* * *

Back at Old Trellick, Violet took off her damp coat and hat, stripped her gloves and dropped them on the hallway table, wanting to remove the lingering sense of Mrs Davey's misery along with them. The second post had been and propped alone in the rack was a letter for Violet. With a sense of fearful longing, she shakily ran the letter opener under the envelope flap and sat with a thump on the bottom stair.

Jack had written the date at the top, but, naturally, not his location, and the censor's black pen had done its work, scoring certain passages and words. But the essence of his message thumped through Violet's head, and she felt her middle collapse, a part of herself giving in.

Doggy claws pattered along the hallway and Jess pressed his wet nose gently against her trembling hands, seeking her attention, giving his own. Violet stroked his worried little brow, wishing Jack could be here to soothe and comfort her in the same way.

But the letter had been written a week ago, and Jack and his regiment had already gone.

PART II
VIOLET, CORNWALL, 1916

17

IN THE LANGUAGE OF FLOWERS: BLUEBELL, CONSISTENCY

Early May, 1916

As Violet left Old Trellick that morning, she caught the sweet scent coming off the moors, the warm, new breath of spring. Bluebells clothed the woodland floor, in delicate promising swathes, and green cow parsley frothed along the verges. Give it a week, or two, and it will ripen, bringing its shimmering veil of white to the lanes. How Violet wanted Jack to see it, to breathe it in, to paint it all; he had not been home in a year, but he will. He will be soon.

'Soon,' she whispered to Aster, who sat up in her pram, facing her, her little pensive gaze turning this way and that as she spotted, past Violet's shoulder, a bird, a flower, a shadow. 'And Daddy will see you, Aster,' she said. 'He will be astonished at how well you are doing. How well you have grown. A fine little Cornish maid.'

The path became too bumpy to go much further with the pram, so Violet lifted Aster out, parked it by the bramble bushes, and carried her the rest of the way down to the cove. Aster seemed to become an ounce heavier every day. Violet spread out the rug at the foot of a dune and set her down. But the little girl clambered straight back up, plucking at Violet's skirt, wanting to walk, to toddle across the sand to the sea.

'Wait a moment, little one. Let Mama at least have a rest for five minutes. How early you were but you're making up for it now,' Violet laughed. 'Oh, come on then.'

* * *

Aster had arrived before her time, slipping out of Violet like a wet fish on a squally spring day of spitting rain. And Aunt Muriel had proved true to her word when she'd said, all that time ago at Montagu Square, that she was very good in a crisis. The baby had caught them all unaware. Violet's father had been called away to a teaching hospital in London only that week, but had assured Violet – and everyone had assumed – he'd be back long before the baby came.

Aster had emerged fragile and raw and as delicate as a kitten, and Violet also was desperately weak. But Muriel, like a reassuring angel, nursed Violet without fuss, knowing exactly what she needed before she did, while her mother could only sit by the bed and worry.

A year ago, the first green specks of hopeful bluebells had emerged under the trees at the bottom of Old Trellick's garden and on Aster's seventh day, Violet watched, exhausted, in bed as Jack – home on precious leave – had held his daughter for the first time, her tiny head cradled in his palm. A watery light had come through the window and glowed around them like an aura. Violet had felt, in that moment, that Aster had chosen to live, and that the world could spin again.

'How light she is,' Jack had said. 'As light as a feather. What shall we call her?'

* * *

At the cove, Violet clasped Aster's plump little hand as they walked in little tottering zigzags across the sand down to the water's edge.

'To think, Aster, Grannie wanted to call you after her own mother,' she said. 'She'd even told the vicar. But I have never liked that name. Too old-fashioned. Daddy and I knew better, didn't we.'

The little girl leant down to pick up a strand of seaweed, limp and luminous green and held it out to Violet, laughing. Her strawberry-blonde hair, and periwinkle eyes were her father's. And Violet could never mistake the brightness of his smile.

'Thank you, my darling,' she said, 'Shall Mama press it and paste it in her *Flower Book*? We can show Daddy, oh, he will be here soon, and he will be so proud of you.'

It had been too long, far too long since Jack had been home. In his letters, he never gave much away, and Violet wanted to cry for missing him. But she wouldn't give in, would not allow it.

* * *

On Aster's seventh day, he had come away from the window, and had sat on the bed, placing her in Violet's arms.

'I was showing her the sunlight,' he'd said. 'She could see it. She turned her head towards it. Her little eyes followed it. And her tongue is going. Look, she is hungry.'

'Aster,' Violet had said, beginning to nurse the baby. 'That is her name. Meaning "star", meaning hope.' She had gazed down at the scrap of a child in her arms and, even though she felt like she had been given a gift that she knew, eventually, she would have to give away, her life felt complete. 'Mother can call her what she likes, Jack,' she'd said, and they'd shared soft private laughter. 'But she is Aster to us.'

* * *

The little girl tugged to let go of Violet's hand, squatting to inspect a miniature crab washed up on the shoreline, the sparkling pebbles, fragments of sea glass, muted and smooth now that the waves had pounded away their shine. Violet gazed along the strand, shielding her eyes. She'd thought she had the cove to herself but a distant figure, graceful and willow thin, emerged from the other side, almost a mirage against the sandy banks behind it. She jolted at the memory. Being here on the beach with Claudia, being met by Weston and his two lurchers. The awkward and pivotal exchange. How they hadn't known it then, but a turning point for all.

Violet, sensing Aster's urge to make a break for the waves, scooped her up, wishing Claudia was by her side as she had been that day more than two years ago, and that she could share the joy of her daughter with her.

'Oh, she would have loved you,' Violet whispered but Aster wriggled in protest in her arms, pointing to the sea. 'No, no, not today.'

Violet glanced behind her again. The person had walked quickly, drew closer, much closer, heading straight towards her. Violet watched, not quite believing her eyes, but wanting to, desperately. And suddenly, gently, Claudia stopped, an arm's length from her.

'I knew I would find you here,' she said. A little boy, some four months or so younger than Aster, chubby and milk-fed, his eyes round and grey, sat in her arms, perfectly balanced on her hip. 'Did you hear it, Violet? Did you have your moment walking down the path?'

Claudia shifted her baby expertly onto her other hip, and they stood facing one another as the spent waves hissed towards their shoes. Her smile was as beautiful as Violet remembered, and yet she could not return it. She held onto Aster tightly, lifted her higher, confusion shattering her instinct for joy. Violet knew she ought to be gracious, and answer her friend's question about hearing the sea as she'd walked down the path, but her own questions stuttered through her mind. And she continued to stare.

Sunlight dappled through the weave of Claudia's hat, sending flecks over her cheeks. Her fair hair was coiled in a great plait, as pale as butter, at the nape of her neck, and she wore lace gloves that fanned out over her delicate wrists. No more let-down school dress and ripped seams for Claudia. She looked as pure and as bright as ever in her finest silk. And Violet, mute with surprise, suffered a peculiar mix of grief and happiness.

'Did you, Violet? Did you?'

'I did,' Violet uttered quietly, feeling compelled to answer. 'I chatted to Aster about it as we walked down. Of course, she didn't understand. But she will, in time.'

'Look at the two of us,' Claudia went on, excitedly, not catching Violet's guarded tone. 'You have a little girl and I have a little boy.'

She seemed oblivious to the space, the time and the estrangement that had stretched between them. Didn't she ever wonder where their friendship – which had disappeared along the way – had gone?

'Yes, this is my daughter. Aster,' Violet said, awkwardly repeating herself.

'And this is little Harry.' Claudia's baby proceeded to dig his fingers into his mother's hair. 'Ouch, Harry.' She delicately extracted his hand. 'I think I will have trouble with you, little man.' She looked back at Violet. 'Do you have time to—? Shall we sit?'

Violet nodded and in a baffled daze carried Aster back to the rug, where Claudia settled herself beside her, bouncing Harry on her knee.

'How different this all is,' Claudia said, breezily looking around her, taking in the sea, the gentle waves, the seagulls wheeling overhead. 'I have certainly missed the cove. London has been an... experience, shall we say. Last time we were here, we were rolling about on the sand like little girls, weren't we? Now look at us. Grown-up ladies. Mothers and married. We're old married women!'

Claudia's laughter sparked frustration in Violet, a horrible hot surge of irritation.

'Come on, Claudia, stop that!' she said. 'It's been two years since we have spoken! We can't sit here and pretend. What on earth happened?'

Claudia's face fell. She stared, her mouth open in surprise. 'Surely, Violet,' she said in half-whisper, '*you* need to tell *me* what happened.'

'Goodness, is that what you think...?' Violet gazed at her friend's placid, puzzled face and felt the gulf between them lurch wider.

'You left Old Trellick so quickly. As if you were running away,' Claudia said, quickly. 'I know that it had been an awkward situation for you and your family. That you turned Weston down. It was a shock, to be honest. All over the neighbourhood, they're all such terrible gossips. But he is too much of a gentleman to say any more about it to me, except that he...'

Violet realised, in that moment, that Claudia returning to Charlecote, meant that Weston would be here too, would possibly cross her path. And Claudia had spoken his name in such a knowing, intimate way, just then, that Violet inwardly shuddered.

'Claudia, I left because of the shame and humiliation,' Violet said when her friend did not elaborate on what Weston might have had to say about her leaving. 'Not my own shame and humiliation, but my mother's. I know I did the right thing for myself. Weston simply wasn't the man for me. They had it all planned out. I felt controlled and was being forced to accept him, live the life I did not want to live. But Mother thought differently. And I had to get away. Thank goodness for my aunt. Mother did not speak to me for weeks.'

Claudia shuffled around to face her, rearranging Harry on her lap. 'You say, Violet, that it wasn't the life you wanted,' she reasoned, 'but there came a point when I realised that I wanted a different life to the one I had been dealt, too.'

Violet opened her mouth to protest, wanting to say: *'with Weston Penruth?'* but stopped herself. She must respect Claudia's decision, however baffling and unexpected it appeared to be.

Claudia cuddled her baby son, blew a raspberry into his chest to make him laugh. In Harry's smooth little face, Violet saw something of Weston, something around the eyes. Violet knew she had made the right decision for herself but what about Claudia? Had she been swayed by a need for security, and comfort, an extraordinary step up the social ladder for her and her family? Had she really fallen in love with Weston? The Weston that Violet knew? Oh, she had no doubt he had fallen for Claudia, for who wouldn't love that genuine, delicate beauty?

Gazing at her now, Violet saw Claudia's happiness, a light shining inside her, and Violet wondered if Weston Penruth had had a complete change of character.

'And look what I have from my new life,' Claudia said, pressing her lips into her baby's hair. 'This lovely little lad. And, there is more joy to come.'

She rested her palm flat on her belly.

'Oh, Claudia,' Violet exhaled and reached over to hold and squeeze her friend's hand.

But Claudia dipped her head suddenly in the way she did when on the verge of tears. She seemed to quail, as if she could not express the thoughts jumping ahead of her. As if she'd been elaborating happiness.

'But, Violet, we have never talked about what happened,' Claudia said, lifting her voice through whatever stifled her. 'I didn't get the chance. In the days after you left, well, you left quite a mess behind you, let's face it, Violet. I was so glad when I received your letter at last. You'd been away a good couple of weeks and it had seemed like forever. But when I wrote back to you, at your aunt's, you didn't reply.'

'But when did you write?'

'Straight away. Return of post, like I always do. You see Weston and I had started courting then, and I wanted to tell you myself. I thought that was only right.'

'I didn't get your letter,' Violet sighed, shifted Aster on her lap, holding her little wriggly body to gain comfort from her. 'I only found out you were engaged when Mother arrived in London specifically to tell me. It was all such a muddle. A misunderstanding. But why, Claudia? Why did you marry him?' she blurted.

Claudia bristled, 'I told you why in my letter. The one that didn't reach you.'

'Tell me now.'

Her friend looked away at the sea, as if seeking the answer there. Violet waited, sensing the delicate nature of her friend's thoughts.

'With Weston, you see,' Claudia said, cautiously, 'I couldn't help myself. It all happened in such a giddy haze. I knew that, in truth, you did not want to be with him. After all, you had rejected him. But I also felt that, like me, you did have feelings... had sympathy for him. I know we used to laugh together about how awkward he always was. How, frankly, a little ridiculous. At first, I wanted to look after him for you, if that makes any sense. Do you understand? He was a broken man.'

'*Broken?* Oh, Claudia.'

'Violet, I know you find it hard to understand. It was such a confusing time. When I heard that you had come back home that winter, almost the same time we moved up to London, I was so happy to find out that you were married too, and were expecting. I wish we'd kept in touch. But I thought that you hated me for some reason. I wondered if it was because I was with Weston. And I accepted that. My guilt didn't help. About Eddie. The whole mess of it. And when I heard he'd been killed...'

Claudia gripped Violet's arm with pale, fine fingers, her eyes glittering with tears.

'I never hated you, Claudia. How could I?' Violet said. 'It has been a terrible misunderstanding, full of cross purposes. But what I have never understood is... Why you thew over Eddie for Weston...? In all honesty, I didn't think Weston was right for me. Or for you. For anyone.'

'Weston is misunderstood by so many people,' she said. 'But I see through it.'

'What is there to see through?' Violet cried, exasperated. 'I heard what he did to the dogs. I can't believe someone would be so vindictive and cruel.'

Claudia took a long shuddering breath, and both children glanced with a trace of fear at her.

'Again, he is misunderstood,' she said.

Violet waited for her to elaborate.

'I was at home as usual, the evening of the soirée at Charlecote,' Claudia said. 'I didn't know what had happened. As far as I was concerned, when Eddie and I left, you were going to continue having a nice afternoon there with Weston, your parents and Mrs Penruth. The lurchers had been kennelled at the farm the day before because Jess would be visiting Charlecote. You see, he was thinking of you, Violet, even then... I was washing up our supper things, looking out of the kitchen window. I saw him, through the dusk, and thought *ah, Mr Penruth has come to collect his dogs*. Didn't think anything of it.'

Violet had imagined the moment for a long time, playing it out in various ways in her mind. But now, with the reality of it being laid out before her, it repelled her more than the fantasy.

'Silly thing is,' said Claudia, and gave a sorry little laugh. 'I didn't notice his shotgun. I just thought he looked unhurried, his usual self. He went into the shed, and I heard him call them. I heard the shots. I can't remember how many. Two. Three.'

'Oh God, Claudia...'

'He came straight back out and collapsed against the side of the shed. I thought someone had shot *him*. I ran out to him. He had curled up in the dirt on the cobbles, his face black with pain. He was bashing his head against the stones, over and over. I knelt beside him, Violet, and wrapped my arms around him, made him rest against me. Shielded him while he wept.'

Violet uttered, shaking her head, saying, 'I still can't believe it,' over and over.

She glanced at Aster and Harry, wondering how much, if anything they might have understood.

'I really can't forgive him for that,' Violet said.

'You don't have to,' Claudia drew herself up, squaring her shoulders. 'I will do it for you.'

'I will try to understand. I know what it is like... when someone you love is not appreciated by others...'

Claudia brightened. 'Mrs Penruth has gone away to stay with her brother in Scotland. Perthshire somewhere,' she said, 'and I've seen even more of a change in Weston. She is frightened of the U-boats. Thought we'd be invaded here in Cornwall. It's uncharitable of me to say, but she is a very *difficult* woman. Really, Violet, there are things I could tell you, but Weston thrives away from his mother and bad memories—'

Claudia broke off and began to fiddle with Harry's little socks. Violet gazed along the beach, realising how such a damaging experience can, eventually, switch into something wonderful. For all of what had happened between her and Weston had led her to Jack.

And how I love him, she thought, watching Aster blithely reach out to Harry, tugging at his sleeve in a questioning manner while he sat nonplussed on his mother's lap.

'And you are married... to Jack,' Claudia beamed at her, as if reading her thoughts. 'He's an artist I hear?'

'Yes, yes, Jack. He's been at the Front for nearly a year, but he will be home soon.'

Claudia's joy snuffed out in that instance. She began to cry.

Violet leant towards her, still holding Aster, and put her arm around her slender shoulders. They rested their heads together, their hats squashed between them, held their children, and supported each other in one embrace. Violet watched Claudia's tears fall silently onto her gloves.

'Hush, Claudia, what is it?' Violet asked. 'Remember, I'm here now. I am always your friend. Why the tears? You're having another baby. Oh, Claudia, it will be fine, and you will be even happier, you'll see.'

Claudia looked at her from under the brim of her hat, her eyes wide and wet, her fair lashes darkened by tears. Her mouth trembled and she uttered one single word, '*Eddie.*'

18

IN THE LANGUAGE OF FLOWERS: WILD YELLOW HEARTSEASE, THE CURE FOR THE DISCOMFORTS OF LOVE

Late May, 1916

The swallows had welcomed Jack home the night before. Sitting in the garden as dusk fell, they had heard the birds peeping high above. Violet tilted her head back to spot the little black sickles against the sky, illuminated and colourless, a pause between day and night.

'First swallows of summer,' she had said, knowing she would cherish that evening, as she would each precious day while Jack was home on leave, daring herself to feel joy.

The next morning, they walked together down to the cove, along lanes rich with green, the cow parsley a froth of white and the undergrowth dotted with tiny sun-bright wild violas. Jack carried Aster over his shoulder, her wispy strawberry-blonde hair caught in a bunch high on her head. She circled her arms around Jack's neck, happily bouncing along, gazing back the way they'd come. Jess trotted ahead, obedient and serene but as spellbound by the world as he had been as a puppy. The path to the cove grew steeper, the gorse tighter.

'Any moment now, Jack,' Violet said. 'Any moment now.'

But he appeared not to have heard. He had pulled his cap down to shield his eyes, a tense and unfamiliar figure, striding ahead of her.

And it came to her then, the sudden hum of voices, the sound of the sea. She longed to ask Jack if he'd listened for it, felt it, but he continued to walk on, his face closed, his eyes brooding. She caught up with him, took his arm, but his flesh seemed to stiffen at her touch.

The sea looked calm today, the sand empty, the tide out, hissing backwards over the glistening pebbles. They settled down in Violet's usual dip against the dune, to any onlooker a picture-perfect family with their little girl and dog. She drew out the flask and sandwiches. Aster, sitting on the rug in her fat nappy, seemed momentarily entranced, but shook herself out of it and began to shuffle across the rug to make her escape.

'Watch her, she'll be off,' Violet said.

Jack scooped her and settled her on his knee, bouncing her tenderly.

'You shouldn't crawl off like that, Aster,' he said. 'For you will be lost. And we will never find you. And it's dangerous out there.'

He fished shells out of the sand and showed them to her in the hollow of his palm, his hand trembling. Aster plucked at the shells and put them in her mouth. She grimaced, on the verge of crying, but not knowing quite what to do with sand stuck to her lips.

Jack sorted her out with his handkerchief.

'There you go, Aster, all better,' he said. He caught Violet's eye, it seemed to her in that moment, with all his courage. 'So, you and Claudia are friends again?'

'Yes, thankfully, we are,' Violet said. 'But we never stopped being *friends* as such. I sometimes wonder if she is still the girl I used to know. But we all change a bit, don't we, as we grow older? It has been a muddle, but we are mending it.'

'Even though she married the Penruth fellow?'

Violet stiffened. 'I can't deny that I still feel shocked by that. But I couldn't care less for Weston.'

Jack winced, and she saw how he wanted reassurance.

'But I do feel,' she said, 'there is something that Claudia is not telling me...'

'Best to let them get on with it, I say,' he said, sounding unusually offhand, and found another shell for Aster. 'Perhaps she can have a sandwich?'

'Ah, she will only chew the bread into a soggy wad. I have stewed fruit for her.'

'Some tea, then. Does she drink tea? Have you tried her with tea?'

'Not yet. But we can try,' Violet said, wishing she didn't sound like she humoured him. 'Although babies her age don't normally drink tea.'

'I didn't even know she could crawl, or that she would have so much hair...' He watched as Aster picked over the shells still held in his hand, her little finger dabbing and exploring. 'You both carry on without me,' he sighed.

'We've missed you Jack...' Violet unwrapped his sandwich for him, feeling ridiculously shy, wondering if a year apart had changed her in his eyes. Certainly, she felt like she had to get used to him again, to *know* him once more, to mend the frayed edges. Jess settled down beside her, resting his snout on her ankle, his tail twitching with contentment.

'I even find it astonishing that it's summer again,' Jack said. 'Isn't that raving mad? I want to sketch the bluebells before I go. Thing is, I'm surprised they're even there. Surprised that life is normal, that everything is normal here. That you all carry on. While all of that...' he nodded at the sea, 'while all of that...'

Violet felt alarmed. Jack never mentioned France, or talked about what had been happening across the Channel, in his letters or if he was home. She hoped, for his sake, that he might. For surely, it felt better to speak of these things. She knew she could not rely on the newspapers.

'I was so naïve, Violet, at the beginning,' he said.

She saw a shadow, something terrible, cross his face, as if cold fingertips had brushed his cheek.

'Remember how I justified my joining up, when we were still in London. What I said about the war being a windfall?'

She touched his hand, noticing how tanned and weathered it looked. 'None of us really knew, in the beginning, Jack,' she said gently. 'How could we? But you're here now, Jack. With us. And I will listen.'

'This little one doesn't want to hear about it,' he said.

Stillness settled between them, punctuated by Aster's babbling and a gentle breeze picking up over the waves. And a brief smile brightened his face as he latched onto a different train of thought.

'Seven whole days, she was, when I first saw her and held her.' He touched the delicate baby hair around her ears. 'My, my... I want to sketch her, Violet. But I can't paint any more. I've lost it. Truly lost it. Only rough sketches, that's all, of the lads on the fire step, perhaps, or the treeline in the distance. Things I dash off in the mess, or my bunker, because I feel I must. But can't possibly show anyone.'

'Why not?'

He looked at her. 'For we are no longer human.'

Violet jolted, felt their connection suddenly break. Frustration, her yearning to help Jack, built pressure behind her eyes.

'Please talk to me, Jack,' she said. 'I'm here. I'm always here. We're both here.' She plucked Aster from the rug and held her protesting little body close. 'Is it that you're missing us?' she tried. 'Missing all the little stages of Aster's life? That it's all broken up like this? That this is the only the third time you've seen her? I try to write it all down, in my *Flower Book*, every little milestone. The news, the little things. I try to convey it to you in my letters. Perhaps I fail.' She paused and the gulf widened. 'But this is hell.'

He gave a short hard sigh. 'Hell, you say.'

'Jack, I'm sorry. I have no idea. Because you won't tell me. What I'm imagining is—'

'You cannot imagine.'

He turned his head and his shoulders away from her, gazing out to sea. His tone lingered, like the taste of bitter tansy on Violet's tongue. The breeze ruffled the sandwich papers. Violet's tea grew cold. Jess trotted off to inspect tufts of marram grass. Aster shivered and Violet concentrated on dressing her in the jacket that Muriel had knitted. Her child curled into her lap, and she held her as she drifted to sleep. How difficult it felt to find Jack's love when he shut himself from her. But Violet knew she must dig deep for it and bring it to the surface. For he needed her. How he needed her.

Eventually, Jack said, 'You remember Captain Welstead?'

Violet nodded. That July day in London, the white terraces, the melting green park, belonged to another age. Sebastian Welstead in his impeccable suit, his elegance and courtesy. And within half an hour, Violet taking tea with Jack in the Pavilion.

'Yes, yes, of course,' she said.

'He's gone,' Jack said, bluntly. 'Couldn't take it at Loos.'

'Whatever do you mean...?'

'You want me to tell you?'

'I want to understand, Jack.'

His eyes turned opaque with memory. 'We were preparing for stand-to,' he said. 'Fixed bayonets. Gas masks on because our boys were sending it over the top of us. In the trench, we're all poised on the fire steps, on the ladders.'

Violet shuddered, inhaled, her ordinary world ripping open.

'I looked left and right. My men hunched with terror. Welstead has his head up first. Leads from the front, always. The whistle blows somewhere down the line, and we scramble up into the storm. Bullets and shells on us. Blasting chaos. Welstead is ahead, ducking, flinching, his revolver held in front of him like a poker. Useless. I glance back. Our line. His men, my men. Scattered like pins along the top of the trench, some writhing, others crumpled. Motionless. Welstead pulls his mask up and screams: "*Orders are to move forward. If in doubt, move forward! Get up, you bloody cowards!*" I scream back at him, although he can't hear me through my mask. "*They can't sir. They're dead.*" They're all dead, Violet. All dead.'

A cold tide moved through Violet's blood. She kept her eyes locked on Jack. She could not flinch from what he told her, for she had to absorb it for him, let him know she heard him, *trying* to understand.

'The rest of us didn't get very far,' he said, his exhale juddering. 'Our own gas was blown back in our faces. The new order was to retreat to our stinking hole. To crouch like animals in our hovel. As I said, Violet, no longer human.'

Violet reached for his hand, but he pulled away. 'Everything slows down out there. Or speeds up at a ferocious rate. Half an hour later, two hours later, I have no idea, Welstead calmly went out of the bunker and put his revolver in his mouth.'

Her cry startled Aster awake, and she snuffled her face into the crook of Violet's elbow.

'With Welstead gone, this is why I have been promoted, fast-tracked to officer training camp,' Jack said. 'There's going to be a big push and I know my chances.'

His words burnt into Violet's mind, branding her.

Jack reached over and plucked Aster from her arms, perching her on his knee. Ponderously, Aster reached a finger and traced the stiff line from his nose to his mouth. Watching her, Violet's vision blurred with tears, her mouth crumpled.

'I can't look at you crying, Violet,' Jack said. 'I shall see you back at the house.'

He passed Aster to her, got up and called for Jess. He walked briskly away across the beach, followed by eagerly oblivious Jess, and disappeared up the path.

'It's all right, Aster,' Violet said, 'We'll see Daddy back at home.'

She tipped away her tea and scattered the sandwiches for the seagulls.

* * *

Later, as Violet drew the parlour curtains against the evening, she noticed in the deepening violet of nightfall the last of the bluebells beneath the trees in the garden. In the past she would have pointed them out to Jack, wondered if he might sketch their delicate fading stems, but now it felt a trivial and patronising thing to do.

The atmosphere in the room seemed so gentle, quiet and natural that Violet could hardly bear it. For no one here, she decided, knew or would ever know what Jack had seen. He played Cribb with her father, Muriel knitted socks for soldiers, humming to herself, counting stitches. Jess lay in front of the hearth and Aster was tucked up in bed. Violet's mother occasionally opened the broadsheet to its full stretch, uttering about some more terrible news. Violet's scalp prickled at her tactlessness. Earlier, she had taken pains to wonder aloud why Jack had come home from the cove alone with Jess, leaving Violet to struggle back with Aster.

Violet went over to sit on the sofa, noting again the outward changes in him: his skin burnished by the Picardy sun, his artist's beard shaved clean, a neat moustache now he'd made lieutenant, and she wondered where his true self, the Jack she loved, had gone. His smile was false, she knew, his laughter a strain as her father teased him, laying his winning hand down on the table.

'For God's sake, I've lost again,' uttered Jack, slapped his own cards down.

'All you need to do, old chap,' said her father, affably, 'is count to fifteen.'

'Can't think straight,' Jack said. 'Honestly, Welstead cops it, I get promoted. But do they really want an officer who can't count, can't win at cards?'

Muriel looked up from her knitting.

'What was that, Jack?' she asked. 'Did you say Welstead?'

'I know that name,' Violet's mother said. 'Isn't Lady Welstead your friend in London, Muriel?'

Violet gave Jack an appealing look, hoping he'd sensed the delicate situation, the link, however tenuous, between the families. And that perhaps he shouldn't elaborate any further.

Jack gave a hollow laugh. 'I'm sorry, Muriel. Gallows humour, I'm afraid. It's how we get through it all.'

'But I didn't see him in the lists. Did they miss him out? Are you possibly mistaken, Jack?' Muriel said.

'No mistake, I'm afraid.'

'Oh, poor Sebastian. Poor Lady Welstead. I must write to her immediately... oh heavens, this brings it right into our homes, doesn't it? There he was, all dashing and, oh, ever so polite. Gave me such courtesies, didn't he, Violet, that time we saw him...?'

'Would a strong drink help, Aunt Muriel?' Violet asked, trying to distract her.

'I think I need one too,' Jack said, his eyes bright with torment. He caught Violet's eye, as if seeking her mercy.

'Right away,' she said. 'Who else? Everyone?'

'Well, I must say,' Violet's mother said, as Violet handed around tots of brandy. 'I barely like to think of it. It is all rather unnecessarily brutal, isn't it?'

'*Unnecessarily*...?' Jack asked, aghast.

'Eleanor.'

Violet turned in surprise to look at her father. She had never heard him say her mother's name with such force, such reprimand before. And from the look on her mother's face, it seemed neither had she.

'That is quite enough of that,' he said with barely contained fury. 'Isn't it all so bad enough, so appallingly terrible, Eleanor, without that sort of careless comment?'

Violet's mother bristled, sipping hard at her brandy, and Muriel dipped her head to her knitting. As the clock ticked on to bedtime, and Jess rearranged himself on the rug, Violet caught the tender look of understanding between her father and Jack, as they quietly shuffled the cards together to deal out another game.

* * *

Upstairs, Violet lit the lamp while Jack loosened his tie by the mirror. He fumbled with his cufflinks and Violet stepped over to help him.

'Shakes again,' he said, and he gave her a crooked smile.

How hard he tried to hide it, Violet thought. His struggle carved a line right through her and she found that she loved him all the more.

'And before I forget,' he said. 'I found this on the dunes on my way back today.' Jack fished in his pocket and drew out a delicate stem of sea holly. 'Oops, it's a bit battered, but there was a little crop of them, tucked away. I thought you had probably missed them.'

'Why, thank you, Jack.' She took the spikey papery-blue flower, turning it over in her hand.

'Not the best specimen ever, but you must press it anyway and put it alongside with that ropey bit of seaweed of Aster's that's drying out up there in your attic room.'

Violet laughed softly, enjoying their spell of intimacy that took her straight back to when they'd first met, when she'd felt that they filled the same space.

'Jack,' she said. 'Please remember. I am always on your side.'

He stood close to her, his fingertips tracing her shoulder and across her collarbone. His face was in half shadow, his eyes darting over her features as if to assure himself of something, to seek a truth from her. Her own expression, she knew, was lit by the glowing lamp. And would, surely, tell him how she felt. When he kissed her, locking her in his embrace, she felt the Jack she knew return to her.

And perhaps this is the way, Violet thought as she led him over to the bed, that it will be for now. By the time the first few days of his army leave had passed, she had him back. But then, he must put on his uniform and become a soldier again. Become a different man. And he must go away, again.

19

JANUARY: THE WOLF MOON; THE BLACKEST MONTH OF ALL THE YEAR

The hammering on the front door set Jess yapping in the kitchen below. Violet sat upright in bed, jolted from sleep, her mind tumbling with bad news and telegrams. Dread pooled in her stomach. She got out of bed in pitch darkness. Fumbling with her lamp, she heard her father's footsteps go past her bedroom door and down the stairs. She wrapped herself in her dressing gown and went out onto the landing. As she peered down into the gloom of the staircase, her father's lamp shadows swayed sickeningly over the walls.

The bolts on the door scraped and clunked, and she walked down the stairs on legs seemingly no longer made of flesh. As her father opened the door, she felt a murderous blast of icy air and caught a glimpse of clouds of stars in the crackling silence of the high midnight sky. And on their doorstep, the boy from Charlecote farm panting and begging for Dr Prideaux. Violet's father took hold of his collar and hauled him into the house, shutting the door.

'What now, what now?' he asked, shivering in his slippers. 'What's this to-do?'

The boy stuttered, breathless, his nose running, his cheeks raw. He'd run all the way.

He squinted in the lamplight, shielded his eyes. 'Master says you got to come quick. It's Missus. The baby's coming.'

Violet gasped, 'Claudia,' and sat down on the bottom stair.

Her father uttered, 'But this is her second child. Where is the midwife?'

'Midwife is sick,' the boy said. 'And Missus took the tansy tea, because the baby wasn't coming. But it's backwards, sir. Someone said to tell you. It's backwards.'

Violet's father set the lamp down and raced back up the stairs, calling for her to fetch his doctor's bag from the cupboard. She held it ready, standing mutely by the front door. There must be something she could do for Claudia. Was there nothing to be done but be hopeless and wait? The boy began to cry, snuffling into his sleeve.

'Pray the car starts first time,' her father said, as he thundered back down the stairs, grabbing his hat and coat. The boy trotted out after him.

Violet closed the door behind them, hearing the engine fire and putter off down the lane, and went through to sit by the kitchen range. Feeling a meagre heat ebb from the fire box, she wrapped her mother's old shawl around her and ruffled sleepy Jess under his chin. But the cold stayed with her, stiffening inside her. She knew she could never sleep, not with Claudia in childbed.

The kitchen clock ticked on to one, to two in the morning, and Violet, her sleepless mind taut with anxiety, could bear it no longer. She went upstairs to the attic room to fetch her journal and sat back down with it by the kitchen range.

'What have you done, Claudia?' she uttered, leafing backwards to find the page from nearly three years before:

20th June 1914. Found by the Regent's Canal, London.

Tansy flower (also known as bitter buttons, or cow buttons).

Flowering time: June to September, grows in hedgerows and wasteland. Highly aromatic. Used by old wives to bring on a birth or menstruation in women. Steep the flowers and use as a tea. Can be dried to use throughout the winter, but care must be taken, as drying intensifies its effects.

Claudia says her mother swears by it.

'Oh, Claudia... Mrs Ainsley,' she uttered. 'What have you done?'

She shut the book, rested her head back and listened to the dark silence outside. And yet it did not feel like countryside sleeping peacefully, but stricken woods, lanes and hedgerows all holding a collective breath under a punishing, hard freeze.

* * *

Violet didn't realise that she'd fallen asleep, cramped in the fireside chair, until the sound of the front door made her jump. The watery light of midwinter dawn had crept its way into the house. Jess pattered round, sounding fretful and hungry, her toes were cold and the fire in the range needed stoking. As the kitchen door opened, she moved to get up, but the look on her father's face pinned her to her chair.

He did not look her way but made straight for the scullery, balling up a shirt in his hands, but too late: Violet saw thick blood had stained the linen in clotted spreading layers.

She heard him lift the lid of the copper, but he must have changed his mind. He came back into the kitchen, opened the fire door of the range and stuffed the shirt into the embers. And he stood, his face blank and grey, staring at the kitchen clock, which blithely ticked on, its mechanics hard in Violet's head. She waited for him to speak, realising that she had stopped breathing.

'I tried,' her father said, his voice cracking the silence. He twitched his blank stare towards her. 'I tried the hardest I ever have. I don't think a man could have tried any more.'

Violet stared at him, the fluid in her body emptying to her feet.

He said, 'And she gave it all she could.'

Violet felt as if he had punched her.

'The baby?' she asked.

'Girl.'

She screamed, 'Alive or dead?'

Her father took a step back, his face ashen.

'Living.'

'Oh god. Claudia...' Violet uttered, her words useless and futile, littering the air.

'I left that poor soul Penruth standing mute in the corner of the room,' her father said, 'with the newborn screaming in the crib and Mrs Ainsley mindlessly rocking it. The poor woman. What more could I do? Was there anything more I could do?'

Violet pressed her hands against her temples, as if to crush the awful scene from her head.

'And little Harry,' her father blundered on. 'Standing at the top of the stairs, thumb in mouth, hair all messy from sleep, asking where his Mama was.'

20

IN THE LANGUAGE OF FLOWERS: RHODODENDRON, BE WARY

Six months later

The approach to Charlecote felt as grand and as sweeping as Violet remembered. She walked along the driveway curving around grand old trees, with morning sea mist veiling curling fern fronds and cushioning the pink flowers of rhododendrons, softening their gaudiness, and sprinkling each glossy leaf with moisture. The chimneys towered above the imposing Gothic house as always, and the upper windows remained curtained with maroon velvet. But, instead of the sleek Penruth car parked outside on the gravel, three ambulances stood in a row, with their back doors open.

Wearing her pristine uniform, hat and fluttering cotton veil, Violet walked up the steps, under the portico, through the front door and turned left into the nurses' quarters to report for duty. Here in the drawing room with its French windows overlooking the rolling lawn and standard roses, the tapestry cushions and silverware – everything that Claudia had admired as a little girl and everything she had presided over briefly as mistress of the house – had been packed away. The old Charlecote armchairs had been rearranged for the nurses to rest and take their tea. Rings from the cups now marked polished surfaces, scuffs appeared on the parquet, and, Violet noticed, a saucer from elder Mrs Penruth's favourite tea set had been used as an ashtray.

Emily, Charlecote's former parlourmaid, snored gently in her old employer's huge armchair, her hands red raw from scrubbing hospital linen and Willis, the long-suffering Penruth butler and now an efficient hospital orderly, walked past the French windows with an enormous stack of blankets in his arms. Mrs Ainsley – 'not quite all there' with grief according to Violet's father – would be helping in the kitchens.

'Morning, Violet,' said one of the night nurses, just off duty, resting by the window and hugging a cup of tea. 'Another day at the coal face.'

Violet offered her a wry smile and signed in at the register lying open on a George III bureau, once Weston Penruth's pride and joy. Matron had taken a shine to it and commandeered it to 'add a sense of decorum to the nurses' room'.

'We had a van load in last night,' the nurse said. 'And Dr Prideaux looked half done-in this morning, I can tell you.'

'I better get to it, then,' said Violet, and hurried off to report to Sister's office in a small room near the orangery.

Weston had quit Charlecote the day after Claudia's funeral and taken his two children up to his mother in Perthshire, handing the house over to the authorities, and in effect, Violet's father, to organise a Voluntary Aid Detachment hospital. And when each morning Violet began her ten-hour long shift, facing the poor souls who needed her care, she did it in Claudia's memory, and in the hope that another girl, somewhere, somehow, would help Jack in the same way, should he need it.

'Start in the main ward,' Sister said. 'And begin with bed baths where you can. Leave the worst of the burns patients to Nurse Peters – you are not properly trained for that sort of work.'

'Any losses during the night, Sister?'

'No, and we have your father to thank for that.' She opened the admissions and discharge ledger. 'This is your new charge: Private Lionel Morgan, aged twenty-two, bullet wound of foot. Bed 42. Came in late yesterday. Large toe destroyed. Second toe can be saved with surgery by Mr Carter, but it is way down the list. This patient also has a severe case of trench mouth.'

The woman pulled off her spectacles, breathed on them and cleaned them furiously. 'It's pretty obvious what has happened here,' she said. 'Surprised he made it this far. Thought he would have been court-martialled at the front. Pure case of PBI in my eyes. Go and see to him, Nurse Fairling and try to make him comfortable.'

'Of course, Sister, I will do my very best.'

Violet crossed the hallway, remembering the silent Charlecote of old, when Weston had shown her, Claudia and Eddie around. Now the elegant rooms and passageways rang with scurrying footsteps, clanking trolleys and muffled, earthy, sometimes piercing, cries of young men shipped home from Flanders and Picardy.

She pushed open the door to the ballroom. Weston's shutters had been removed, too cumbersome to deal with in a busy ward, but the chandelier always caught her eye, glinting incongruously over two rows of metal beds. Where there were means to do so, men turned their heads, or offered a flinching smile as Violet walked past. Some raised a hand in greeting, while Cartwright in Bed 36 lifted his bandaged stump and waved it at her.

Violet said good morning to each and every one, seeing faces brighten, seeing some crumble in agony. She gazed into eyes desperate to live, and others that wanted to die. The man in Bed 40 had spewed up stinking blood down his pyjamas and she added it to her list of things to attend to, convinced that every general, instead of sitting behind his desk in a Picardy château, should take a turn around this ward.

Private Morgan lay with his foot propped, wrapped with a festering field bandage. He tried to haul himself up at her approach but grimaced and shrieked like a child.

'Would you like a cup of tea?' she asked. 'I will also get you salt water. You need to gargle hourly to help your teeth and gums.'

'Sounds like a punishment, Nurse,' he uttered and pointed down the bed. 'But aren't you going to see to that first?'

As Violet began to unbind Morgan's foot, he grew as pale as sour milk, pain cracking up his leg. He began to struggle and writhe, and Violet froze as his screams grew louder and more violent, reaching the intricate plaster carvings on the ceiling. Nurse Peters hurried down from the far end of the ward, unceremoniously turned him over and, her thin face pinched in concentration, stabbed his buttock with a syringe of morphine.

'That should do it for now, but the foot's a mess,' the nurse said with an earnest glint in her eye. 'Mr Carter will see to it in surgery and will make sure he can rejoin his battalion within the month.' She turned abruptly to respond to a sudden keening cry from another bed.

Morgan continued to pant and rage, his fists clenched over his eyes, until the drug started to take effect. Violet studied his notes on the clipboard hung over the end of his bed, waiting for him to return to a more human shape.

'Thank you,' he said at last, breathless, resting back on his pillow, his face shining with a film of sweat. 'That will do it for a while. May I have a cigarette? In my pocket there.'

Violet took one from the packet, lit it for him, placed it in his mouth and returned to his notes.

'You look confused,' Morgan said, inhaling deeply, relishing temporary absence of pain and blowing smoke towards the ceiling.

'Sister mentioned something about PBI to me,' said Violet. 'I'm new, you see, and I'm just trying to find out what it could stand for...'

Morgan snorted in despair, his face fixed with a memory of something Violet could not hope to understand.

'PBI? I know what that is, all too well,' he muttered, sucking hard on nicotine. 'That's what we all are, us fellows. Poor Bloody Infantry.'

***

A week later, Violet pushed Private Morgan in a wheelchair through the double ballroom doors, across the hallway, along the back corridor and out into the garden. She negotiated the ramp, crossed the patio in front of the French windows and parked him by a bench with a view of the lawns and the mighty chestnuts beyond.

'Nice 'ere, isn't it?' Morgan said.

His cheeks looked a better colour that morning but his eyes retained dull chips of misery and his hands constantly twitched at his dressing gown cord.

'Having a nice holiday, I am, in a nice posh house in the country. Except the holiday will soon be over. That surgeon, Carter, is pleased with himself. He's too good, isn't he? Should have cut my foot right off. Then I wouldn't have to go back. Rehabilitation ought to take months but not from where I'm sitting. Commanding officer's been in touch, did you know? I'll have my orders soon. Back into the thick of it.' He paused, his eyes narrowing. 'I say, Nurse, my big toe's really itchy, could you just...? Silly me, it's not there any more.'

Violet indulged him with a sympathetic smile and sat down on the bench, gazing at the overgrown flower beds and the molehills in the lawn. Bees sipped at swathes of clover, and she knew full well what Weston would have to say about that. Her lower back burnt with the strain of lifting patients, bending to wounds and spillages. Her marrow ached and her temples throbbed, but she must keep going for the men like Morgan.

'Don't feel you have to stay,' muttered the soldier. 'I'm not going anywhere. Just going to sit here and rave.'

'I'll push you on in a moment, I just need to sit.' Violet felt in her pocket for Jack's latest letter, wanting to read a snippet to feel close to him.

Morgan said, 'That's all I do, sit – ha!'

Violet checked her watch. Five minutes, that's all she needed. She longed to be with Jack and Aster. The three of them, at the cove. She closed her eyes and held the dream in her grasp, almost smiled as it began to feel real.

'Do you know what it is that I cannot face again?' Morgan said.

'What's that, Private?' Violet sighed.

'It's the smell. There's this sweetness in the air over there. Rotting bodies. Men and mules. And then there's the pear drop smell, you know, just like when you were a kid in a sweet shop. That's gas. Every time a shell drops, well, you can imagine how it's all stirred up.'

Violet stared at Morgan, wondering how any of them manage to survive it, to tell the tale.

'Bullets you can take. The wound is clean enough. And we both know how this looks to the Brass.' Morgan pointed to his foot. 'But shell shrapnel is another matter. Jagged, deadly. Can rip a man apart. They come over, sounding like water trickling into a tub. Keep your bloody head down. My pal standing next to me. I think, if he can take the fear then so can I. Talking to me one minute. Blown to pieces, the next. And I mean... pieces.'

Panic sparked in Violet, drenching her insides with cold fear. How could she ever understand any of it? How could she ever know what Jack went through? A few months ago, he'd been home on leave but barely spoke, his eyes haunted. After they'd made love once, silently and swiftly, he got out of bed and slept alone in the spare room. He stared at Aster as she chattered and played, growing into an adorable little girl, as if taking a photograph in his mind. His fingertips buzzed and fidgeted; he could barely hold a pen long enough to do the crossword.

'Jack,' she'd said, that one time. 'Do you want to talk?'

'I can only talk in charcoal and paint, Violet. And sometimes, not even then.'

Morgan noticed the letter in her hand. 'Your sweetheart?'

'My husband. He's at Ypres.'

'What rank?'

'He's lieutenant.'

'Glad to hear it. Still one of us PBI. Just about. I don't like to say this in polite company, Nurse, but we Tommies hate the red-tabbed staff more than we hate the Boche.'

'Come on, Morgan,' Violet said. 'Let's do a circuit.'

She pushed the wheelchair around the corner of the house towards the front and trundled along the drive a little way. A flash of sunlight on metal caught Violet's eye; perhaps it was the postman cycling in on his bicycle, that beleaguered soul and the constant bearer of bad news. Like many folks, Violet imagined, she had grown accustomed to the headlines about pressing on at all cost. Another big push. The revolting lists of casualties. She felt dangerously separated, as distinct as the living are from the dead. She living; Jack among the dead.

'Ah, it's quite the family affair here for you, isn't it, Nurse? We have your eminent doctor father, and you, such a sterling nurse. And here comes your aunt to grace us with her presence.'

Muriel appeared around a corner in the drive pedalling her sit-up-and-beg bicycle, on her daily mission to read to the soldiers giving them both a cheery wave as she passed.

'What a woman,' sighed Morgan. 'Such a pleasure. Someone who looks at you like you are human. A bit formidable but immensely kind.'

'She is all of those things,' Violet said, thinking that morning of the little spat between her aunt and her mother, about who would be able to look after Aster.

Her mother had wanted to go to Looe to speak at a rally, along with other armchair patriots, to get more support for the war effort. In other words, Muriel had said, to persuade more mothers to send their sons, even if in reserved occupations. Her mother had only the day before taken a delivery of leaflets with the headline:

Women of Britain say 'Go!'

Spotting a car rounding a corner through the trees, Violet turned the wheelchair off the main drive to take Morgan back to the house the long way.

'Busy today, isn't it? Like Piccadilly Circus,' the soldier said.

'Perhaps it's another doctor coming for an interview,' Violet said.

'Well, we bloody need one. Oops, here comes Sister down the steps to greet this one. Look out, she's very keen.'

Violet grasped the wheelchair handles tighter and sped up. 'Come on, Private, let's get going. I've got a strong feeling I have been out here for far too long.'

'You'll be for the high jump,' Morgan said.

Violet bent to it, pushing faster. 'She'll have to catch me first.'

Morgan chuckled. 'Something tells me you're a little bit of a rebel, Nurse Fairling.'

'Did I ever tell you—' she laughed, 'about the time I ran away from school?'

* * *

With Morgan installed in bed and Aunt Muriel poised to read to him from *Jane Eyre*, Violet headed for the nurses' room to take her morning break. But Nurse Peters stopped her before she'd even crossed the hall.

'Nurse, can you fetch the enema equipment from the first floor bathroom? Cartwright's in trouble again and I need your help.'

'I was just about to—' Violet looked at the Nurse Peter's tired, watery eyes and remembered how difficult nursing Cartwright could be because, as well a stump for an arm, the nurses had to account for his two amputated legs. 'Of course, right away.'

She walked up the marble staircase and skirted the carpeted gallery landing. Most of the rooms on the first floor at Charlecote had been shut up since it opened as a hospital, with a few used as the doctors' offices. But the bathroom, reached through one of those rooms along the passageway, proved handy for the walking wounded.

Now that paintings had been removed and the carpet rolled up, the corridor felt neglected and bare, with grubby shadows on the walls where the frames had been highlighted by the sun streaming through a parade of elegant windows. Violet could only imagine how it might have once looked, with statuary and plant stands thick with specimens cut from Weston's hothouse to enhance his collection of art. Claudia would have loved it, she thought, for the brief time she'd lived here. She pictured her strolling along here with little Harry, making up stories about each of the paintings in turn. How sad the grand house seemed now, without her. A sorry version of itself.

Violet paused by a window, enjoying an elusive moment of peace away from the clamour downstairs. She gasped. There in a gap in the trees beyond the grounds, lay a fragment of clear blue sea. Remembering how she'd once thought she would never have a chance to see that view from Charlecote, she chuckled softly to herself. But grief found her, stinging at the back of her throat, as she carried on towards the doctor's office. She hoped that Claudia had enjoyed the view too.

Violet opened the door and stopped abruptly, uttering 'I'm sorry, I didn't realise...' Her blood seemed to change direction, clotting with shock inside her skull.

Weston Penruth had his back to her, naked from the waist up, his shirt in his hand. And her father stood behind the desk, busily rummaging in his doctor's bag.

Violet stepped backwards, reaching behind her for the handle but knocked her elbow on the door instead. She knew she must leave. She must go and shut the door, but she could not stop staring at the scars the colour of butcher's meat scored into Weston's back, his flesh raw and contorted, as if he'd recently come back from the Front with a terrible injury. But he hadn't. He had been in Perthshire with his children.

'Oh, it's you. Do give us a moment,' said her father. 'I meant to put the engaged sign on the door.'

Weston turned, livid at the intrusion, a half-snarl around his mouth. But his eyes softened, blinking in disbelief when he saw her.

'Violet?' he said, holding his shirt in front of his chest with a nod to modesty. 'I didn't realise you worked here.'

Violet saw lacerations, old scars now, stretching over the front of his shoulders and down his arms. No wonder he held himself in the way he did, she thought, as if concentrating on every move, disabled by the tightness of his skin.

'Ah yes, Violet makes a very good nurse,' said her father, retrieving a bottle of tincture from his bag. 'Although she ought to learn to knock before entering a doctor's office.'

'I'm sorry...' she uttered again.

'Was there something you wanted, Violet?' Weston said.

She caught the trace of sadness in his voice, with a bitter inflection on its tail.

'I came here to fetch some equipment. Cartwright will be waiting.'

'Fetch it then, dear. Be quick,' said her father, clipped and professional, although he gave her a sharp look of apology.

Violet peered around the room, loath to take another step into it. She felt petrified with shock. Encountering Weston so unexpectedly, and the gracelessness of the situation, the utter embarrassment of blundering into her father's surgery, seemed to load the air with shame.

But she spotted what she'd come for, darted to the shelf to grab it and scooted out of the room.

* * *

Walking home through the tranquil summer evening, breathing new air and feeling a fresh freedom in her limbs, usually revived Violet and salved the horrors of her working day. But today, the sight of Weston blinded her to any hope of forgetting.

The car pulling up while she pushed Morgan in his wheelchair had been his arrival, she realised, with Sister greeting him like she would any lord of the manor. Charlecote belonged to Weston, after all, but the shock seemed to have ingrained itself into Violet's bones, bringing back uncomfortable memories of his proposal three years before, the scandal of her departure, and Claudia's violent, sudden death.

She heard the puttering of a car engine approaching behind, breaking up the peaceful dusk in the lane. A creeping fear gripped her as it grew louder. Had he followed her to berate her for bursting in on his privacy? She shook herself, remembering her reaction to the doorbell on her first evening at Muriel's, hating him for provoking such extremes in her.

The vehicle eased itself alongside her with its passenger window down and she began to walk faster, feeling ridiculous at trying to outpace it. But she stopped, giddy with relief when her father called her name.

'Violet, hop in,' he said from behind the driver's wheel. 'I can't have you walking home. Not today.'

She slipped gratefully into the passenger seat, and he drove on.

'You don't usually finish at this time, Papa?' she said, sensing an oddity in his voice, as if he spoke to her as a doctor might, and not her father.

'I owe you an apology, Violet,' he said.

'I shouldn't have walked in like that, Papa. I should have knocked and waited. I'm sorry. It's very unprofessional.'

'Not for earlier, Violet. For keeping secrets from you. For everything.'

Violet turned her head to stare at him as he kept his eyes on the road, driving on as the hedgerows full and green with high summer rolled past on each side of the car.

'Papa?' she asked, hearing her childlike tremor.

'Weston Penruth,' he said.

She waited, stupefied, her blood hammering in her temples.

'You saw the state of him,' her father said. 'I was examining him because, as you know I have been studying the effects of scarring and burns, and how we can help heal them. My work at the London hospital, remember?'

'But Weston hasn't been to the Front. When did this happen?'

'He was a boy. And I first treated him then.'

A blackbird flew sharply across the lane, making Violet jump, shrieking its alarm call as it vanished into the hedge.

'But, Papa, the scars are horrific,' she said, aghast. 'I never seen anything like it. I realise... I realise now that he has always held himself in that curious restricted manner. He cannot walk without flinching. Was he burnt in a fire?'

'No, Violet.' Her father slowed the car as the lane narrowed on its approach to Old Trellick and he drew to a stop in his usual spot outside. 'His father tortured him.'

She sat still, staring through the windscreen at her home. A lamp glowed upstairs in Aster's bedroom, and a thin line of smoke rose gently from the chimney into the pale evening sky.

'*Tortured*, Papa?'

'His father, you may not remember him, was a brute.'

Violet caught movement in the corner of her eye – Muriel holding Aster up to the window, laughing with her, both waving down at the car. But her instinct to wave back had been crushed. She remembered something Claudia had said, a suggestion that all with Weston may not be as it seemed. And so, possibly, the place where Claudia's love for Weston had sprung from.

'Claudia said something to me once,' she said with difficulty, her mouth parched. 'About Weston... but I had no idea.'

'It started when he was quite young,' said her father. 'He said he could not remember a time when it didn't happen. Routine, as it were. Not for misbehaviour. Weston told me that he did not know how to behave, for whatever he did, he was punished.'

'Dear God...' uttered Violet.

'And in the end, it wasn't about the pain that piggy-backed him day and night, and the wounds that he had to hide, but of course, it was about power. And cruelty.'

'What about Mrs Penruth? Did she know?'

'I think she may also have been on the receiving end, from time to time. Although she never let on to me.'

Violet glanced at her father, hearing his despair.

'She came to me with him. He was about ten years old. You were just a baby, Violet. The wounds had become infected. His shirt stuck to his back with pus and bleeding scabs. I took care of him here at Old Trellick, treated him as best I could.'

'Oh, Papa, of course you did. But couldn't you report him – Mr Penruth?'

'He was our landlord, Violet. He had great power all over this corner of

Cornwall. What could we do? Go to the constabulary? They may well have been in his back pocket, like the magistrates and the mayor. And, as you can imagine, Mrs Penruth was eternally grateful to me, unable to express it properly to be frank, for keeping her counsel and helping her son.'

Violet thought of the elder lady, her difficult behaviour, and imposing presence, all the result of much unhappiness.

'And when Penruth died,' said her father, 'when Weston was about twenty, he and his mother pledged to help us. Promised to do whatever they could. They waived our rent for years. They offered to pay for your schooling.'

Violet felt nauseous as little scattered parts of her life began to fall into line. And yet, she still could not take it all in.

'But Papa, he shot his dogs.'

Her father sighed, his regret a heavy presence inside the car.

'We did not handle any of that properly. We knew he was keen to marry you. Perhaps that was all part of his gratitude, paying us back. And, of course, your mother was beside herself with joy. For, on the surface, what an eligible young man he was.' Her father gave Violet a rueful glance. 'Weston wanted things to turn out so neatly. Marrying you, he felt I'm sure, would secure the happiness that he'd never had. But he didn't account for your spirit, did he, Violet? I don't think any of us did,' he said with pride. 'And I think in a way, Weston also felt entitled.'

'He didn't know me,' Violet said. 'That was the problem.'

Her father glanced at her in admiration. 'That evening, after the afternoon tea debacle and his failed proposal, I was called up to the farm by Claudia's mother. Claudia was with him, helping him. She was so kind, so *good* with him. Stayed by his side until she knew he was all right. Eventually, weeks later, long after you'd gone up to Muriel's, Weston told me that the shotgun was meant for himself.'

Violet slumped back against the car seat, wrung out and exhausted by everything being beyond her control.

'Ah, here comes your mother,' her father said, 'wondering why we are still out here. Come on, Violet. We better go inside.'

21

IN THE LANGUAGE OF FLOWERS: HONEYSUCKLE, AN EVERLASTING BOND

The next day Violet could barely manage her breakfast. She'd had a restless night. The shock of seeing Weston's wounds and being told how he had received them kept her from sleep. And finally, when she dropped off, the complications of the whole situation cluttered her dreams. Even her slice of morning toast, browned to perfection and spread with good Cornish butter, clogged at the back of her throat.

'Come on, Violet, eat up,' said Aunt Muriel, pouring her another cup of tea. 'You need to keep your strength up for another day at Charlecote.'

'Thank you, auntie, but today is my day off,' she said. 'And thank goodness for that.'

'I must say you do look a bit peaky,' Violet's mother said. 'And before you say anything, I know it is totally understandable, all things considered.'

Violet caught a look between her parents, a sort of wary but blatant communication that they perhaps thought no one else noticed.

Her father folded his newspaper into a neat rectangle, laid it ponderously on the table, and said, 'Violet, we have something we would like to discuss with you.'

'Is it Jack?' Violet blurted.

'No, no, nothing like that,' Muriel said soothingly.

Violet glanced at her aunt. 'Well, what is it?'

Muriel looked around the table. 'If you will all excuse me, I think this is best left to the three of you,' she said, and went out of the room.

Violet waited. Her mother took great pains to wipe toast crumbs from her fingers, not catching Violet's eye.

Her father cleared his throat. 'So, this is the situation,' he said. 'As you know, Violet, I had dealings with Weston Penruth at Charlecote yesterday. And during our discussion, something came to light... a suggestion as it were, which I talked over with your mother last night after you'd gone to bed, and Muriel too, who happened to be still up, and I welcomed her input. We both did.'

Her mother sat up a little straighter and gave Violet an emphatic nod.

'And I would like,' he said, 'to put it to you, Violet.'

'What is it, Papa?' Violet said evenly, irritated by his drawn-out explanation.

'You may not have realised but Weston returned to Charlecote yesterday with his children. They are at the farm now with the Ainsleys, but Mrs Ainsley can't cope.'

'Someone told Muriel that she's become a bit of a broken-down Annie,' Violet's mother chipped in.

'Hardly surprising, Eleanor.' Her father gave her mother a sharp look, and went on. 'But as you know, Violet, Charlecote is no place for children at the moment and until Weston can make other arrangements, he asked if we would take them in here.'

'Here?' Violet said. 'Harry and the little baby?'

'Kate,' said her mother, who seemed to be swelling with delight the more Violet's father elaborated. 'And I think it would be an absolute honour and a pleasure to have the Penruth children living here. Under our roof, and in our care. Don't you think, Violet? After all, they are Claudia's children.'

'That goes without saying,' said her father, wanting to keep to practicalities. 'Weston explained that having been away from Charlecote previously for so long in London, and then leaving so abruptly for Perthshire in January, after poor Claudia's funeral, he has neglected the farm somewhat and wants now to work towards having the biggest and best harvest next year that Charlecote has ever seen. He is planning to move into one of his cottages, and do whatever he can for the war effort.'

'They will be our little refugees, bless them,' Violet's mother said. 'It's the least we can do. I think it will suit everyone all round, don't you think?' She gazed at Violet. 'Well, you're very quiet.'

'Why are you not surprised, Eleanor?' her father said. 'Let the girl think.'

Violet took a sip of fortifying tea, but it had gone cold. She let out a wry laugh.

'With all of the horrors taking place across the Channel...' she started carefully, not quite sure exactly what she wanted to say, 'the things that Jack has told me, and the soldiers at the hospital, I think everyone must do the right thing here back at home. I think giving a home to the children is the right... is the proper thing to do.' But a small voice inside her head kept asking what Jack would say. 'After all,' she said, 'it's only temporary.'

'I should say so,' said her father.

Her mother tapped her hands together. 'I never thought you'd agree to this, Violet, after everything that has happened.'

'Something tells me that you didn't need my approval, Mother. It sounds to me that you had, all of you, already made up your minds.'

'Just think of Aster,' said her mother, 'she will have new little playmates right here.'

'I expect you will let Jack know in your next letter, Violet?' her father asked.

'Yes, I will,' Violet said hesitantly. 'And I am sure he will be supportive about it.'

'It's not really up to him, though, is it?' her mother said, curtly.

Trying her hardest not to feel annoyed with her, Violet said, 'One thing's for sure, Mother, Claudia would have loved the idea.'

* * *

Towards the middle of the afternoon, Violet stood by the front window with Aster in her arms and watched as the Penruth car pulled up outside Old Trellick; a smaller model, she noticed compared to before the war when Weston had a chauffeur and didn't have to drive himself.

Violet's mother gave a cry of joy, and hurried down the path to the gate, trailed by Aunt Muriel, and Violet heard the chattering hum of their excited welcomes as Weston got out of the car. He gave them a humourless yet polite welcome and bent into the back seat to pick up Harry, who at shy of two years old, held tightly onto his father's lapels and gazed about with a discerning glare. Her mother fetched the bassinet containing baby Kate from the footwell and walked back towards the house with a triumphant spring in her step. Muriel followed with Harry, who clutched a ragged posy of honeysuckle and dog roses.

Watching Weston busy himself unloading suitcases, Violet saw the stiff way he moved, his buttoned-up gestures, in a whole new light. She sensed she understood him a little better, knew what lay beneath his exterior. And she felt sorry for him, as Claudia had admitted she did herself, all that time ago at the cove when the gorse had torn her dress.

Aster wriggled in Violet's arms and shot her hand out, pointing through the window. 'It's a boy.'

'Yes, yes, little maid,' Violet said. 'Do you remember him from the beach? Ah, no you won't. You're all still so young. But he and his sister are coming to live here at Old Trellick. Look, Kate is only a little baby.'

The children arrived in the hallway, and Aster twisted her little body, wanting to be put down. Violet set her gently on the floor and watched as she trotted to the door and peered around it.

'Ah, now here she is,' Violet's mother said. 'Here is Aster. Say hello to Harry, dear, that's it.'

Muriel set Harry on his feet. He did not appear as chubby as he had been when she'd last seen him. He had lost his puppy fat, becoming as lean as Claudia had been. In the bassinet, still cradled by Violet's mother, six-month-old Kate looked like she needed a good sleep. Her rosy cheeks, reddened by teething, were tear stained. Her baby hair, sneaking out from under her lace bonnet, appeared the colour of corn, the exact match of her mother's.

Violet expected Harry to make a beeline across the hallway to giggling Aster, but he toddled straight past her, and came up to Violet, sitting down with a plonk in front of her. He held the bunch of flowers up to her, one or two stems escaping his tight little grasp.

'Are you a mummy?' he asked.

'I certainly am,' she said, accepting his gift, and felt something crack inside her.

A shadow darkened the front door and Weston hesitated on the threshold.

'Come in, come in, Mr Penruth,' said Violet's mother. 'We won't stand on ceremony. Let's get the children settled in the parlour and we can all have tea.'

'I'll take the suitcases upstairs, shall I?' he asked.

'Oh, George can do that when he's home from the hospital,' Violet's mother said.

Weston came in, closed the front door, and offered Violet an apologetic look, which she returned with a smile. She understood, now, how his abrupt manner disguised his pain, his general lack of social grace echoed the insecurity beaten into him as a child.

'The roses and honeysuckle, Violet,' he said, as her mother ushered them all through to the parlour. 'We stopped on the way over, and Harry picked them from the verges. We thought you'd like them... the lovely wildflowers.'

'I do,' she said, 'and I will put them straight into water.'

The two children settled down on the floor together with their backs against the sofa. They touched fingertips, cocked their heads to gaze at each other, and exchanged their whispered subliminal messages of childhood.

* * *

As Violet sat down in her bedroom that evening to write to Jack, she heard it start to rain, pattering against her opened window. She pushed it wider, breathing on the new wafts of fresh tangy air, hoping it would refresh her and clear her mind.

After the commotion of the past two days, she needed a little time, a little space to gather her thoughts. The children all slept now, to everyone's delight. Weston had left after one cup of tea, repeating his thanks, managed a warmer, wider smile, his façade loosening to reveal a strange, humble sadness.

But in her letter to Jack, Violet left all of this out. She reminded him about

Charlecote becoming a hospital for soldiers, and told him of the Penruths' return. She wrote that her parents wanted to take care of Claudia's children for the time being, and that she thought it might be nice for Aster to have them around. She did not mention Weston, thought it best to leave him out. For it did not seem fair to let Jack read about him while he sat in his bunker at the Front. She signed her name and told him she loved him. That she always would.

Turning down the lamp, she twitched the bedroom curtains closed, and wondered if it was still raining 'somewhere in France'.

22

IN THE LANGUAGE OF FLOWERS: NETTLE, SLANDER

Weston Penruth's wheat fields shimmered cloudy gold in the dawn light, knee-high to a man, with birds darting over the ripening ears. They all sat in the back of the wagon on bales of straw, Violet clinging tightly to Harry and Kate as it bumped and jiggled along the lane, the carthorse's hooves ringing a steady beat. Jack held Aster on his knee, his hair army-cropped and his skin brown from four summers on the battlefield, tanned so deeply that his features seemed unreadable. But as Aster giggled and squealed with each lurch of the wheels, cautious happiness emerged like a film of sweat over his face.

Violet caught his eye, offered a smile and the invisible cord pulled her towards him, as it had done the first time she saw him in Regent's Park. Jack returned a guarded smile, little more than an acknowledgement, and his detachment, his silence, crippled her.

Around the field the mighty oaks wore deep-summer green and the light behind them rose milky and ethereal. But what about the mornings over there? What did dawn look like in the valley of the Somme? How did evening fall along the Menin Road? Jack had told her once that time seemed to work in a different way. But how did those hours pass for him? She could not imagine, and she knew she couldn't ask. But she would do her best to understand should he ever feel he could tell her.

The driver reined the horse in, the wagon drew to a shuddering stop, and the sun eased itself up over the fields, like a promise.

'I think it's going to be a beautiful day,' Violet said.

'Come on then,' Jack said, brightening suddenly, undoing the back of the wagon and leaping down. He held out his arms to Aster. 'Come on, then. Shake a leg, all of you.'

He lifted each child in turn, giving each one of them a whoop and a playful flourish, setting them gently on their feet in the stubble of wheat. His acceptance of Weston and Claudia's family, perhaps, Violet thought. He had not responded to her letter last year when she broke the news to him that Harry and Kate had come to live at Old Trellick, and she half wondered if it had been lost; it surprised her that her letters reached him at all. But on his return home on leave last autumn, and now, his acquiesce seemed to come from indifference. And, still, they had not discussed it; Weston's name unspoken. It felt like one more burden Jack could not endure.

He took her hand now as she stood at the back of the wagon and helped her down, his grip firm but careful, as if he did not know how to hold her.

Weston's farmhands, old men, boys and women from Lansallos, had started harvesting yesterday, and stooks stood in the far corner ready to be loaded onto the wagon. Violet spotted Mrs Davey and her younger children. They all must have arrived before dawn this morning, bending to it with their sickles, already into their rhythm, their songs high on the still air.

Jack went to join them, and Violet took the children along the edge of the field and spread the rug in the shade of an oak. She unpacked tea pails, baskets of sandwiches, and water bottles. End-of-summer heat began to rise through the air already, disturbing odours in the earth: tangy roots, pungent soil and the dry, dusty scent of the felled wheat.

'Now, Aster, Harry, stay where I can see you,' Violet said, as the children scooted off to explore the hedgerow, and its margins speckled with poppies and cornflowers. 'You're not to go into the field. The harvesters have sharp blades.'

Harry, who always stuck close to Aster's side, gave Violet a solemn nod, but Aster said, 'How do I know where you can see me, Mama? If you can see me? And, what if I want to go and see Daddy?'

'You can't do that, darling. Not while he's working. I'm sure he will say hello each time he reaches the end of his row.'

Aster stared into the field, giving a little shake of her head as she tried to pick Jack out among the figures bent to their work, her anxiety tangible. And Violet had become used to her daughter's worried little expressions. Each time Jack returned for a brief spell of leave, Aster's days revolved around him. They gravitated towards each other; a joy to witness. Whenever Violet worked at the hospital, he took Aster on walks to the cove and into the woods and they basked in deckchairs in the garden at Old Trellick, side by side, their chattering conversations ebbing and flowing, while the days for Violet and her time with Jack slipped all too quickly by.

'Watch out for nettles, Aster!' she called, sounding cross when, really, she felt the usual creeping fear. 'There's a big patch right there!'

'Yes, Mama.'

Violet watched Aster and Harry play, and little Kate, an eighteen-month-old replica of Claudia, leant against her, seeking a cuddle. Violet wondered if the child wanted reassurance as well as attention, for the wheat field must feel as empty and as big as an ocean to her, and likely to swallow her up.

'Your mama would have loved today, Kate,' Violet said. 'She would have loved you.'

But Kate could not understand, and concentrated on tracing the stitching around Violet's skirt with her tiny forefinger.

Aster mooched back with a handful of flowers and leaves, trailed by Harry, and they proceeded to scatter them on the rug around Violet and Kate like a sort of offering. They sat down together, a serious little pair, and began to sort the flowers into colours and size, their still-babyish skin flushed from the sun, leaning their heads together as they played, as if absorbing each other's thoughts.

'Mama, is Daddy going to have a picnic with us?' Aster asked. 'We have enough for him, don't we?'

'Of course we do,' Violet said, 'That's why we are here. So he can rest with us, have his lunch with us. Oh look, there he is.'

Jack had come to the end of his row. He lay his sickle down and stood for a moment, wiping his face and around the back of his neck with his handkerchief.

'Pop over, Aster, and ask him if he wants his water bottle,' Violet said. 'He must be thirsty already. Even though it's become overcast, the sun will be strong behind the clouds.' She turned rearrange Kate's bonnet, to make sure it shaded her face.

But Aster must have heard incorrectly. Violet looked up to see her lugging one of the bottles across the stubble, struggling to keep hold of it, but wanting so hard, trying so hard, to take it across to Jack.

'Aster, no, I didn't mean that. It's too heavy for you,' Violet called. 'Put it down, darling. Aster!'

Hearing Violet shout her name, Aster spun around. The bottle slipped from her hands, hit a stone in the stubble and smashed into pieces.

Jack thundered over to her. 'What do you think you're doing!' he yelled, standing over Aster and the broken glass, sounding hard and livid, and not like Jack at all. 'Aster, you've wasted it. It's broken. What a terrible waste.'

Aster flinched, gazed up at her father in disbelief, fighting confusion and pain. Her mouth trembling as she began to cry.

'Oh, for goodness' sake, Aster, no tears please,' Jack muttered. 'That won't help anyone.' He turned away, back to where he'd left his sickle. He picked it up and walked back into the standing wheat.

Violet told Harry to watch Kate and hurried over to her, gathered her up. Aster pressed her face into her neck making it damp.

'Come, come,' Violet soothed. 'Daddy is not cross with you. He is just very busy. It is hard work, you know, harvesting the wheat. What about the flowers you and Harry have picked? Let's have a look at them. Shall we use them to make Kate a crown?'

Aster nodded tearfully, rubbing her face with the back of her hand, in that instant suddenly so baby-like again. Violet could see the effort she made, sitting back on the rug, as she tried to shake off the creeping trauma of Jack's anger, to pretend it didn't matter. And Violet knew exactly how she felt.

'Papa's here!' Harry cried suddenly. 'Look! He's here!'

The little boy scrambled to his feet and dashed over towards the gate as Weston came through and walked up the side of the hedgerow towards them. Propped over his shoulder lay something peculiarly long and heavy, and he held a heavy leather case in his other hand.

'What do you have, Papa?' said Harry, darting around Weston, his joy at seeing his father unexpectedly, almost painful to watch. 'What's this?'

'Ah, give a man some space, my boy,' Weston said, coming towards the little gathering. 'My, my, this looks idyllic. Good morning, Violet. This vignette could be from any time in the last five hundred years. Immortal. The harvesters at work in the field, and the families gathering with their sustenance.'

Violet returned his greeting with a tight smile, and the atmosphere shifted, like a sudden change in the weather. She hadn't seen Weston for a good while, or really, had managed to avoid him. Whenever he came to Old Trellick to collect his children to take them out for the day, she lingered in the back garden or upstairs in the attic room. And when she was at Charlecote her work caring for the injured soldiers left her with no space to even consider him. And she certainly avoided going up to the first floor.

But this was Weston's field, his wheat, she thought. He had every right to be here. More than a right. It was his privilege. And she saw how happy his children were.

He set down what Violet could now see as a folded-up tripod, and the case which, she guessed, must contain a camera. Harry buzzed around him, excited beyond measure.

'You can have tuppence, Harry, there you go.' Weston dropped a coin into the little boy's hand. 'And one for Kate. And Aster...'

Harry doled out the coins, and as the children inspected each other's gift, Weston gave Violet an enquiring glance.

'I've got a new hobby, Violet,' he said, standing the tripod on its feet and undoing the buckles on the case. 'Had this lot sent down especially from London.'

As he had done with the forced flowers, the roses, lilies and peonies, Violet thought grimly, the bouquet that started it all.

Weston reached down to cluck Kate under the chin.

'There's my sweet little maid,' he said.

But Kate looked simply bemused. She barely recognised him.

'Can I have a go with the camera, Papa?' Harry asked, the coin now secure in his pocket, and wanting something else from his father.

'You're too young, my boy, but stand there properly, pay attention and I will show you. Look, Harry, but don't touch.' Weston began to unpack the camera, setting it out on the rug. 'See here is the shutter and the lens. Now that is the costly part of the whole thing, so no dirty fingerprints please. Watch Kate, don't let her...'

Violet pulled Weston's daughter on to her lap and Aster retreated to her side, as unsettled as Violet by Weston's intrusion, the strange equipment taking over the rug, and the new rules.

'Jack has thrown off his military hat for today,' she said, conversationally, to point out his presence to Weston, forewarn him in a way, and help ease the discomfort she felt with both men being near each other. To somehow make it normal. 'He's busy with the harvesters over there.'

But Weston glanced with disinterest over his shoulder and carried on setting up his camera.

Aster nudged Violet. Her tears had dried, and she wanted her attention, pulling at her hands as she held little Kate.

'Mama, the flowers, remember. Which ones shall we choose?'

Aster began to gather the scattered cornflowers and white mayweed, the tiny petals falling away between her fingertips.

'Oh, they are fading already in the heat, Aster,' Violet said. 'But look, you found some mint. We can make it into a tea if you like. Shall we ask Auntie Muriel to do that for you later? She likes mint tea. It'll help you sleep.'

'What are these yellow ones?'

'Ah, they're tansies,' said Violet. 'Bitter buttons.'

At the corner of her eye, she saw Weston flinch, grimace, and turn his head away.

'We don't want those, Aster,' Violet said. 'Let's throw them back into the hedge.'

'Why, Mama?'

'They're... they can be poisonous.'

Weston gave an odd half-laugh, grief glittering in his eyes. 'I hope they're keeping up the pace out there. We can't have them slacking, can we Harry? We can't fight the Hun if we're hungry.'

Violet glanced at the field. Jack had stopped. He stood knee-deep in the wheat, staring at them all sitting on the rug: Violet holding Kate; Aster with

Weston and his children. He looked closed-in and rigid with shock. He looked like a different man.

'Daddy!' Aster cried, waving, suddenly luminous with joy. 'Over here! Here I am!'

Her call, high and thin over the stubble, broke the spell. Jack shook himself, renewed his grip on his sickle, lifting it, and bent to slash through the golden stalks.

'Why didn't he come over to see me, Mama?' Aster said. 'Is he still cross?'

'I expect so,' Violet said, but how could she be sure? She'd glimpsed his anger, certainly, and his despair flaring behind it, radiating towards her. 'But don't worry, Aster. He is possibly all hot and bothered in this muggy weather. I'm not surprised. Now what about this crown of flowers for Kate?'

Weston glanced at Violet, and seemed to appraise her.

'Ah yes,' he said, 'but now it's turned cloudy, the light is good. Perfect for a photograph. I think all of you on the back of the wagon, children. What do you say, Harry? You, too, Aster. Come on, would you like to be in the photograph?'

He strolled over to the wagon with his tripod and camera, Harry dashing after him, and began setting up, pacing out distances over the stubble, and adjusting his position. He fiddled with the lens, pressed his eye to the viewfinder.

'Mama, come on.' Aster tugged at her hand.

'That's right, Violet,' Weston called out, 'you, too.'

'Yes, Auntie Violet,' Harry mimicked. 'You too!'

Violet noticed Jack stop again in the field, halfway along his row. She was further away this time, and could not make out his expression, but the way he stood, the way his body seemed to strain against itself, filled her with a strange and creeping fear. Something did not feel right, as if she had not heeded a warning. But the children kept up their excited appeals, filling her head with their chatter. She picked Kate up and walked over to the wagon, ushering Aster in front of her, wanting to please her, to make her happy.

'Here you are, Aster,' she said, and Aster ran towards the wagon to join Harry. Still holding Kate, she turned to Weston and said evenly, 'I don't want to be in the photograph.'

'Why ever not, Violet?' Weston muttered, and took Kate from her arms. 'I will make sure you have a flattering light.' He glanced across to the harvesters in the glimmering wheat. 'Is it Jack? Is your husband becoming a little rocky upstairs?' He tapped his finger against his temple.

'He's been at the Front for years,' Violet snapped. 'You must have heard what it does to a man?'

'I dare say.'

Weston walked off with Kate, and set her on the back of the wagon, then lifted Harry and Aster in turn and sat them with her against the bales.

'Hotch up, Harry,' he said, 'keep a good hold of Kate. Aster, squeeze in, that's it.'

Aster and Harry giggled, nudged each other, shuffling their bottoms in the scattered straw. Kate looked like she might burst into tears. Violet drew back from the wagon, wanting to move out of the way, but knowing she must keep an eye on the little ones. Weston went behind the camera and peered into it, holding his finger aloft to attract the children's attention.

'Come on, Violet,' he said, gesturing irritably, 'it's one for the family album.'

'I said no, Weston, I don't think it is appropriate,' she said, her annoyance turning to anger, firing darts inside her head.

'There, I have taken a photograph anyway,' he said. 'Just a test shot, but you're in it. In the corner. But we shall see when I have it developed. Now, the children.' He bent back to his viewfinder.

'Weston, really, I...' Violet's patience broke with a painful snap, and she walked towards him, her rage rising, wanting him to undo what he done, to erase the photograph. To have not done it in the first place. She didn't want to be captured like that, without her permission. She wanted Weston to stop encroaching on her life, to be forever linked with her. If he hadn't married Claudia, Claudia would still be alive. Violet wanted him gone, wanted him to leave her and Jack and Aster alone. She hated him and wished he'd disappear.

But Jack moved more quickly than her. He came out of the dusty dull gold of the wheat field with dreadful purpose, as if he had no weight in his body, his strides long with force and intent. The muscles in his arm wiry but as sharp as blades. He swung the sickle, and it glinted in the light. He bellowed Weston's name. Weston glanced up from his camera, bewildered and blind-sided, and Violet saw the bright flash of metal for a brief, poised second.

'Jack!' she cried.

Aster screamed, 'Daddy!'

But Jack kept walking, straight up to Weston. He raised his arm, brandishing the sickle and, caught in an eerie, massive balloon of silence, swung it down.

Violet heard a sickening crunch and Weston's intake of breath. And a strange, crushed stillness. No one spoke. They had forgotten how.

The children's screeching shattered the silence, like the sound of Aster dropping the glass bottle. And Weston's scream drowned them out, surging violently up and out across the broken wheat stubble, hanging in the hot muggy air and branding itself inside Violet's mind.

* * *

She found him huddled in the lee of the dune. A breeze had picked up here at the cove, and a hundred voices rattled in the marram grasses. She knelt beside him in the sand, wrapped him in her arms, and he leant against her, curling himself around her, his teeth chattering, exhaling long shuddering sighs.

'When will this end, Violet? When will this end?' Jack rubbed trembling fingers over the stubble on his chin. He glanced down at Weston's blood on his shirt. 'If he's dead, then it will be over. I will be spared the Front.' He broke into a bitter laugh. 'You can kill whoever you like over there, you know. Kill the men that have done no wrong, just happen to have been born in Dusseldorf or Berlin. But here, now, it's the noose for me, isn't it?'

Violet wanted to tell him no, it cannot be, but her ability to reason with him dissolved, the struggle over. She gently pulled his head on to her shoulder, rested her face on the top of his head and let her hot tears soak his hair.

She asked Jack why... why had he done it, but thought he can't have heard her.

Eventually, he shifted around so he could look her in the eye.

'A broken love affair, that's what your mother said. In the garden at Montagu Square,' he said, and she saw the hollowness in his eyes, as if his soul had been erased. 'And there you were, with him. With his children. Looks like he thinks he still has a chance. Does he?'

'Jack, no. Please, believe me.'

'Is it over?' he asked.

'It never began,' Violet said weakly.

How unbearable it felt, the consequence of her father's one act of kindness towards Weston all those years before. One act that changed the course of her life. She smoothed Jack's hair, still dusty from the wheat, over his forehead, and remembered, also, that Jack had changed her path. From the moment she walked into the rose garden at Regent's Park, the sunlight glorious, the flowers a blur of colour, not aware that he watched her, took note of her.

How differently she had felt, earlier, when Weston had wanted to take her photograph. She had felt uncomfortable, trapped and cornered. But with Jack, when she saw his painting of her, although angry at first, she had been released. The memory pulsed like a beam of happiness. *Violet in the Daytime* lay tucked away in Muriel's cellar in London. We send for it, she decided, it should be framed and on display for everyone to see. For even before she walked into that rose garden, in her mind, they had already met, had been in love for years. And she'd known him then, at once. Had recognised him. Jack, beside her now, wrecked by the war. Always Jack.

'What's that you say?' she asked.

'I said... I couldn't bear it, seeing you with him, sitting on the rug with the children,' Jack spoke with apology. 'You looked like your own little family. And I might as well not be here.'

His words floored her. Earlier, last year when she had told him about the plan for the children, Violet had worried that Jack might feel this way. But she had reminded herself then that they were also Claudia's children. Seeing him staring at them across the wheat field, she understood the gravity of his fear.

'I realise that now, Jack, and I am so sorry,' she said, but that single word did not sound enough. 'We will leave Cornwall, you, me and Aster, go to live in Camden, or go down to Kent where your father is, when all this is over. Get away from *him*.'

'It is never over,' Jack said in surrender. He shuffled around and lay his head on her lap, his body slumping. She rested her hand behind his ear and gently stroked his hairline. 'It won't be over until I can sleep,' he said. 'And I can't sleep. I dread the night, but the days are worse. What can a man like me do, but go on with his sickening fate? The wheat field—'

'What, Jack? The wheat field? What do you mean?'

Shifting a little to catch her eye, he said, 'I thought it would not get any worse than Loos. And what happened with Welstead right at the start. But in Picardy, on the Somme...' Jack winced.

Violet braced herself; she had asked Jack the questions, and he seemed ready to answer her.

'We had prepared for this, my God,' he said. 'This is what everything since 1914 has been about. This is what we came for. We were the boys who had trained together, remember? All that time out on Salisbury Plain. The Pals. Civilian life had become a foreign country. Remember how difficult it was for me to be back home?'

'I do, Jack, of course I do,' Violet whispered.

'It was our purpose, our reason, all of us together. I remember thinking this as we crawled along in darkness on our bellies through the wheat. The farmer, his house was just over the hill, had left it to the weeds.'

Violet sighed, realising. 'Ah, I see...' she said, 'the wheat field...'

'It was perfect cover for us. We waited for the dawn. But not wanting it, even though this was our *purpose*. Never wanting it. The hour.'

Violet held her breath, her flesh icing over. She had wanted to know, and reality began to play out for her, presented as a picture by Jack, the artist: dawn on the Somme.

'The whistle, somewhere along the line,' he said. 'Hundreds of us, identical, rise out of the wheat, but each one of us separate, a distinct life. We each have our lives, our ways, our homes. We emerge like we are being born. Row upon row of us. We want to apologise to the farmer, wherever he is, for ruining his crop. And yet it stands, and we have the advantage, the element of surprise. An adventure story. We'll win, of course. They told us we will win.' He stared at Violet and she saw the pain of deception in his eyes. The breaking of trust.

'The ground is dry and stony. And birds start to dip past, like they do in Weston Penruth's field. Yes, amazing the birds are still there, feasting on the seeds, taking their fill. But they're soon gone when the noise starts. It comes from nowhere: metallic, mechanical, persistent hacking. Brutal, man-made. They fall to their knees on my left, rifles still brandished, useless. The men to my right bow, a strange salutation to the morning light. And they keep on falling, some silently, their lives cut before they hit the ground, harvested, falling. Some scream like children. Over in the copse, the little knoll of trees we did not notice, did not reckon with, the row of machine gun nests keep up their sickening strafe. No matter how many of us fall, it keeps on going. And I hear the swelling screams, the swearing, cursing God. I hear chaos. This is what death sounds like. I hear a cry, "Why, why, why?" Remember what Welstead said, "Go forward, at all costs." We lose our humanity in that farmer's wheat field, dying like cattle. Shrapnel turns the sky silver. They're sending in the shells. We have no means of protection against this... this. Let me tell you about the noise, Violet. The sound of men dying like this is not human. It is a revolting momentum, a revolting inevitability. They got it wrong. Got it so wrong.'

Violet leant forward, her mouth gaping, dumbstruck. She pressed her face to his. She didn't know what else to do.

Jack whispered, 'Tell me, Violet, how is it I am still alive?'

'I cannot answer that,' she uttered and held him, trying to contain his shivering, hold his trembling hands in hers, while the waves continued to wash over the shore and the sun crept out to sparkle on the sea.

'I tried to stop it, earlier at the harvest,' Jack said, after a little while. 'Knee-deep in the wheat stalks. I tried to control the feeling, the immense tearing feeling of being lost, being insignificant. Having no control. But I saw you with him, you see. Him taking photographs. Our little family. My most precious things. My Violet and my Aster. The things I stay alive for. But he was taking them away from me. He nearly took them from me.'

'He hasn't taken us, Jack,' she said. 'We are here.'

* * *

An hour later, possibly two – Violet did not know, for time seemed to expand generously through the afternoon, giving them more moments together than they deserved – Muriel emerged from the path down to the cove and made her indomitable way across the sand towards them.

'He's in bad shape,' she said, before Violet could ask, her eyes darting between her and Jack, dark and unreadable. 'They took him on the wagon to Charlecote. Your father is with him now. They're waiting for the surgeon to finish what he's doing so he can operate. The wound in his thigh is gaping. Your father said he saw the ligaments.'

Jack uttered a groan, and Violet pulled him closer, but he moved away from her.

'Your father says they have to keep an eye on gangrene,' Muriel said. 'But he said he'll live.'

'Where the hell are the police?' Jack said. 'I thought I'd be in cuffs by now.'

'It's been reported.' Violet's aunt, usually good in a crisis, seemed to struggle. 'Someone, Mrs Davey I think, went straight to the station at Looe.'

'As soon as the Red Caps hear about this, I will be done for,' Jack said.

'And...' Muriel said. 'Weston, despite his incapacitation, ordered that a car go from Charlecote to Old Trellick to pick up Harry and Kate. I don't think Aster realises what has happened. Any of it...'

'We must get back to her, Jack,' Violet said. 'She needs us.'

23

IN THE LANGUAGE OF FLOWERS: SWEET PEA, DEPARTURE

But Jack, when they eventually made their way up to Old Trellick, did not want to go in.

'Will you sit with me, Violet, outside for a while?' he said. 'I should pack up my kit, but I can't face them, any of them, yet. Probably never. They have never approved of me, accepted me, not truly.'

'Jack, it's only Mother. Papa and Aunt Muriel, they...'

'But this should put the tin lid on all of it. Imagine what your mother must be saying about me in there.'

Violet gazed at her home, embedded so deeply in the landscape, in her life, and yet she too felt that she did not want to cross its threshold. Not yet.

She walked with Jack around to the back garden and sat on the bench by her father's unruly end-of-summer border. Her father would understand, and he would be the voice of reason, for he had seen at close hand what war does to a man, to his body and inside his head. She wished he would come back from the hospital at Charlecote, for him to be here, offer Jack his support and to her, his calm no-nonsense counsel.

'I will have to go inside at some point,' Violet said, spotting her mother and aunt through the open French windows sitting down to play cards. She wondered how they could carry on with such trivialities. Perhaps, they tried to keep up appearances for Aster's sake. Aster sat curled up in the armchair, fighting tiredness, Violet could tell, tracing her finger over the newspaper crossword that Jack had started the day before. Jess lay on the floor in front of the chair, looking after Aster in her absence.

Violet heard the faint chimes of the clock in the hallway.

'Aster should be in bed by now,' Violet said as Jack lit another cigarette.

'What have I done?' he uttered, his words trailing and pointless. 'Do you think she will ever forget what she saw?'

'Will any of us?'

As dusk settled, the scent of her father's sweet peas, rambling up the bamboo frame behind them, intensified. Violet left Jack and walked over the lawn towards the house. She stopped at the French windows, leant against the doorway and watched Muriel deal cards into a circle. Jess lifted his nose to greet her. Her aunt snapped the final card down and her mother inhaled sharply.

'We shouldn't be doing this now, Eleanor,' said Muriel, quickly gathering the pack together. 'We really shouldn't.'

They both looked up to see Violet at the doorway and Muriel seemed to shrink into her guilt. But her mother turned to Aster in the armchair, projecting whatever embarrassment or shame she felt onto her, saying that she ought to be in bed.

Wishing they'd not decided to play Muriel's fortune telling parlour game, not tonight of all nights, Violet came into the room and knelt by Aster's chair. Her little girl sleepily struggled with her yawns, noticed Violet and reached up to touch her tear-stained cheek.

'Grannie's right,' Violet said, 'it's time that little girls were in bed. And it is high time Aunt Muriel put the cards away.'

'But where is Daddy?'

'He's taking a stroll,' Violet said lightly, despite the pain expanding wide across her chest. 'He will come up and tuck you in, he won't be long.'

'Where's Harry? It's his bedtime too.'

Violet hadn't the strength to tell her that Harry and Kate had been taken back to the cottage at Charlecote. And that her father would soon be gone too.

* * *

Violet and Jack sat up in the parlour after everyone else had gone to bed.

Her father had returned earlier from Charlecote and they had all gathered in the hall as he told Jack that Weston had had an operation and appeared to be stable.

'But,' he had said, 'the policeman from Looe visited Penruth when he came round. And he is going to instigate the full force of the law.'

'Inform the Military Police?' Jack had asked, although he already knew.

'Indeed.'

Violet had glanced at her father's sorrowful face and saw his allegiances stretching and tearing. Her own distress seemed to melt her bones.

Muriel placed her hand on Jack's arm.

'Jack,' she said, 'is there anything any of us can do?'

'Nothing, Muriel. Thank you, but there is nothing anyone can do,' he said, and Violet felt the humiliation in him. 'When you have been at the Front, things like this seem not to matter... it's inconsequential... I could walk out any morning... and be dead. I've seen it far too many times—'

'Listen to the man!' Violet's mother had cried. 'He thinks this is inconsequential. I don't know why you are bothering to comfort him, Muriel. He needs punishing.'

'He means inconsequential to *him*, Mother,' Violet had responded in fury, in dismay, 'don't you understand?'

'I don't want to hear any more about it,' she'd said. 'I want nothing more to do with you, Jack. I hope you are listening to this, Violet. I trust that by the time I wake in the morning your husband will be gone.'

Violet's had mother turned and walked up the stairs, trailing her blistering rage in her wake.

And now, they waited, while the parlour darkened around them, night creeping in to fill the corners, shadow upon shadow. Jack, sitting in the chair opposite, began to disappear into the gloom, and panic blossomed inside Violet, like a stain of ink over a page. Immense fatigue dragged through her limbs and her mind filled with a strange tugging blankness. But, like Aster had done earlier, she fought sleep.

The perfume from the flower beds thickened the air. A nightjar called from beyond the garden wall, and another creature, a fox perhaps, shrieked across the valley. And below, the sea murmuring, its sighs drifting up the path from the cove, across the cow meadow and along the lane. Violet jolted. She must have fallen asleep. She must have been dreaming. For the sea, everyone would tell her, could not be heard from Old Trellick.

Jack had lit the oil lamp and she saw that he'd been gazing at her.

She wanted to tell him what she had heard, the sound of waves as if she had pressed a shell to her ear. It had felt hypnotic and soothing, proving everyone wrong, visiting her like a wonderful old friend. But it felt wrong, too hopeful, at that moment. Perhaps, one day, she would tell him in a letter.

'Remember Regent's Park, Violet,' he said. 'The rose garden?'

'Always,' she said, tears rolled silently down her cheeks.

They both looked around at the door. The sound of a cry. Aster above them in her bedroom, calling out suddenly, calling for Jack.

He hauled himself up from his chair.

'Sounds like she's having a bad dream. I'll go to her,' he said. 'I didn't get a chance to wish her goodnight.'

As he walked past Violet, she closed her eyes and breathed in the scent of him. He rested the back of his hand lightly against her cheek and went upstairs to Aster.

* * *

Violet woke with a start, the hard fierce hammering at the front door knocking through her head. And in the background, the throb and rumble of a motor car.

Jack stood in front of her in the grey dawn light. Buttoned up in his khaki-brown officer's jacket, belt tight, puttees laced, he looked shaved, clean and smart, his cap pulled firmly over his eyes. The uniform seemed to increase his height, straighten his shoulders. But he felt remote, and no longer *her Jack*. And whatever waited for them outside Old Trellick seemed to have already broken them apart.

'It's time,' he said.

Violet drew the back of her hand over her eyes to dash away the tears. Her longing for Jack made her mute; all her resolve fixed on standing up, bracing herself, and keeping herself from screaming his name.

'Take care of Aster, Violet, and both of you, be happy,' Jack said, and walked out to the hallway to pick up his pack, hoist it onto his shoulder.

'Not yet, Jack,' she said. 'It's too soon. You can't go now. I simply won't let you.'

'Violet, I must go.' He opened the door, and two men, the policeman and a Military Police officer sprang forward. One of them warning Jack, his words grave and foreboding. One of them picked up his pack, and they both marched him swiftly out of the house to the waiting path.

'Wait, oh, wait!' Violet cried, burning suddenly with the need to move, to run to his side.

Halfway down the path, she stopped, appalled, as they stood Jack by the car and handcuffed him.

He glanced around to look at her. Her heartbeat blazed in her throat, her body straining with the need to run to him, to pull him back from being swallowed again by the war. But he remained still, trapped now, and surrendering to consequence and Violet knew that he was already a world away from her.

She stared at him, her blood thundering with an intensity that made her shudder.

Jack glanced up at the sky, at the ground, at the tall trees, unable to look at her.

'I love you, Jack, I always will,' she whispered, unsure if he ever heard her.

PART III
ASTER, CORNWALL, 1936

24

The memory snared Aster as she kicked her pony on and ducked beneath the trees. Gripping Starbright's mane, her hands trembling, she wondered, as she often did, which part of the evening before and the morning her father left had she imagined and made up over the years until it became her own legend. And which part was real?

However she remembered it, Aster's sore, unhappy truth proved inescapable: she'd lost both her father, and her mother, before she was five.

Earth-and-stone walls rose either side of the bridleway, enclosing Aster and her pony in a tunnel of green. Sunlight dappled her hands through the leafy ceiling and ferns curled among ancient roots. The late-spring day could not be more beautiful, but Aster let the reins hang loose and slumped in her saddle, dazed and swimming through grief. She let Starbright make her own way, the pony's hooves ringing on chunks of flint, the rhythm chiming her loss.

Aster knew that something terrible had happened during the Great War. Something besides the slaughter on an imperial scale. She'd seen the flickering brown film footage in documentaries at the cinema showing regiments going jerkily over the top, stumbling into oblivion. She knew about the wastelands and the notorious mud. And the war lived on all around her, even now, twenty years later, with the men she saw in wheelchairs, the wooden legs, the burnt faces, and empty sleeves pinned by a medal. And the ranks of older unmarried women who had lost sweethearts, or who would never find them.

But violence had happened, closer to home.

Her grandparents had sat her down when she had been still quite young, and had told her about the telegram that had arrived at Old Trellick after peace had been declared:

MISSING IN ACTION. PRESUMED DEAD.

'And what about Mama?' she'd asked. And her grandfather had said, 'You know, young lady, we have told you before. She died in London when you were a very little girl.'

Instinctively Aster squeezed her knees to encourage Starbright through the shallow ford and into the pinewood beyond. She sat up straight, forced the grinding cycle of thoughts to stop, breathing the clean spruce-scented air as if it might cure her. Starbright walked along the woodland floor, winding between trunks cushioned by ferns and pink foxgloves. Far, far below the stillness, came the trickle of the stream in the crook of the valley, invisible, on its way to the sea.

Aster lifted her chin, willing herself to feel better, to put aside things out of her control, as her grandmother often advised her, and noticed Starbright pricking her ears.

Two riders, way along the path and merging with the fabric of the wood, approached, straight-backed and strong-armed. Of course, Aster smiled: Harry Penruth had mentioned that he and his father had recently taken to riding out this way. She pulled Starbright up and waited as Harry kicked on across the soft pine-needle carpet, trailed by his father.

'So we meet again, Miss Fairling,' Harry said, by her side in moments, their horses greeting each other with snuffles and snorts. He doffed his cap with humorous ceremony, laughter mapping his eyes. 'What a glorious morning. Aren't we lucky? We have just spotted a kestrel out on the top field, and a kingfisher down by the stream. Everything is coming out at last. But it's far too good to enjoy alone. All this glory needs sharing.'

'Sharing? But I like to be alone,' Aster said, with gentle humour. 'Everyone knows that.'

'In that case, we'll ride on by. We'll keep our own company.' Harry gave her an exaggerated shrug, making ready to kick Sparrow on. But his smile told her he understood.

'Good morning, Miss Fairling,' Weston Penruth stopped his own horse a polite distance away, took off his hat and nodded in her direction, his eyes not quite meeting hers.

Aster knew all about Mr Penruth's surly closed-off manner. His profile, rugged and weathered handsomely, always looked inscrutable, his mouth permanently set in a grim line. But Harry, leaning forward to rub Starbright's neck, could not be more different.

'How is the old girl?' he asked.

'Doing really well,' Aster said, directing her answer to his father for he had gifted her Starbright when she had turned eighteen. The gesture had been astonishing to Aster, for even though Harry had been a friend for years, his father had always been the aloof landlord from the Big House. She remembered overhearing her grandmother say to her grandfather that it had been one way to mend the past. And she knew, as always, not to ask too many questions.

'Glad to hear it, Miss Fairling,' Weston said, distracted by the loud scolding of a blackbird in the pines. 'Well, Harry, come on, we best be off.'

'You're not going anywhere until you've told me all your news, Harry,' Aster said softly. 'I have nothing to tell you, of course, and that is quite normal for it is always so quiet over at Old Trellick. But you, you must have something to tell me. How is everything over at Charlecote? How is Kate? Is she enjoying school? Mr Penruth, I heard you had a poorly lamb? What about the red barn roof? Can you see daylight through it yet?'

'All fine, all fine. Kate is fine,' said Weston, forcing charm.

Harry said, 'My little sister will be home soon for Whitsun. There is nothing else to report, to someone who shuns our company, who shuts herself away. It has to be a fair exchange. It was your birthday the other week, wasn't it? I was expecting a little tea party, if nothing else. And until you have something exciting to tell *me*, Aster Fairling, then I will also stay quiet and mysterious.'

He reached again to pat Starbright. 'Doing well, aren't you?'

Aster watched him concentrating on rubbing her horse's neck, noting the fine cloth of his jacket and admiring the cut of his fair hair. She had known Harry forever, it felt, and there had even been a time when Harry and Kate had lived at Old Trellick during the war, although she didn't really remember. But she'd always felt a lightness and ease talking with him, a pleasant settling of her spirit. They used to see each other from time to time, as they grew up, and when they had each come home from school for the holidays.

'All right, then, how about this, Harry,' she laughed. 'I warn you, it's not exactly groundbreaking. My grandmother dug out an old recipe for saffron buns, my mother's favourite, apparently. She told me my mother would make them once a month as a treat, when there was saffron to be had. Grannie was putting a batch in the oven as I rode out this morning.'

Harry gathered his reins, adjusted his seat. 'Buns? Saffron buns? You'll have to do better than that, Aster Fairling.'

She glanced past him at his father, who stared resolutely into the pinewood as if he wished to make his escape.

'Come back with me now, Harry, have some tea and try them for yourself. Call it a belated birthday celebration. And you, Mr Penruth,' she added, 'of course.'

'Oh no, oh no, no.' Weston looked startled. 'And I'd rather you came back with me, Harry. We need to sort out that paperwork.'

'Surely, Father, it can wait one afternoon?'

Weston gazed at his hands resting on the saddle and Aster and Harry waited in uncomfortable silence.

'Go if you must,' he said. 'I'll see you at home.'

He turned his horse away and trotted off.

* * *

They rode side by side back the way Aster had come, out of the trees and along the bridleway, following the track that skirted the side of the hill. Beyond the wooded valley where the sea was hiding, the sky widened in a watery arch. Old Trellick emerged from a dip in the hill, centuries old and recorded in the Domesday Book. Aster's home, the woods, the sea: her security, the constants in her life. She glanced at Harry.

'You know,' Aster said. 'I don't think I've ever seen your father without his horse.'

'He hates walking anywhere. His leg gives him trouble. It was injured during the war. And it's getting worse. These days he would rather ride. Takes the pressure off. And he has other ailments and troubles, which he prefers to keep to himself.'

'He always seems so preoccupied,' Aster said.

'Oh, that's normal,' Harry laughed. '"Cantankerous" is the word.'

'Well then, that's perfect, isn't it?' Aster said. 'Everything is normal, and thank goodness for that. What quiet, peaceful lives we do lead.'

She kicked Starbright on and rode home through the freshening breeze, with Sparrow's hooves ringing out behind her and Harry laughing, catching her up. His company, as always, diluting her dark, unsettling memories.

* * *

'Look who I've brought home for tea,' Aster announced, walking into the parlour.

Her grandmother stood up and Aster noted her still-firm frame and well-cut shoulders. She'd had grey hair until a few years ago when it began to turn as white as moonlight; her hair may have softened with age, but she had the same steely interior that Aster found quite unfathomable.

'Well, good afternoon, Harry,' she said. 'I must say. What a surprise... You must be home from university?'

'That's all finished now, Mrs Prideaux. Home for good now, trying to find my way in the world.'

'Glad to hear it. I'll put the kettle on. We have saffron buns, you know.'

'It's all right, Grannie,' said Aster. 'I've filled Harry in on your morning of baking.' She glanced again at her grandmother's hair. 'But do you realise, you have what looks like a cobweb in your hair?'

'I shall pretend I did know.' Aster's grandmother forced a laugh and patted at her hair with a handkerchief. 'Is it gone now? Good. Apart from baking, Grandpa and I were up in the attic room this morning having a clear-out. Having a good old rummage. Place is sixes and sevens now. Perhaps that's what wore Grandpa out.'

'Where is he?' Aster asked.

'Having his constitutional nap. Though he should stir when he hears the kettle whistle.'

Her grandmother left the room, and Aster went over to the French windows.

'Take a seat, Harry. Will be nice to get a little sea breeze in here,' she said, opening each glazed door wide. 'Grannie does tend to like this room warm.'

Aster paused for a moment to admire the garden, always her grandfather's pride and joy and more so now he had retired. The ruby-red hollyhocks that he'd planted over Jess's grave against the stone wall looked taller than Aster now.

'Ah, what's this?' She said, picking up the brown envelope on the card table. It had never been sealed, and had no name or address written on the front. Turning it over, she pulled out an old sepia photograph and held it towards the windows for a little extra light. She peered at it.

Three little children – a girl in a smock, a boy in short trousers and a smaller baby girl in a bonnet squashed between them – sitting on the back of a farm wagon. The older children looked the same size, the same age, and both tilted their heads to the side as the shutter clicked.

'Goodness me, Harry, look at this,' Aster said, holding it out to him.

He came over. 'This isn't...?' he began, examining it. 'I say, is this *us*?'

It surged back to Aster, the memory blinding her, like the burning sun over the wheat fields. Her father sitting with her in the back of the wagon as it rumbled and lurched along. Her father hoisting her up and out and setting her down on the ground. He was laughing and she had felt as if she was flying. And another thing. Someone screaming. Someone in pain. Something terrible happening.

'I think I remember...' she said, picking carefully over her words, not sure what she recalled. 'A harvest time...?'

'I can't say I remember this being taken,' Harry said. 'I can picture a harvest, the scratchy straw, the warm smell of it. But perhaps I'm remembering later years. Do you get that sometimes when you can't tell if you are remembering a memory or the actual event?'

'This...' she whispered, as if sharing a secret with him. 'This seems so familiar.'

The door pushed open, and Aster's grandmother came around it with the tray of tea.

'Well, here we are,' she said. 'Tea and the fabled saffron buns. I hope you're hungry, Harry.'

'Grannie,' Aster said. 'What's this photograph?'

'What photograph?' Her grandmother set the tray down with a tinkle of crockery and took it from Harry. 'Oh!' She waited, staring at it, gathering her thoughts, her lips compressed as if to stop another exclamation erupting. 'I told him to throw it away, or put it in a drawer, at least.' Her face closed, cold and secretive. 'Honestly, he's getting worse.'

'But why would you ask Grandpa to do that?' Aster asked. 'It's a nice old photograph?'

'Really, there are some things best forgotten. Left in the past. I can't believe that photograph still exists. You young people don't want to be bothering with silly old pictures, do you. Sit down, Harry, come on, and I will pour the tea.'

Harry, the perfect gentleman, the perfect guest, did as Aster's grandmother requested, but politely took the photograph back. Aster's instinct told her not to ask any more questions, but Harry would not be brushed off so easily.

'What is best left in the past, Mrs Prideaux?' he asked, gazing at the picture. 'Who's that standing to one side? She's nearly out of the photograph. Goodness me, Aster, is that your mother?' He passed her the print.

Aster's grandmother set the teapot down with a clatter.

At one blurred, spectral side of the picture stood a young woman in a loose linen dress, her face half-shielded by a huge sun bonnet, staring past whoever was taking the photograph, staring beyond what had been captured in the frame – the wagon and the children – at something none of them could see. Violet. Caught unknowingly in a moment one summer afternoon. Looking beautiful and ethereal and, as always, completely out of Aster's reach. She stared, shock and sadness colliding inside her.

'I had no idea we had this photograph,' she said. 'I mean, I have seen some photographs – Mother as a little girl – and there's the painting in the attic, Grannie, but not this.' She caught Harry's eye. 'I have never seen a picture of me and my mother together.'

'I had forgotten we had it,' her grandmother said, bristling and discomposed. 'We found it earlier, in the attic, Grandpa and I.'

She gave Aster a minute shake of her head, a caution to be quiet about it. Aster read her expression: they have a guest and really should being talking about the weather.

In silence, Aster's grandmother poured the tea and passed a cup to Harry. He took a sip and began to laboriously slice a bun in half and slaver it with butter. Aster sank back, mute and bewildered. She wanted to cry.

She could feel Harry stealing glances at her, as she drank her own tea; her saffron bun had taken on a stale taste.

Harry put his cup down. 'Ah, now I *do* have some news,' he said, making Aster jump.

'Goodness,' she said, feeling grateful for him simply being there. 'You are a rotten tease, Harry.'

'I have bought a new motor car.'

'So, you will be tearing up half the countryside, then?' Aster's grandmother asked, still sounding prickly.

'Well, if I do, it will be with Aster by my side in the passenger seat.'

'Well, if you do, it will be you on your own,' Aster teased him, hoping he hadn't noticed her teary eyes. 'What is it? I mean what type of motor car? Is it very big? You must show Grandpa. Take him for a spin.'

'Oh, don't encourage him,' Aster's grandmother said, a cautious smile sliding over her face. 'His motoring days are over. That old car he had before the war is now crumbling away in the barn making a fine home for the mice.'

'I will gladly take Dr Prideaux out if he wants,' Harry said.

Aster's grandmother rolled her eyes, conceding the inevitable, and Aster felt affection for Harry blooming, and deepening. For he simply knew how to ease any situation.

* * *

After tea, Aster walked with Harry out to the stable where Sparrow rested with Starbright.

'Are you quite well?' he asked her, his hand on her arm. 'I know, it has been a shock to see that photograph.'

She nodded, giving him her best, bright smile.

'You in your breeches,' she said. 'How funny.'

Harry tightened his grip on her arm, his fingers moving over her sleeve.

'Talk to me, if you like, any time, Aster,' he said. 'You know where I am.'

Aster fought the strange urge to gently touch the skin above his collar.

She said, 'And the saffron buns? Do they pass muster? Were they as good as any you'd find in Cornwall? What shall you be telling your father? Marks out of ten?'

'You know what he's like. He only cares about things with four legs.'

'You mean tables and chairs?'

He laughed. 'Your home baking, Miss Aster Fairling, is most definitely up to scratch.'

25

Aster woke to the chattering of birds along the eaves, the sunlight clear and pure, finding its way around her curtains. A sweet warm fragrance came straight off the moors through her open window – the perfect day for her trip out with Harry in his car. She would sketch, and they would take a picnic. How wonderful it will be up there in the gorse and heather, the wildness and freedom. She and Harry, alone.

'Ah, so you are awake,' her grandmother came in with a morning tray. 'Thought I'd treat you to breakfast in bed.'

'Goodness, Grannie, what have I done to deserve this?' Aster said, sitting up in bed.

'Surely, I can bring my granddaughter her tea and toast once in a while?'

She set the tray over Aster's lap and walked to the window to draw the curtains, arranging them just-so.

It had been a few days since Aster had found the photograph. Her kind gesture this morning seemed to be some sort of apology. For what exactly, Aster felt unsure. But she sensed her grandmother had not properly explained her unsettling reaction. After Harry had left, her grandmother had secreted the photograph in her bureau. And there it remained, out of sight, as if it had never been unearthed from the attic in the first place.

'There's some post for you on the tray there,' her grandmother said, opening the window wider. 'Now I must get back upstairs. We're tackling the attic room again today. If you feel inclined, perhaps you'll give us a hand.'

'Have you forgotten Harry is coming by?' Aster said. 'We're going for a drive.'

'Ah yes.'

Even with her back to her, as she tugged at a loose thread on the edge of the curtain, Aster could see her grandmother's thoughts colliding.

'Harry is a super fellow,' her grandmother said at last.

'He is indeed.' Aster tipped a splash of milk into her teacup.

Her grandmother turned. With the light behind her, her face a shadow, Aster could not read her expression. 'And he does seem rather keen on you. He always has done.'

'I know,' Aster said, feeling herself blush. 'We've always been friends. Our mothers were too. I think it is wonderful.'

'Grandpa and I...,' she began. 'We can certainly see it. But, Aster, remember, you are still so young.'

'Grannie, I've just turned twenty-one!' Aster laughed. 'I am *of age*! Surely, you wouldn't want me to be an old maid.'

'Isn't it a little bit too... easy? Convenient?'

'Oh, Grannie! Harry and I are *friends*.'

Her grandmother returned a little hesitant laugh, and left the room, apparently satisfied. Aster poured her tea and buttered her toast, gave a baffled shrug as she licked crumbs off her fingertips. The birds outside set up a racket, distracting her as she sipped, musing on what she should wear since the weather looked so wonderful. She set the tray aside and got out of bed, went over to her wardrobe, remembered she had some post. She picked up the envelope, postmarked London, and turned it over in her hands, weighing up the expensive heavy-grade paper.

Aster hadn't a paperknife, so she wiped her butter knife on her napkin and deftly slit the envelope open.

'Goodness,' she uttered, as she pulled out a letter typed on a solicitor's office headed notepaper, with an address in Cavendish Square, W1. 'This looks rather official.'

Why on earth would a London solicitor be writing to her? Standing by her open wardrobe door, she read quickly the succinct and formal contents.

She covered her mouth with her hand, her cry muffled. Prickling ice formed a cap over her scalp, tighter and tighter. She tried again to take in the typed words, her eyes widening in horror, nausea raking her stomach.

Upstairs in the attic room, her grandparents' footsteps resounded across the ceiling. And the memory returned: a summer evening long ago, her grandmother and great aunt playing cards, the snapped photograph on the back of the wagon, the wheat field. Could it all have happened on one day? Calling for her father in queasy sleepiness in her darkened bedroom; the far away sound of the sea.

Aster pressed her palms to her face, her fingers cold and damp, her legs shaking.

'They have got it wrong, utterly wrong,' she uttered, fumbling for her dressing gown, the letter crushed in her hand, trembling as the news kicked her, and kicked her again. 'How could they? How could these solicitors lie to me and say that my father is alive?'

Aster went upstairs to the attic room and pushed the door ajar. A trestle table that should have long ago been firewood had been moved out from the corner and a battered cardboard box stood on it, spewing old jigsaws, a threadbare quilt and a stringless tennis racket. Stacks of crumbling books, their backs broken, were ready for the bonfire. Tarnished candlesticks, thick with wax, a jar of broken nibs, and Aster's old dolls' house had been assigned to a corner. Balls of dust collated and spun across the floor.

Her grandparents seemed unaware, engrossed in the dusting, filing, putting away of things. Her grandfather had lit a cigar and forgotten about it, and it lay in its ashtray. A stream of blue smoke rose to the sloping ceiling. Her grandmother tickled a framed picture with a feather duster, saying how much she loved it, and why wasn't it on the wall downstairs?

'That's only fit for the scullery, Eleanor,' Aster's grandfather said. 'Or the outside lavatory.'

Their chattering, their industry, excluded Aster. She felt unwelcome. She did not know them.

Her grandfather noticed her. 'Ah, there you are, Aster. Good morning. Still in your dressing gown, I see. Never mind, roll up your sleeves and get stuck in. Rag-and-bone man will have a field day with this lot.' He stooped to lug a drawer open. Whatever lay inside it made him swear under his breath and he closed it again.

'Oh, Aster, I'd rather you got dressed first,' her grandmother said, barely glancing at her.

'Do you know that my father is still alive?' Aster said, raising her voice to counter their chattering. 'Do either of you know? Of course you do. How silly of me. You *must* know.'

The stopped talking, turned startled faces to her and the noise of their flurrying exclamations and denial rose like dust from the floor.

'What have you there?' her grandfather asked, straightening up, his face stiffening.

'It's only a letter,' said Aster, waving it frivolously, working hard to restrain her anger. 'From a Messrs Baldwin and Son of Cavendish Square. It appears that on the occasion of my twenty-first birthday, since past, I am to be bequeathed a series of paintings by Mr Jack Fairling. Works that he has accomplished over the past twenty or so years and that are being exhibited in London at the... let's see, the Regent's Gallery.'

'What on earth...?' her grandmother took steps towards Aster.

'Oh yes, astonishing, isn't it, the way that he has been able to produce, let's see, fifty-odd paintings, when he died years ago in the trenches? But he did not die, according to these people. Except you... you and Grandpa, told me that he did.'

'Missing,' interjected her grandfather. 'Missing in action.'

'But that's not *killed in action*, is it?' Aster looked at her grandfather, with sudden and unprecedented distaste. Her own clarity chilled her blood. 'According to Messrs Baldwin and Son, he is alive and well and living in Camden, and looking forward to the retrospective of his life's work. But why didn't I know? This isn't what I... who I... how any of this can be—'

Her grandfather held her by the elbow and propelled her to the old chair in the corner. 'Sit, sit. That's it.'

'But what *is* this?' Aster's legs felt like straw. The letter dropped from her hand to the floor. She felt her tongue stiffen, as if she could no longer speak.

'Brandy,' her grandmother said. 'I will fetch the brandy.'

Her grandfather stooped to pick up the letter.

'Well, I'll be blowed.'

Aster looked up at him in horror, staring through chaos. She wanted him to say something to save her, something to right this, set her world straight.

But her grandfather tutted, shaking his head as if he had come across a bad case of hives.

'Oh, Aster, I suppose this had to happen one day,' he said. 'So much time had passed, so many years. We honestly thought he'd been lost to the war.'

Her grandmother returned with a tumbler of brandy and pressed it into her hand.

'Drink this,' she said.

'But he is my father,' Aster uttered as the crystal tumbler grazed her teeth. 'Why didn't he want to see me? Why didn't he get in touch?' Her voice jerked in her throat. 'I don't understand. I just don't understand why you would keep this from me.'

Her grandmother knelt by the chair, her knees cracking like gunfire.

'Time moved on,' she said. 'After your mother died, he did not get in touch. It was a strange and terrible time. My sister Muriel died soon after, you see, and, frankly, I could not cope with any of it.'

Aster's grandfather mutely patted her grandmother's shoulder.

'I think in a way, in the confusion, we left it to him to get in touch,' her grandmother said. 'And then, for a long time, thought it had been a mistake. That he hadn't made it home. To all intents and purposes, dear Aster, we thought your father was dead.'

Aster took the letter back from her grandfather. Its cold formality and her grandmother's meaningless words *to all intents and purposes*, spun in her head, rocking her insides. She pressed icy fingertips to her brow, screwing up her eyes.

'But he is my father,' she whispered. 'And he is *alive*?'

'I think we may have handled this entirely the wrong way, don't you think so, George?' her grandmother said.

'We did the best we could...'

'When your mother died, Aster,' her grandmother said, 'that just about finished us off. The telegram... when did Violet get that, George, just after the Armistice? It said he was missing, remember, *missing presumed dead*. We didn't lie. After all, how many of them ever came back?'

Aster stared at her and felt an astonishing spasm of anger. She thought of her mother and how she'd had to face that news, typed out on a little chit of paper. She stared at the letter clutched in her grandfather's hand, and grief slumped through her, a great weight over her head.

'But why did he not contact me?' She set the glass down and wiped at her mouth with the back of her hand. 'Why did he not come home and find me? Why has he ignored me all this time?'

'Looks like he has written his will,' her grandfather said, sounding infuriatingly rational. 'Handed his paintings over to you, Aster. It sounds like a very generous gesture. Don't you agree, Eleanor? An olive branch?'

'But I don't need an olive branch.' Aster let out a hard laugh. 'I just need my father.'

* * *

Harry parked his little blue Morris on the lane and parped the horn. Aster buttoned her jacket up in front of the hall mirror.

Her grandparents crept out of the parlour, repeating their apologies, her grandfather reminding her, rolling his hands together, that they thought they had done the right thing. All that they had been thinking of had been Aster.

'And if Violet hadn't gone up to London to look for him that day,' her grandmother said, with a crack of despair, 'she would still be here.'

'It's all so terribly complicated,' her grandfather said. 'Muriel had sent her a telegram, you see, but we never saw it. We were away at the time. Before we knew it, Violet had taken the next train to Paddington. There's so much we did not understand.'

'Please don't talk to me,' Aster uttered, putting on her hat. 'Because everything you say to me sounds like a lie.'

She gave them a devastated look, shut the front door behind her and hurried out to the car.

'Steady on, Aster, there's no rush. We have all day,' Harry said as she climbed into the passenger seat. 'Oh, whatever's the matter?'

'Just drive. Please,' she said.

Harry drove in astonished silence along the tight lanes where birds darted out recklessly from the hedges either side. Every now and then

Aster caught glimpses of sublime views through farm gates, suddenly, a portion of blue sea. All of this, her home and her life since she could remember. *Had* been her home, her life. The new leather interior of the Morris was scented, cushiony and comfortable, but Aster felt pinned and trapped. She wound down the window, and inhaled a sudden trace of the sea.

'Stop the car! Stop!'

Harry slammed on the brakes, jolting them forward. Aster opened the door and fled. She raced along the lane and ducked down the steep footpath that led to the cove, her mouth open, a sob clotting her throat, her grandparents' voices rattling in her head: *If Violet hadn't gone up to London to look for him that day, she would still be here.*

Aster made it to the sand, stumbling over the shifting hollows, and she sat down, her insides numb and stretching with loneliness. The waves tumbled as they always did, as familiar as a trusted old friend. Her mother used to come here with Harry's mother; her mother's flower journal told her. They had been happy, young girls, loving everything around them; the beauty of the turning seasons, the countryside and all that it gave them. A new and vigorous sense of grief folded around her, while the seagulls called and wheeled overhead in flickering currents of air.

Harry found her. He sat by her side, out of breath and red in the face.

'I've had shocking news,' she stated, sounding flat with disbelief.

Harry listened, but did not speak, his profile fixed in distress. He reached out to hold her hand, trying his best, but it did not feel enough to comfort her. Presently, he drew out his large handkerchief and she used it to mop her face.

'Such a filthy huge shock, Aster,' he said. 'But we will dig out the truth one way or another. I will do whatever you want me to. If you want to go and see your father, I will come with you, if you like. I will talk to you, or I will shut up. I will stay by your side. I will go away. Aster, whatever...'

His kindness swamped her, but she could not respond. She felt as if a steel rod had plunged through her core.

'You know, Aster,' Harry went on, 'there is no need for me to get to know you again. Somewhere, deep down, you're part of me. There's something about that time we had together as children, a shared memory... yes, we grew up apart. I blame boarding schools, university. I haven't been around much. But now I'm back...'

He moved closer, put his arm around her shoulder. The warmth of his body shielded her from the freshening sea air but, inside, she wriggled with discomfort.

'You're so very nice to me,' she said. 'But you must understand how I... Until this morning, I thought I was an orphan. Now, I don't know who I am.'

'You are Aster to me.' He turned her so that she would look at him. His face, firm and determined, and bright in the sunlight. 'You'll always be—'

She stopped him with a hard look. 'We're friends only, Harry. Please don't say anything else.'

***

The afternoon was fading into evening when he dropped her back at Old Trellick. Aster walked into an empty house. Her grandmother's note on the hallway table told her that they had gone out to a long-standing arrangement, a bridge party at Looe Town Hall. She hoped they'd not be too late. She hoped she'd had a nice day with Harry.

They had left a lamp burning for her in the parlour and a plate of sandwiches covered up in the larder.

Aster sat in the kitchen to eat. Since that morning, shock had delayed her hunger, made her nauseous. Now she felt ravenous. But as she chewed, she barely tasted her food. She gave up, put the kettle on the range to make a pot of tea and went into the parlour.

She slid the book out from its slot in her grandparents' collection and returned to the kitchen, cradling it, treasuring it. Could almost not bear to touch it. The dark-green leather cover of her mother's flower journal reminded Aster of the most secret corners of the pinewood; the spine cracked, the corners worn. She lay it on the kitchen table and opened it.

Inside the front flyleaf, her mother had written:

Violet Prideaux, aged 10, her book.

A pressed violet – perhaps the first she'd ever gathered – its purple faded, transparent, had been pasted down next to her name. Below, underlined for emphasis, young Violet had written:

So long as the leaves are not picked or too much trampled.

Aster closed her eyes and imagined her mother: thick auburn hair in Victorian ringlets, dressed in bloomers and buckles, studiously recording the flowers she gathered – violets, and heather and lady's smock and periwinkles – along with her thoughts and her dreams.

The kettle sang on the hob as Aster turned the pages. Her mother's handwriting started as a child's in the summer of 1906, looped and faded, improving as the years slid by as she documented flowers of the wayside as and when she found them. Aster took her time, browsing and revisiting the pages. Her mother's words felt like a balm seeping into her blood.

'I really never knew you,' Aster whispered, in wonder at the amount of pain she felt, 'but you left me your legacy. Here in your book, the buds and blooms you collected ever since you were a little girl speak to me now. Our very own language of flowers.'

She turned pages of round-faced daisies, innocent blue forget-me-nots, and yellow marigolds, the paper crinkled and aged. All her mother's passion and wisdom, her legacy passed down to her. Aster shook with longing, felt dazed and exhausted.

Sea Holly,

her mother had written, and under it the delicate specimen, plucked from a crook in the dunes, perhaps, and so familiar to Aster.

A day on the beach with Jack and Aster.

She had written beneath it.

We took a picnic. Later on, I met Claudia, expecting her second child. I hadn't seen her in a long, long while. Aster and Harry met for the first time.

Aster found some seaweed and we brought it home for pressing. Jack to go back to France soon. May, 1916.

'Oh, Mama,' Aster uttered, 'why did you go up to London on *that* day? Why not another day, any other day? You'd be here now. We'd all be here now.'

She could not sit still. She shut her mother's journal and returned it to the shelf and climbed the stairs taking the lamp with her. Her grandfather had yet to put electricity into the upper floors of Old Trellick and so the yellow glow set shadows dancing around her. At the top of the second set of stairs, she opened the door to the attic room, noticing how tidy it looked now compared to that morning.

Aster set the lamp down on the trestle table and went over to the cupboard in the alcove next to the chimney flue. Years ago, her grandfather had asked her if she wanted to keep her father's portfolio, but she'd been young, had not quite understood. She'd never linked her father – who resided only in her memory – to the drawings and paintings stowed away in the dusty attic. She hoped, with all the strength she could muster, that her grandparents had not taken it upon themselves to throw it out; either today, or any other day.

Her relief felt visceral, when she found the portfolio, right at the back of the cupboard, its cover stained, and a little crumpled She pulled it out, releasing a puff of musty dust, and carried it over to the trestle table. He had written his name in the corner:

Jack P. Fairling

Night birds began to call outside in the garden, and she breathed in a short flare of memory, the odour of his cigarette. She opened it, revealing a dozen or so loose pages. Sketches and pastels. Her father's doodles and imaginings. Her sense of loss compounded. It felt like this was just the beginning.

26

Aster set her mother's journal down on the bedside table in the London hotel room and, next to it, the old photograph of the day of harvest. She had found a frame to fit it. After all, it had been neglected for so long, stuffed in a drawer in the attic room, and needed protection. She took the invitation card from her handbag and propped it alongside. It had arrived a week ago from the solicitor's, the scrolled wording saying simply:

Jack Fairling: A Retrospective, The Regent's Gallery, W1.

A neat parameter of dates declared that her father's paintings would be on display for two months only.

She went to the window and gazed down at Portland Place. All looked busy and unfamiliar, and strangely reassuring. Cars and buses and hurrying folk distracted her, and yet she still felt fragile with uncertainty, wishing she could turn a corner in her mind and not feel lost any longer.

Aster lifted the telephone receiver and dialled Harry's room number.

'Would you like to pop in for some morning tea before we go?' she said when he answered.

'Sounds like an excellent idea,' he said, his voice cheerful at the other end of the line. 'I shall order it straight away.'

Harry had insisted on paying for their trip, assured her it would be a belated birthday present. They each had a room at the fine and elegant Langham Hotel, a short walk from the gallery.

'Your grandparents must think you are running off with me,' he had joked.

Aster had laughed, but said, 'I'm twenty-one years old, Harry, and it's 1936. I feel that I can do what I like. Lots of girls come up to London to be secretaries and live in flats with other girls. Perhaps that's what I'll do.'

Sitting together at the round table by the window, Harry said, 'I'm glad you brought the photograph with you. Did you grandmother ever explain why she had been so prickly about it?'

'Not really, not about that,' Aster mused, stirring her tea. 'But perhaps the revelation about my father has shocked them as much as it has me. And knocked everything else into a tin hat.'

'Possibly,' Harry picked up the photograph. 'This day now seems to be coming back to me. My father was there. Of course! He must have taken the photograph. He still has all his old cameras and tripods. Every time a new model comes out, he has to buy it.'

An uncomfortable memory crept around Aster's mind. 'The more I look at my mother in the photograph,' she said, 'the more terrified she looks.'

'Ah, but perhaps she was about to sneeze,' said Harry. 'Perhaps she thought she wasn't in the frame. Or was exasperated by my father. He is very difficult at the best of times. I do tease him about being a recluse – gently, mind – but I do believe he lost his mind when my mother died. We were carted up to Scotland then. I was too young to remember of course. And Kate has been no comfort to him – she is too much like our mother – and I'm no use, really. And him being injured. He nearly lost his leg, you know?'

'But he didn't go to the Front, did he?'

'I assume it was a farming accident,' Harry said. 'He doesn't talk about it. I said before, there are many aspects of his life he keeps private. I often feel I am living with a stranger.' Harry looked away from her, took a breath, 'We have a lot in common, Aster. We both lost our mothers when we were very young. And I cannot remember her. I've tried, God knows.'

'Ah, I know someone who can help,' Aster said. She fetched her mother's journal from the bedside and handed it to Harry.

'Your mother's in here, have a look. Turn to March 1914, "*the gorse that tore Claudia's dress,*" and then two years later – May 1916 – when my father found the sea holly and I found the seaweed. Our mothers became friends again that day right there on the beach. And we met for the first time. It's all in there. There's a gap of two years when she isn't mentioned, but perhaps that's when they both got married.'

Harry's cheeks reddened, his eyes watered as they leafed through Violet's warm and snappy entries.

'Look here,' Aster said. '"*Heard today in the village that Claudia's little boy delivered safely. An August baby, born in the heyday of the year. Beautiful by all accounts.*"' She giggled. 'Bless little Harry!'

Harry laughed and suddenly embraced her, holding her close. Aster surprised herself, relaxing into his arms.

'You're being so very brave about all of this,' he said, resting his head against hers. 'It makes me admire you even more, you know, which is very dangerous indeed.'

'Is that what I need in my life, Harry, more danger?' Aster laughed, and they went back to the journal.

Turning a few pages, Aster paused.

'This always bothers me, this one,' said Aster. 'This pressed peony. I'm no expert but, really, a peony in spring. Mama dated it March 1914. It looks like a bloodstain spreading across the page,' she said. 'It's my least-favourite flower. Seems like it was Mama's too. She obviously wasn't keen on it. Listen...'

'"*A deep-red Peony means honour, respect, kindness, and compassion, but these are the things this man does not possess. And yet he gave this flower to me, in March, thinking I'd believe him, thinking I'd want the Peony, and all the other forced, premature, incongruous blooms he offered. And give myself to him in return. He could not have been further from the truth.*"'

'And listen, she wrote this in London in June 1914. I assume that was when she met my father: "*A week ago, among the roses of Regent's Park, I glimpsed beyond the shame, I glimpsed a new beginning. I discovered a new day. A new self.*"'

Aster began to cry. 'So why didn't he try,' she uttered. 'He knew where I lived. He didn't *try!*'

Harry gathered her in his arms again. 'You've seen what the war did to people, Aster, what the war has done,' he said tentatively. 'Did he have shell shock? So many of them did. Perhaps he went into an asylum. A lot of the soldiers were put there, you know? They removed them from society. It's a terrible thing to say, but they were often an embarrassment. Perhaps your grandparents were only trying to protect you.'

'He still managed to paint, though, didn't he?' she mumbled petulantly. 'You know, when I was a little girl, my grandfather told me all about the Unknown Soldier. How, after the war, his body had been taken from the battlefield and brought to England. How the coffin was draped in the Union Jack and taken on a gun carriage drawn along the streets of London. They buried him in Westminster Abbey. I was only five when this happened, but I have seen pictures from newspapers. The stunned and weary crowds watching the coffin going past. I was convinced that the soldier was my father.'

She faltered, covered her face with her hands. Harry held her while she cried, and continued to long after she stopped. Eventually, he released her and pulled aside the gold-braided curtain.

'Will you look at that sky,' he said, wiping the back of his hand over his eyes. 'We're going to get drenched.'

* * *

Harry was right. As they walked down the Langham's steps, the large grey clouds burst, the rain began to fall. Car lamps glowed in the sudden half-darkness and buses rumbled by with an enormous swoosh as they glided up Regent Street. Aster's best bottle-green cloche and matching gloves were soaked within moments, her stockings splattered and her umbrella dripping a steady stream onto her shoulder.

'We'll get a taxi,' Harry said.

But Aster wanted to walk to the gallery. It was only on the other side of Cavendish Square and she could do with the fresh air to clear her head. How kind Harry was; how wonderful. But she suddenly craved privacy; wanted to do this on her own.

'How are you feeling?' Harry asked, struggling with his umbrella, hunched under the downpour. 'I can see you're nervous.'

'There's no need to ask, then, is there?' she snapped, stalking off down the street, clutching her umbrella, head down. The rain fell in long silver strings around her, and she felt her life, everything she knew, peeling away in great painful layers. In her handbag lay the invitation. And she thought, what daughter on earth receives this sort of thing via a solicitor? She pounded along the pavement with Harry trying his best to keep up with her, chattering, throwing well-meaning phrases at her. And she realised her fury was aimed at her grandparents and the false world they had built around her. As beautiful and as sacred as Old Trellick had always been, it had only been half of her life. The other half was one huge secret.

A car drove past sending a scoop of water over the kerb towards Aster's feet. She very nearly laughed. Surely, she could not get any colder and wetter. So much for looking smart and well turned out for her father.

They stood in the gallery's vestibule, holding dripping umbrellas at arm's length, thankful to be inside out of the rain. Aster's face was wet, her hair in tatters. Harry eased her coat off her shoulders and prised the umbrella out of her hands, passing them to the cloakroom girl. He gave Aster her ticket, which became soggy and crumpled even before she put it in her pocket.

Aster remained where she stood, making a puddle on the marble floor, her eyes fixed on the poster on the wall. She squinted, feeling a strange coldness trickling down inside her. Beneath the title:

Jack Fairling: A Retrospective

was the reproduction of a sketch in brown ink, dashed off hurriedly, she suspected, between roll call and stand-to. At the bottom sat his signature and:

Hope, 1918

A shaking began inside her chest. She reached for Harry and held onto his hand. And his strength came to her once more, his warmth returned. No longer bothersome or irritating Harry. Simply Harry.

The hammering of the rain on the skylight above them ceased like the abrupt turning off of a tap, and sunlight glanced down through the glass.

The sudden warmth sent a shiver through Aster's bones. There seemed to be an aching seriousness to the hush in the room beyond where, she guessed, her father's paintings must be hung. Aster stepped forward still holding Harry's hand. She kept her gaze ahead of her, away from the poster, away from the inked sketch, for she could not take it in. *I am Hope*, she thought. *My name means Hope.* The drawing was a portrait of a little girl, barely three years old.

27

According to the brochure for which Harry paid thruppence, her father's paintings had been divided into three periods displayed over three rooms of the gallery. They traced his growth and development as a painter and visitors were encouraged to start in the first chamber, with the *Camden Series*, to witness the fascinating evolution of such an underrated and little-known artist.

Aster walked in with Harry by her side into the space where more skylights beamed down, illuminating a dozen works. Her father depicted the city of London in a stark yet plainly beautiful way: pavements, plane trees and railway lines shimmered with rain; the oily canal glided past the rickety stables at Camden Lock; terraces of houses were aligned in smooth blocks of colour; chimneys belched smoke over crowds of bent and hurrying people.

As she waited for a couple to move away from the last of the paintings she caught the back view of a man on his own wearing a coal-black suit and pondering the room as a whole, his hand scratching his chin. Her stomach leapt in curiosity. She stepped backwards, treading on Harry's toe.

'It might be him,' she hissed in his ear.

Harry, always keen to please her, asked, 'Do you want me to find out?'

She broke into a giggle. 'For goodness' sake,' she chided herself. 'He's got a brochure in his hand, and he's got dark hair. My father had fair-reddish hair, apparently. And he might not have any left by now... Who knows? He might be bald, he might have a beard. How will I know him? I won't, will I? I won't know my own father.'

Harry took her hand and lead her into the next room. Here, frames the size of pages torn from a pocket sketchbook, compared to the confidently generous Camden paintings next door, snaked around the walls at eye level. There must be fifty of them: identically dark, charcoaled and scribbled, hard to make out until Aster went over to take a closer look. She stared at each intricate and unique sketch in turn, absorbing it and moving on to the next, horror expanding inside her with each step and each ragged breath she took.

With bald and intimate strokes of his blunt pencil, her father had drawn soldiers in trenches, wearing tin hats, their grins breaking dirty faces. In these miniature sketches, they fixed their bayonets, cooked over fires, gathered around braziers, ate from metal plates, were fed their rum ration off a spoon, burnt lice off their seams with matches, marched around unburied bodies being devoured by rats, stepped over skulls blown up out of the ground, were blinded by flares, witnessed guts hanging from between tunic buttons, saw screaming agony on faces grinning, this time, *in* agony, they cut their pals from the wire, drowned in mud, drowned in gas, begged to die.

Aster reeled as if punched in the stomach, but felt herself dragged closer, compelled to stare. She wanted to know, to feel what her father her lived through, what he had seen, things that he would never be able to forget.

A notice on the wall told her it was a miracle any of the charcoal sketches of the *Trenches Series* had survived, stowed away for many wretched months in Lieutenant Fairling's kit. Some creased and torn and soiled, others more pristine, but each one depicting a darker view of hell.

Mesmerised, Aster came to a stop in front of the last picture. Enormous, a hundred times larger than the others and obviously a work done in oils in a studio, not crouched in a sodden trench. Its size forced her to step back, lift her face and stare upwards until her neck began to ache. The painting glistened, illuminated by the skylight, and became alive as she flicked her eyes from top to bottom and side to side, unable to take it all in in one glance. A lone tree, bare and stark, stood out against a sunny blue sky. A peculiar calm washed over Aster as she smiled, in blessed relief. So much easier on the eye compared to the confined abyss of the trench sketches.

But she shook her head, closed her eyes, took another step back and stared again, raising her palm to cover her mouth. Cold sweat coated her throat and her stomach caved in. The tree, obviously long dead but somehow still standing in the blown-up wasteland of battle, stretched jagged branches like contorted arms, hung not with fruit or leaves but with rags, flesh, torn limbs, parts of men, shapeless festoons of what once had been human, what had once been a son, a brother, a father.

Aster felt Harry's arm around her shoulder, and she wanted to turn away. But she could not peel her eyes from the painting, as if she had become addicted to its horror. Swaying on her feet, her knees ready to buckle, Aster leant forward to read what her father had written in the corner: his signature, then:

Somme, July 1916.

And, according to the little typewritten sign tacked to the wall beside it, he'd given the painting one simple word as a title:

Monument

* * *

Aster felt Harry's hand on her shoulder, his voice in her ear, assuring her that they could do whatever she wanted. 'Do you want to go home now? Go back to the hotel? I'll order a cab.'

She shook her head, her voice a whisper. 'No, I want to see them, see them all.'

They walked through to the next gallery where a group of people spoke with murmuring voices near the exit, flicking over the pages of their brochures. Aster fumbled with her own copy, her blood running like ice as the hell that her father had lived in and recreated burnt into her memory. She pressed her fingers over her eyes, wishing for it to go away, waiting for a quiet blessing of strength to help her carry on. She hid her face, realising her tears had only just started.

Harry took her arm and guided her forward.

'I think he's still here, Aster, over by the door. See the man in the black suit, talking to that couple? He looks like the Press. I expect he's doing an interview, look.'

Aster glanced. The man flipped through a notebook, pencil poised, listening to a well-dressed older man, in a mackintosh coat and trilby, who spoke softly, his companion, a handsome woman of a certain age, nodding attentively.

The distraction of the trio cleared Aster's mind.

'I didn't realise how much I need him,' she said, turning to the new set of paintings in this, the third gallery. She wiped her eyes discreetly and her mother's face came into focus.

Aster's blood began to thump absurdly around her head. Violet appeared in the painting taller than *Monument* and wider still. Violet, sheltering under a parasol cradled delicately in her hands, her complexion lit by unearthly tranquil light. Deep layered daubs of oil colours shifted constantly, breathing and glimmering, her mother alive, walking through the park... *under dappled silvery willow trees; star-like daisies bright at her feet. Her face is half in profile, the line of her cheek exquisite. Her parasol the colour of luminous water, protecting her, separating her in her own world. Her eyes, even in shadow, are lucid sea-green. As she walks, she isn't aware of the artist as he sees her; just of the light that comes from below her, reflected from his direction, to illuminate her and set her apart. She lifts her pale hand quickly to shield her eyes.*

'Seriously, Aster, are you all right?' Harry broke the spell.

But Aster smiled, she did not mind.

'I'm fine, I'm more than fine,' she said. 'This is wonderful. Can't you see, Harry? This is more than I have ever had in my whole life. I have Mama's journal, and a few grainy old photos. But she is a ghost there, so fleeting. And my mother wrote in riddles. She was a curious, secretive little girl and a rebellious young lady. I try to understand her, understand what she means by swarms of bees in July, and April showers. All that country lore. I try to understand because that helps me believe I know her. She wrote down all the days and all the seasons and all her years, but what did it really all mean? It is beautiful but what was she trying to say?' Aster gazed back at the painting, breathless. 'And now, just look. You can see her. My father knew her. He understood her, and it shows. Can't you see? This is Violet.'

Aster's voice rose high, a sing-song pitch and a tiny echo responded from the ceiling. Suddenly conscious of her outburst she stopped, laughed a little, her hand over her mouth.

The couple with the journalist glanced in her direction. But she turned back to the painting and found the magic again, filled her vision once more with light.

Harry kept his arm around her waist, and calmly read from the brochure.

'This painting is entitled *Violet in the Daytime*,' he said. 'There are only three paintings in this last series, all executed in your father's Camden studio during the mid 1920s. There is a smaller version of *Violet in the Daytime*, painted in 1914, but he reworked all three in this series, in huge proportions, each given its own wall here.'

Aster glanced around but she wanted more time to take in each one of the paintings, for they lit the room with colour and deep beauty beyond what she could possibly see.

'She's life-size,' she uttered in pure understanding. 'Violet is life-size.'

After some minutes, she pulled herself away and walked with Harry over to the next painting.

'How safe she looks, so safe and happy,' Aster said, her words trailing in wonder.

Harry read from the brochure: '"*Violet in the Evening*, completed in oils 1923. Taken from an original sketch in pastels, 1914."'

In the painting, the window had no curtains, its frame bare wood. Beyond lay a London skyscape, a tumble of chimney pots and grey slate roofs. Little globes of dust bowled along floorboards under the chaise beneath this window. A gas lamp in the corner spilt tentative light over naked green walls and onto the sleeping form of Violet, curled on the cushions, oblivious to her effect on the observer. Any observer.

'Even asleep, she looks happy,' breathed Aster. 'They were happy, weren't they?'

Harry's arm around her waist pressed firmly, supporting her. He rested his face against hers and they gazed together, drinking in the peaceful scene of twilight in a Camden artist's studio.

'We can be happy,' he said, quietly into her hair. 'We can be too.'

She reached for his hand at her hip and bound her fingers around his.

'Yes. We can,' she said, and her own bravery almost floored her.

Who else but Harry? Who else would bring her here, would stand by her side while her world fell away to smithereens, and brought itself together again in such irregular, misshapen pieces?

Aster remembered. At Old Trellick, the presence of a little boy, bobbing up to the surface while she swam beneath it. The recollection there, like a snatch of a tune, or the odour in a long-closed cupboard. She gazed at his face, her thoughts settling into place. And she must get used to this new, sensible way of thinking, to move on from the troubling news in the solicitor's letter, for Harry, speaking quietly and earnestly close to her ear, asked her to marry him.

She took his hopeful face gently in her hands. 'Yes.'

* * *

The third and final painting made Harry blush, and Aster laughed gently with him, feeling her own cheeks smoulder as they gazed up at *Violet in the Night-time*.

'Stop giggling,' Harry teased her. 'You're spoiling it.'

'Did you know that when you're embarrassed your ears also go red?'

'Well, the tip of your nose has gone all shiny.'

She laughed, couldn't help herself. In the space of a few moments, they'd made their decision, their lives together resolved. She wanted to run right into their future with open arms.

'I say, this is rather risqué,' Harry uttered. 'Perhaps we better stand a few feet apart while we view this one.'

'I don't know where to look,' Aster said, but stared directly at her mother's face as she relaxed on a window seat, with her body reclined luxuriously against a pile of cushions, the hinting glow of streetlamps through a gap in the draped curtains. Her father had used caressing paint strokes to capture the light and shadow over her skin, the silk of her grey dress that had slipped artlessly from her shoulders, the fascinated flicker of her smile, a dot of mischief around the lucidity of her eyes. At first glance, her mother's face looked open and innocent, but Aster spied a mystery in the deep green of her eyes. It charmed her, made her look again.

'"...completed at the Camden studio in 1925." First time it has ever been exhibited in public...' Harry said, looking at the brochure. 'From a sketch executed at the St Pancras Hotel. On their wedding night. Goodness, it is rather something, isn't it?'

A laugh bubbled from Aster. She grabbed his hand and kissed it. 'Trust you to help me through this,' she said. 'This is why I will marry you, Harry Penruth.'

She sense someone else standing near her and turned around. The older gentleman and his companion had finished talking to the reporter and stood at her shoulder. He tipped his hat, dipping his head with old-world courtesy. His lady friend looked noticeably younger than he did, with lots of black hair, piled precariously under her hat, threads of silver adding to its wild beauty. She patted the man's arm gently.

'You must say it now, Peter, or it will forever drive you mad.'

'We couldn't help ourselves, you see,' the gentleman began, as if Aster and Harry had been party to their previous conversation.

Aster stared at him, at his fair-grey hair, and sparse neat moustache. A familiarity came to her, some sort of inherited wisdom, a feeling of knowing her own kind.

'But when I heard you speaking, sorry to admit, I overheard you... you seem, young lady, so familiar. You seemed to know so much about... I had to come over. We both had to. This is my wife, Cecelia, and I am Peter Fairling.'

Aster swayed backwards as if hit by a blast of hot air. Harry grabbed her, held her steady.

'Fairling, you say?' he said, and Aster, shuddering to her bones, felt his arm like a dead weight across her shoulders.

'Yes. That's right, the artist's father,' the gentleman said. 'We were on a little trip around Europe, Venice, Florence, you know, when the exhibition opened, so thought we'd better catch it, or we won't hear the end of it. Of course, we've seen the paintings before but to view them here... This is a grand space, isn't it? Perfect size for what Jack wanted. But I must say, my dear, are you quite all right?'

'Of course she's not,' Cecelia Fairling dipped in and held Aster's hand. 'It's as if you've seen a ghost, isn't it, my dear? We need to take her outside. Look at her face. White as a sheet.'

Aster felt herself propelled forward, Harry assuring her that this was the best thing, to leave this place, get some air. The other voices, the gentleman and his wife, puttered around her, offering empathy and understanding. She stepped over a rain-washed pavement, with the smells of tar and rain combining as puddles dried out in the sun, hearing Harry telling her not to worry, that he had her coat and hat, and the older man informing them that there was a good tearoom just around the corner.

'Honestly Peter, at a time like this?' Cecelia said. 'We'll go to the Crescent Moon across the road.'

As they ducked into the warm wood-panelled and mirrored embrace of the public house, Aster at last managed to pin down the words spinning in her head.

'Excuse me,' she said, tugging at the gentleman's sleeve, 'are you my grandfather?'

28

The landlord brought over the four brandies and set them on the table in front of them. One by one, sitting in collective shock, they each picked up their drink and took thoughtful sips. But Aster gripped her glass, knocked it to the back of her throat and squeezed her eyes tight as the alcohol scorched through her. They waited while she composed herself.

Harry said, 'You must understand, Mr and Mrs Fairling, what a blow all of this is to Aster. Up until a month ago, she understood that her father went missing in the war, had *died* in the war. Her grandparents seem to have been economical with the truth, I'm afraid.'

'It all does sound such a muddle,' said Aster's grandfather. 'Were Violet's parents ashamed, perhaps, about what happened? People just didn't talk about such things.'

'They still don't, Peter,' his wife said.

Aster looked from Cecelia back to her grandfather, her confusion deepening.

'What things?' Harry, reading Aster's expression, asked. 'What do you mean?'

'You see, Aster, your father was terribly injured and then captured in the last week of the war. We, also, thought he had been killed. The telegram would have been sent to your mother at Old Trellick. But she would have known as much as we did. God knows what that did to her. Simply awful situation. To have Jack *missing*, and her never knowing. And when he came back, by golly, it was as if the dead *had* returned.'

Aster planted her tumbler firmly down on the table.

'Please tell me what happened,' she said, 'for I am going out of my mind.'

Her grandfather seemed to take a ludicrous amount of time to gather his thoughts.

'Your father was in no man's land just before the Armistice when the shell hit him,' he said, 'and he was taken prisoner by the German Army. We got him back eventually, thanks to the Red Cross, by summer 1919, back on English soil. He returned to his studio in Camden. But he couldn't stay there. He couldn't be left alone. He was in a very bad way. We put him in a hospital in Sidcup for a year where the specialists were.'

Aster blurted, 'But why did he not come and find me when he got back? Why did he forget about me...?' A blunt shaft of pain stopped her speaking. She wanted another brandy.

Harry rested his hand on her arm. 'It sounds like he was far too poorly, Aster.'

'You are right young man,' her grandfather said. 'Years passed and it seemed we were all silenced by the shock of it. Oh, the bright young things all got roaring drunk and danced the night away through the Twenties. But they were too young to know, or chose not to know. The ones who came back, like Jack, well, they didn't want to speak about it. And we kept our heads down and ploughed on. I, to my shame, never felt truly able to understand what Jack went through. Although we did hear the guns, oh yes, didn't we, Cecelia, from our house in Kent? Did you know that, Aster? The roar of the guns in Flanders like distant thunder, across the Channel, but never moving on as storms do. But we never heard from Violet. We wondered if she might write to us? We didn't know what to think. Perhaps, Violet, like her parents, felt ashamed of him. And the silence became normal.'

Aster struggled to maintain her composure, holding on to it by the thinnest of threads. Her earlier clarity, with Harry in the gallery, began to slide away. And all the questions she wanted to ask blended into chaos in her mind.

Cecelia gazed broodingly at her. 'You are the image of your mother, you know,' she said. 'I met her before they married. She came to his studio. I called her "the girl in the painting". You are just like her.'

'People do say that,' Aster said. Only Harry's hand in hers kept her planted in her seat, ensured she didn't leap up and run outside to cry. 'Although I understand I have my father's reddish hair... But why,' she asked, feeling utterly beaten, 'why would my mother feel ashamed of him?'

Aster's grandfather gave her a worried glance. 'Jack was a changed man, his injuries severe. He thought Violet had decided it was for the best for them both that they went their separate ways. But we've supported him, haven't we Cecelia, in everything he wanted to do?'

'I was his landlady in Camden,' Cecelia said. 'I saw him struggle as a young artist. I was his patron, I suppose. When he met your mother a huge flood of creativity opened. He was crazy about her, passionate, as you can see from his work. And with this retrospective, of course he wanted you to have the paintings, as a peace offering. A way of saying sorry.'

'After the war, Jack's painting went downhill. Didn't pick up a brush for a few years. It's a miracle we have these wonderful paintings at all,' said Aster's grandfather. His eyes shone with pride, of what her father had achieved despite everything. 'And, by golly,' he said, 'what a stroke of luck that we happened to be at the gallery at the same time as you. We weren't even going to come today because of the rain.'

Aster gave Harry a frustrated look, a plea for help.

'But why would Violet not want to be reunited with him?' Harry pressed. 'This isn't making any sense.'

'Yes, why would my mother be ashamed?' Aster cried, her flailing hand knocking a tumbler over on the table. 'That wasn't the case, surely?'

Her grandfather reached across to right the glass.

'Perhaps this was your grandparents' way of protecting you. You see, dear Aster, towards the end of the war, the summer of 1918, when he was home on leave, he assaulted a man, was arrested and court martialled. They told him either to go to prison or go back to the Front. I always argued that he must have been horribly affected by what he had seen in the trenches, to make him behave like that. For he really was, and still is, a passive, thoughtful man. And he assumed, as did we, that because of this, the shame of what he'd done, Violet left him.'

Aster shook her head in confusion. 'No, you're wrong! She wouldn't abandon him.'

Her grandfather looked from Aster to Harry and back again. 'We understood she left him for another man. Jack said that there was a local Cornish landlord. Dash it, I can't remember his name. Pen... something.'

Harry's gave a short sharp laugh. 'My father? She certainly did not! My father was widowed during the war, but this is ridiculous. He had been married to Violet's best friend. How did Jack come to *that* conclusion? That Violet wanted to be with my father?'

Aster turned to Harry, calming him. 'It's not possible. It sounds ludicrous, a horrendous misunderstanding...' she uttered.

'It was what Jack told us,' Aster's grandfather said, 'But of course, he was in a terrible way when he came back from Flanders. Perhaps we shouldn't have taken that as gospel.'

'I think perhaps you are right,' Aster said, quietly. 'You see, what you don't understand... Do you not know...? Does my father not know? Do any of you know? The reason for my mother's silence. The reason she did not get in touch.'

Cecelia leant forward. 'Oh, my dear, *what?*'

'My mother is dead,' Aster said with all simplicity, her own calmness beginning to worry her. 'My mother died in an accident in London, a year after the war ended.'

Aster's grandfather and his wife sat back, as if slapped, and turned to stare at each other. Aster watched their faces stretching wide and flat in astonishment.

Her grandfather spluttered, his voice thin and reedy, 'We had no idea. Dear God, no idea.'

Aster clawed her strength back, 'It was the summer after the war. Yes, 1919. Of course, I was still very young, I—'

Cecelia whispered, 'Jack *doesn't* know. He *never* knew. He... he thought Violet didn't want to be with a man maimed like he had been. Because he never heard from her... because, oh my goodness, he thought she'd decided to be with this Mr Penruth fellow.' She glanced at Harry. 'With apologies.'

'My mother died on her way to see my father. She loved him, I'm sure of it...' Aster drew in a shuddering breath. She faltered, knowing the truth hurt everyone, not only herself. 'And my father never knew? All this time. He did not know.'

29

The taxicab squeezed over the bridge through the jam of motor cars and buses, all tooting quite comically as they jostled for space and braked for pedestrians. Aster watched from the back seat as the scene ran like a newsreel compiled to show how any ordinary day should look. And it felt strangely comforting that all this normal activity should carry on while her own world continued to spin and crash.

A few weeks ago, she had been an orphan. Only yesterday she'd been admiring her father's paintings, unfolding her parents' story at the gallery and the truth of what had happened had been laid before her. And, as she got out of the vehicle on this busy Camden street, she stepped into a new present-time, another life.

Aster waited outside the pharmacy that her grandfather, Peter, had told her to look out for, while Harry paid the driver. The little shop looked like it had not changed in years, an old-fashioned charm preserved in its serene interior, and yet she herself had changed with the simple opening of a solicitor's envelope.

'Here we are,' Harry said, his arm around her as they walked to the entrance tucked around the corner.

Standing under the porch, Harry put his hands on her shoulders, holding her steady.

'I can't stop trembling,' she said. 'Is this so unbearably silly? I shouldn't be like this, brimming with dread. I should be ecstatic. But I'm scared, Harry, I am really scared.'

He began to speak low and calmly to her, reminding her he was with her now, would always be, but she barely heard him.

'Are you ready?' he asked.

She managed a half-smile.

Cecelia opened the front door, ushered them into a narrow hallway ending in a staircase. Aster caught a vague smell of paint, of artist's chemicals, as they followed Cecelia up to the first floor landing where her grandfather waited mutely his face stiff with nerves, and ushered them into a front parlour. He asked them to take a seat.

Aster fumbled for a handkerchief to wipe the sweat from her palms. 'Dear God,' she uttered.

She sat, although she didn't want to, feeling Harry's – everyone's – concerned gaze on her.

'You must also remember, Aster,' her grandfather said, 'that your father had been severely injured. You must prepare yourself.'

Aster had longed to see him for so many years. For such a long time had thought he was dead. How could she possibly prepare?

'I'll be with you,' Harry reassured her. 'I'll come in too.'

Aster looked from her grandfather to his wife, from one anxious face to another and the uncertainty and misery that had been darkening her mind began to evaporate. Her reason to be here, right now, at her father's home became clear. She felt liberated, that she had grown up, in that moment, no longer the little girl trapped in a world of falsehood and shame.

'No,' she said. 'This is something that I must do on my own.'

'Darling, I—' Harry began, but Aster's look silenced him.

* * *

Her grandfather showed her along the passageway to a closed door at the end.

'This is your father's studio,' he said with quiet reverence, and went back to the others.

Standing by herself, on the threshold, Aster's burst of strength foundered. She tightened her fist and raised it, waited, gazed at her own hand, as if it belonged to someone else. She inhaled, wanting to rekindle the clarity she longed to feel. Even though it did not return, she knew she must do what she'd come here for. She knocked on the door, turned the door handle, and opened it onto a bright, wide beautiful room.

In an instant, she recognised the window overlooking the street, with escalating views over the rooftops and the chaise in front of it. *Violet in the Evening.* Her gaze travelled around the room, over canvases, pots of paint, fans of brushes, the detritus of an artist's work. Everything new to her, and yet so very familiar. As if she had already visited here, over and over in her mind.

He sat in the armchair with its back to the door, facing the old-fashioned hearth, remaining quite still, as if examining the cold ash in the grate. She wondered if he had heard the door open; perhaps he had lost his hearing in the war. His hair, that soft-sandy colour that she remembered, or told herself she did, looked flecked with grey. And, like his paints and his palettes, she knew him already, in a tiny forgotten part of herself. Aster felt drawn across the room towards him, the reality of being here, within touching distance, scorching her bones. At last, through years of craving, she felt as if she woke from a long, long sleep.

'Dad?'

Her father turned in his chair, holding a handkerchief to the left side of his face, gesturing for her come closer with his other hand. Aster saw brightness in his eyes – oh, those laughing eyes in the back of the wagon on the way to the harvest – and realised that he was crying.

He stood up, surprisingly energetic, his demeanour at odds with the devastated, crippled man that her grandfather had suggested or that Aster had built in her mind. He wore a collar and tie, a pleasing shade of blue, his trousers loosely gathered in the baggy smart new fashion that Harry and so many men wore these days.

'Oh, Dad,' she uttered.

He lowered the handkerchief and Aster drew in her breath in a long excruciating gasp.

'You are just like her,' he said. 'And I am so glad she never got to see me like this for I would not have wanted to see that look on her face. The look you're giving me...'

She tried to focus on his eyes and the smile that lay within them, but the jagged, brutal scar running along his hairline snared her attention. And above his collar and tie, where that side of his jaw would once have been, lay a deep hollow of mutilated flesh, the skin an odd yellow shade, taut like parchment. Her mind emptied of all her memory. Rudely, and finally, her father and what she had remembered of him, disappeared. This shattered mask in its place. Aster wondered how he had the ability to speak at all, his mouth being so torn and crooked, and yet his eyes gleamed like stars in a storm.

'Sit, Aster, please. Good God, you are as white as a sheet. It is a terrible shock, I know. They didn't have mirrors at the hospital in Sidcup. Would have been too grisly to bear.'

Aster knew that he wanted her to laugh. But she could only slump into the other armchair by the hearth, her energy, her courage all spent.

He gazed at her for some moments, and then went to the door. He called out to his father or Cecelia, to please bring them some tea.

'Or perhaps,' he turned to Aster, 'Something a little stronger.'

'No... no,' she uttered, knowing that there wasn't anything that would make her feel better.

Her father came back and sat down opposite her, gesturing with his handkerchief to establish whether she wanted him to keep it in place or not.

She shook her head, and gazed around at the studio, at the light shimmering through the generous windows, streaming through jars of paint, highlighting flecks of dust, and dropping blocks of gold across the old worn rug.

'I realise now,' she said, catching his eye. 'That the last time I ever saw you, Dad, was also the last time Mama saw you. Is that right? There is so much I don't understand. We've been strangers all these years, and I am still reeling. Receiving the solicitor's letter, and bumping into my grandfather yesterday was a shock enough. And now this... to be here, with you...'

Cecelia came in with a tray. She kindly, tactfully, said nothing and left it with them.

Aster instinctively set out the cups and poured the tea.

'Ah,' her father uttered, 'You are just like her. Even the way you hold your teacup, and check the temperature of the pot.' He stirred his tea three times, tapped his spoon twice on the rim. 'All the years, all that time. Wasted. I can't believe she is dead. How can she be, when she's been alive in my mind, alive all this time?'

Aster watched in breathless silence as tears spilt out of his brilliant eyes and ran in strange and unfamiliar channels towards his ruined chin. He put his hands over his face and bowed his head, his breath shuddering as he uttered visceral groans.

Aster waited. She knew that whatever she wanted to say to him would make no difference to his pain.

Eventually, her father wiped his face with his handkerchief.

'You see,' he said, grimacing. 'This has many uses.'

A rush of affection flared inside her. How her father tried to make light of his situation, of hers too, to try to help her feel better.

'I wished I'd known, Dad, that you had survived the war,' Aster said, and felt a quietly futile fury surge, directed at those she'd left behind at Old Trellick. 'All this time, wasted.'

'And, all this time, I thought that your mother didn't want me,' he said. 'There had been so many obstacles in our way, I almost expected it. Her parents who didn't approve of me, perhaps more so her mother; my behaviour, admittedly. Offering you my paintings when you reached twenty-one was my peace offering to you both. To you and Violet. She didn't think much of me, Violet's mother. Oh, she was perfectly polite to my face, to some extent. But I was a poor artist scraping a living. And then there was Weston Penruth.'

'Ah yes, Weston...' Aster began but stopped, hungering to hear her father speak further, for him to put everything right. Harry and Weston could wait.

'I was jealous of him,' her father said, 'what a thing for a grown man to admit. And I think your grandparents secretly preferred him, rubbed their hands with glee when I went off to war. After all, what was my life expectancy?' His voice broke. 'I became a cold stranger to Violet. That's what the war did to me. And all this time, these past two decades more or less, I thought she was happy, taking care of you, and living her life... which was what I told her to do. It was the last thing I said to her when I left.'

Aster watched her father's private pain creep over his features, altering them as each fresh reality gripped him. He picked up his teacup, his hand juddering, changed his mind and placed it down with a clatter.

'I must take you to the Pavilion in Regent's Park,' he said, recovering a little, grasping on to a happier time. 'Let's go there tomorrow.'

'Is that where you and my mother met?'

'Nearby...' On reflex, he lifted his handkerchief to his face.

'Dad,' Aster said, 'what happened to you?'

He looked past her, down into a deep memory, and winced.

'A shell passing overhead emits a whistling sound,' he said. 'If you hear it, the reckoning is that you're safe. That it has passed over. Of course...' he cocked his head. 'I didn't hear this one coming. And when shrapnel hits bone, it sounds like me smashing a glass jar into my porcelain sink over there.'

Aster recoiled, waited, open mouthed, not wanting to listen but knew she must, for her father.

'We were at Ypres, October 1918. It's true when they say you don't know what hits you. My father told you, didn't he, that I was captured and sent to a prisoner of war camp near Berlin with half of my face missing? The German surgeons were unfeeling but efficient,' he said. 'A month later, I was too busy drowning in morphine to realise that peace had been declared. It took six or seven months for me to be able to come home to England with the Red Cross. I came straight to London, dropped what was left of my kit here – Cecelia by this time had married my father and was living in Kent – and headed straight for Montagu Square.'

'Great Auntie Muriel's?' Aster asked.

He nodded. 'Knocked on the door. I seem to remember the housemaid being struck mute, staring at me. She wouldn't let me in at first. I was off the morphine, disorientated by pain. My scarf must have slipped, I must have looked like a madman. Then Muriel thundered down the stairs, took one look at me and ushered me inside. She had just returned from Cornwall. Was unpacking her Meissen. I remember, we laughed at her love of German porcelain and made a joke about it making it through the war intact. Unlike some of us.'

Aster smiled, remembering little of her great-aunt, but that she was a kind and energetic, if somewhat formidable, presence at Old Trellick.

'I was frustrated, impatient,' her father said. 'I wanted to see Violet. And you, of course. But I knew what I had become. But Muriel didn't flinch. Muriel understood. She was a great fixer, Muriel. She said that she would send a telegram to Old Trellick, and tell Violet that I had made it back and was here in London. She said she would warn Violet about me as best she could and as gently as she could. I thought it would all be fine by the end of the week. That Violet and I would be together. We'd live together, the three of us, in Camden or Kent or Cornwall, it didn't matter to me. We could start again. Rebuild our lives. Have the time together we deserved.'

Aster struggled, wiping her eyes. 'With the war over,' she uttered, 'you had so much hope. And Mama did come up to London. I know that much. That's when the accident happened.'

Her father turned away to stare out the window, covering his face with his handkerchief.

'I don't think you realise, Dad,' Aster continued gently, 'that Aunt Muriel caught the Spanish flu around that same time. She passed away. Their funerals were within a week of each other.'

Her father exhaled. 'So many thousands died,' he said. 'I remember thinking, how much worse could things be for this nation, for Europe? The world?'

They sat quietly for some moments, taking time, gathering strength to absorb all that they'd told each other. Presently, Aster asked, 'What did you do, then, once you'd visited Muriel?'

'At my father's insistence, I went to the hospital in Sidcup where they specialised, or learnt to specialise, in this sort of injury. They had me on the list, and I felt duty-bound, to be honest. I met the kindest surgeon who repaired my face as best he could, made me a tin mask.' He nodded his head in the direction of a bureau where a cardboard box sat. 'Go on, take a look.'

Growing up, Aster had certainly caught sight of men over the years, wearing large hats, their faces wrapped in scarves, and a glint of metal where their face ought to be. She went over to fetch the box, sat with it on her lap and tentatively lifted the lid. Her father's mask lay nestled in cotton wool. It looked eerily immobile, like an effigy of the dead, its hard metallic form following the curves of his now shattered cheek and once firm jaw, a replica of her father's face.

'This is to spare the nightmares of ordinary folk on the streets,' he said. 'But I never wore it. Go ahead, Aster, you can touch it.'

Aster lightly brushed the smooth cold edges and realised, with a jolt, how a mask such as this would have given so many men new hope, new confidence, a new life, perhaps.

'Thank God my nose is still intact,' her father said, wryly. 'Got a good Fairling nose.'

They both laughed together, relief verging on hysteria spilling between them. Outside a vague hum of traffic and day-to-day voices kept Aster's nerves remarkably steady. She put the box away and went back to sit by the hearth.

'Again, my recovery at Sidcup took many months,' he went on, 'and all the time I kept thinking that any moment Violet will appear at my bedside, or surprise me as I walked the grounds. She'd have got Muriel's telegram and will have made her way to London, found out where I was. Muriel would surely have given her the details of the hospital that I left with her. I wondered, should I wear the mask, or should I let her see me? Some days, my courage was better than others, you understand. And still, Violet did not come. And then I made up my mind. She must have gone to Weston.'

'But how would you even *think* that of her?'

Her father sighed, sounding like a man dying. 'So many reasons, Aster, so many reasons.'

'But, Dad,' Aster said, the chaos and frustration returning. 'I need to tell you something. You mention Weston Penruth, as Grandpa Peter did yesterday. But do you remember his son, Harry, Harry Penruth?'

'I do, he was a quiet little lad, as I recall. I only saw him a handful of times...' he stopped and stared at her, understanding. 'Oh, Aster,' he said, 'something tells me...'

'Yes,' she said, brightening. 'Harry and I are engaged. I haven't had a chance to tell you. It seems inconsequential news, really, along with everything else. And it has happened quickly, but it feels wonderful and right, he has been such a support to me. He's sitting now with Grandpa and Cecelia, out there, and...' She stopped, seeing the uneasy look on her father's face.

'Oh, Aster,' he said, 'I am happy for you, I am, but you obviously don't know—'

'What, Dad, what else?' she cried, thinking for a moment that he was about to make another joke.

'I tried to kill his father.'

She gaped at him. A sheet of ice sliced through her middle. Her scalp tightened and sweat broke out on her upper lip.

'Why...? When...?' she spluttered, staring at him. And when she could no longer look at his stricken, mutilated face, she got to her feet and walked over to the chaise where he'd once painted her mother sleeping. 'Oh, Dad, why?' She sat down on it, feeling her middle give way. She leant forward, resting her face in her hands.

'Harry Penruth's out there?' her father asked, calm in the face of her turmoil. 'Please, Aster, go and fetch him in.'

She got up at once to do as he asked, but hesitated at the doorway.

'Dad, are you sure?' she said. 'Do you want to speak to him, *now*?'

'Aster, think about what has brought all of us here,' he said. 'It has to be done. I have been wanting to make it up to Violet for what I did to Penruth for such a long time. For she saw me do it, she witnessed the horror of it, my arrest, and she had to deal with the shame it brought to her and her family. I shall face Harry now, Aster, and I will ask for his forgiveness. And perhaps one day, I will travel down to Cornwall and visit the man himself, and make whatever amends I can.'

30

London basked under the benign summer sky. The rain of the past few days had moved on that morning and along the Outer Circle of Regent's Park, the white mansions looked resplendent in the sunshine, sparkling with elegance and discreet wealth. Huge trees in the park, vigorous and green, released drops of rain into the air.

Aster and Harry walked under the leafy canopy, heading for the Pavilion.

'We've had quite a week of it, haven't we?' Harry said.

'Always an understatement with you, Harry,' Aster laughed. 'It is something I should get used to, I suppose. Like your always obvious observations about the weather. And, I realise,' she said more cautiously, 'your father will have to get used to you wanting to marry the daughter of the man who attacked him. He will have to get used to *us*.'

'I will write to him tonight,' Harry said. 'And also to Kate separately. She often knows how to handle our father despite the distance between them. She knows exactly what to say to him whereas I, frankly, struggle at the best of times. But she seems to have a gift for it. And I am sure that was one of my mother's many talents – to temper the fire in him. And I think it was that very trait of his that drove your father to distraction.'

They walked on a little further, Harry checking the time: 'Two o'clock we said.'

'Harry,' Aster stopped him. 'Do you remember it? The harvest? My father's outburst? Him attacking your father?'

'No, thank goodness. Perhaps I was too young, perhaps I have blocked it out like you do with bad memories,' he said. 'Do you remember?'

'I have a feeling, that's all,' she said. 'That something terrible happened, and yet it all seems to be caught up with the war, and my father not being there all the time. And when he was, it still didn't seem right. I remember disruption and unease. A sort of grinding anxiety. But always, my mother taking care of me. And my father, too, when he could. In the only way he knew how.'

They walked on through the leafy London park. The recent rain had intensified the scent of the cut grass, and it lifted in fresh waves around them with each step they took, reminding Aster of the smell of hay and straw. The harvest nearly twenty years ago. She felt that the sepia image in the photograph she found of her and Harry and Kate, with her mother unknowingly captured and almost cropped out, belonged to a different age. An entirely different lifetime.

'Look, Aster, I forgot to say,' Harry said, plucking the rolled-up newspaper from under his arm. 'I picked up the first edition of the *Standard*. The review is in here.'

'Oh, let me see.'

Harry found the page for her.

'The reporter – remember him? – in the black suit. He's the one we saw speaking to Peter and Cecelia. Got a very nice quote from them. Here it is.'

The headline was under the paper's 'Arts Review' banner. Aster read: '"*Jack P. Fairling: A Retrospective*. A message of love from the trenches."'

They'd printed the sketch of her as a three-year-old child and *her* eyes gazed solemnly out of the page at her.

'How serious I look,' she said, overwhelmed by the joy she felt seeing the column inches given over to her father's work. 'Oh, I won't read it now. Let Dad read it first. After all, it's all about him, his work, his life.'

They found him waiting outside the Pavilion, wearing a particularly perky trilby and a peacock blue silk scarf around his chin.

'I can be as flamboyant as I like with these scarves,' he said, greeting them with his crooked smile. 'I have a whole wardrobe of them.'

As Harry and her father shook hands, Aster peered into the tearoom. 'It's rather busy in there. We'll never get a table.'

'Then let's take a stroll first,' her father said. 'The roses are looking exceptionally beautiful today.'

'Well, we have had a lot of rain,' said Harry, laughing, and winked at Aster.

'And mercy,' she said, when they reached the Rose Garden, 'the seat is empty.'

Her father sat down under the clambering roses, exhaling a mighty sigh and taking in the banks of flowers in the garden, their wide faces open to the sunshine.

'This is where she was sitting, under this canopy,' he said, rearranging his scarf. 'I was over there, sketching in the corner. I first saw her walking over the grass. She looked so angry and bewildered and beautiful. She came and sat here – just for a moment or two – and I didn't miss my chance. She was done in a matter of minutes. Perfect.' He paused. 'I thought I'd never see her again.'

'And that became *Violet in the Daytime*?' Aster asked.

'The start of it all,' he said, looking steadfastly at the roses blooming around them, and then at Harry. 'I want to apologise to you again, Harry, for what happened. Assaulting your father. Whatever madness came to me at that moment, I should have been more resilient. I lost my dignity.'

'Nonsense, Jack,' Harry said. 'I won't hear of it. What you went through, it is hardly surprising. And, in all honestly, I know he is my father, but he can be infuriating at the best of times.'

'We understand how much Weston being linked to Old Trellick and my family must have troubled you, Dad,' Aster said. 'But we want to set your mind at rest, once and for all. Move up a bit,' she said, 'and I will show you.'

She sat down next to her father, opened her bag and drew out her mother's journal. She passed it over, and he held the book in trembling hands, caressing the battered green leather cover, and ran his fingers across the pages.

'Goodness, here she is,' he uttered, his eyes ablaze.

'Yes, she certainly feels alive in this book,' Aster said, looking at him full and unflinching in the face. 'May I?'

She turned pages hastily, trying to find the entry. 'Oh, it's here somewhere. Something she wrote, which meant she loved you. She wanted you, and not Harry's father. Oh yes, she often spoke in riddles in here, all her rhyme and wisdom, but to me this was clear.'

Her father's face brightened. 'Your mother was so damn secretive sometimes, and yet there were times when I could read her, and I knew exactly what she was thinking. I wish I had understood more. Asked her more.'

As Aster fumbled with the book, her father gently took it from her and opened it towards the back.

'I'm curious about her last entry,' he said. 'You see, I want to know what she was thinking right up to the end when... Ah, I see.'

'That was me,' said Aster. 'I pasted in those rather limp and sorry-looking daisies. I've dated it June 1919, in my rather poor four-year-old handwriting, look. But I simply don't remember doing it.'

'What you're looking for will be around the summer of 1914,' Harry said, he held out his hand for the book and found the page in an instant, and Aster understood exactly why she wanted to marry him.

'Weston's peony, Dad. She pressed this flower in the spring, but wrote this entry in June 1914.'

'Ah, soon after we met,' her father said.

She settled next to him, and glanced over his shoulder as he read: *"'Today is not the day I pressed and pasted this flower, but today is the day I wish to record how I have found a new meaning to myself, to my life... A week ago, I walked for the first time in Regent's Park among the roses... a week ago, I saw beyond sorrow, and shame – the only things offered to me by a person from my past. For everything else he offered proved to be false, a charade... the gestures, although gallant, were not for me, but were only for that person's self-interest. The proposal had been in arrogance, an effort to squash me, and stop me being Violet, the person I am.*

"'A deep-red Peony, like the one pasted here, means honour, respect, kindness, and compassion, but these are the things this man does not possess. And yet he gave this flower to me, in March, thinking I'd believe him, thinking I'd want the Peony, and all the other forced, premature, incongruous blooms he offered. And give myself to him in return. He could not have been further from the truth.

"'A week ago, among the roses of Regent's Park, I glimpsed beyond the shame, I glimpsed a new beginning. I discovered a new day. A new self.

"'Violet Prideaux, Montagu Square, London, 15 June, 1914.'"

Her father pressed his handkerchief over his face.

'Oh, my beloved Violet,' he said. 'How did I doubt you?'

'We will leave you for now Dad, so you can be with Mama and read in peace,' Aster said, 'We will see you later on, over at the Pavilion.'

She leant down and kissed her father on his hollowed-out ruined cheek.

As she took Harry's arm and walked away, she brushed passed the roses and caught their lightest and sweetest breath. Her father sat quite still at the centre of the garden, surrounded by cascading colour that shifted and blurred as the breeze blew. He unwrapped the scarf from his ravaged face so that he, too, could breathe more deeply on the scented air.

He settled her mother's journal on his lap, turned to the first page and began to read.

31

KENT, A YEAR LATER, 1937

Aster watched from the upstairs window as cloud shadows chased across hop gardens and orchards, patchworked in gold and green. Starbright and Sparrow shook their manes in the sunshine, wading through the long grass in the pasture, pricking their ears to Harry's whistle as he worked in the garden. Such a different land, such a different world here, Aster thought, compared to the miniature wildness of Cornwall. So ordered, serene and secluded. Exquisite peace seemed to be borne on the clear empty horizon, with only the occasional little plane buzzing out of the airfield at Manston on the far skyline. And beyond, of course, the sea.

The breeze through the window ruffled the letter in her hand. Her father's despair ebbed and flowed with crushing inevitability, he wrote. Sometimes, he struggled to contemplate the unthinkable: that her mother had been dead for almost twenty years. But when he thought of the joy that she brought him, the enduring spirit of his muse, he felt revived and ready to face another day. He wrote:

I paint and I paint!

Aster and Harry must promise to travel to London to view his new exhibition, he said. He also welcomed their own exciting news and would come down to Kent to visit before the summer was out. He loved coming home, was looking forward to seeing his father and Cecelia. But that wasn't all...

Aster pressed her fingers back inside the envelope and pulled out another sheet, an old drawing, her father explained in his letter, that he'd chanced upon recently, dashed off, he said, towards the end of the war in a Flanders trench.

On the paper, soft with age, tatty and stained, lay the drawing of a single crimson flower, clinging precariously to life, gasping and vulnerable, its petals still blood-red but surviving amid the chaos. And beside it, so many years before, he had written:

Darling Violet, Here I am hemmed in by wasteland, walking with death at my shoulder, but I found this flower growing, living, one bright moment in hell and it reminded me of you – for the thought of you conquers my fear of dying... and I will get through this. I, too, will live. And I will see you again.

But her father had not been able to send the drawing to Violet, for the next day the German shell fell.

Aster stared at the sketch as it first swam out of focus and then re-emerged, her falling tears in danger of soaking it. A memory nudged her: lying in her bed at Old Trellick on a late-summer night and, incredibly, hearing the sea. And, again now, even though it had been impossible then and would be impossible now for the Kentish coast was over five miles away, the sound of waves filled the room, swaying her gently, moving in a cradling embrace.

Aster fetched her mother's journal from shelf and slipped her father's sketch inside the pages. It will become, she decided, the beginning of a new journal. The child inside her kicked her twice and she soothed it, telling it to hush, stroking her fingertips over her stomach.

'If you are a boy,' she told the baby, 'We will call you Edward. Because a long time ago, so everyone tells me, Daddy's mother once loved a man called Eddie. Before she loved your grandfather, Weston.'

She gazed out of the window at the sublime peace of the Garden of England.

'And if you are a girl,' she said, 'I will call you Violet.'

EPILOGUE
IN THE LANGUAGE OF FLOWERS: WHITE ROSES, I AM WORTHY OF YOU

Violet, London, June 1919

The night train from Exeter had been delayed and Violet did not reach Montagu Square until mid-morning. She had expected to arrive early with the milk cart and the baker's van, but the day had already begun with whistling window cleaners and the sweep setting up his ladders next door. The serene square and shady garden appeared unaffected by the last five years, but perhaps, thought Violet, behind chintz curtains and spilling window boxes, dwelled brooding grief, disbelief and tenuous, fading hope.

On the train, Violet had read in the newspaper how, this summer, poppies spread themselves over the churned-up filth of the silent wastelands. How quickly and swiftly nature swooped in to disguise devastation, she thought, stepping out on to the sunny pavement. It seemed to want to put right what we have done, and dress it up as if it had never happened. To show us that life moved on, with us or without us. As indeed it had done at Old Trellick.

Violet paid the driver and stood for a moment by the railings of Muriel's house, thinking of home. Since the news had come through about Jack last October, *missing in action*, Aster had grown another inch, had learnt cat's cradle and hopscotch. And she'd developed a good eye for picking out willow herb and cow parsley; daisies now her favourite. How happy Aster had looked, merrily pasting the daisies she'd picked and pressed the other week onto a fresh new page in Violet's journal when Muriel's telegram arrived.

> JACK HOME IN CAMDEN. PLEASE COME. PREPARE YOURSELF. MURIEL.

* * *

Violet walked up the steps to her aunt's house, daring the hope sparking in her mind to shine a little brighter. She rang the doorbell and waited, trying not to give into fatigue. It would be hard to describe the night train as the 'sleeper' for she'd not had a wink. And she must keep going. She must, as Muriel's telegram said, prepare herself.

The front door opened a fraction and Smithson peered through the narrow gap, a linen mask over her nose and mouth.

'Good morning, Mrs Fairling,' she said, her voice sounding as if she spoke down a telephone line. 'We are expecting you. But it's probably best you don't come in.'

'Whatever's the matter?' Violet felt a snap of irritation. Smithson, efficient and rather pedantic, had left Muriel for better-paid work in 1914, and only returned now, for a price. Muriel had said that she'd wanted all sorts of new labour-saving devices that she'd seen advertised in the *Evening Mail*. And a pay rise.

'Madam is very ill. She has the influenza,' Smithson said. 'Came back from the post office yesterday, when she sent your telegram, shivering with cold despite it being such a warm day. Went straight to her bed. Doctor's been once. Says he can't come back 'til tomorrow. Too many people coming down with it. A new strain or something...'

Violet heard the catch in the housemaid's voice; saw her frightened eyes widening above the mask.

'And how are *you* feeling, Smithson?' she asked.

'I am well. I will do what I can for Madam,' she said. 'She's delirious. I've never seen anything like it. It has happened so quickly. It's hardly her any more. She's so very ill. Her face has turned a sort of... *purple*.'

'I will call the doctor back,' Violet said pushing the door and stepping into the vestibule. 'We can't have that.'

'No, Mrs Fairling!' Smithson's shout stopped her. 'You have a young child. I don't think you should come into this house.'

'Yes, you're right.' Violet didn't want to catch Spanish flu and take it back to Old Trellick with her. 'But may I leave this here, for now?' she said, putting her small suitcase down by the plant pots. 'You see, I need to go...'

'Of course, Mrs Fairling,' Smithson said, and Violet sensed a new kindness, an understanding in the woman. 'One more moment...' The housemaid dipped back into the hallway, and reappeared with Muriel's parasol. 'Here, take this. It's a warm day, and I'm sure Madam would not want you to be out in the sunshine. Oh, and this post arrived for you the other week.'

Violet took the parasol and slipped the letter into her bag.

'Thank you, Smithson,' she said, hurrying back down the steps. 'Tell Muriel I will be back to see her soon.'

She wondered if her taxi might still be parked on the square, but, out of luck, she began to walk towards Baker Street.

Oh, poor dear Muriel, she thought. But Jack may know a better doctor. Jack will know what to do.

Violet paused at the busy road to check the queues of jostling buses and cars for a free taxi, but, glimpsing the entrance to the park beyond the traffic, it seemed it would be quicker to walk.

She crossed into the Inner Circle, and the tranquil beauty, the delicate peace, of Regent's Park embraced her. People strolled, walking dogs, nannies pushed prams and a young couple in a buggy, pulled by a handsome black pony, scooted around the main pathway. They had all survived, Violet thought with tender hope.

She glanced around at the sound of a dog barking, a bit of a hubbub. The pony with the buggy rose in its harness, pummelling the air. But the young driver reined it in, settling the matter, congratulated by his sweetheart, who laughed and clutched his arm. How happy they look, as we will be, Violet mused, as soon as she got to him. She hurried on, both joy and tiredness making her light-headed.

But she must prepare herself, as Muriel had said in her telegram. Perhaps Jack had the flu? So many soldiers came home with it. Ah, but he was home. He was over there, beyond the rose garden and across the stretch of green. If she quickened her pace, she would soon be passing Cumberland Terrace where Lady Welstead sat, no doubt in all her finery, mourning her son. Then she'd be crossing the bridge over the railway and walking up Parkway. And there, past the pharmacist, and round the corner. She would soon be knocking on the little shabby door.

And then Violet remembered, the letter in her bag.

How odd, she thought, drawing it out while she walked, that someone would write to her at Muriel's after all this time. The envelope appeared old and unduly crumpled, and she inhaled with shock. Claudia's handwriting. Postmarked July 1914.

'Oh, my dear friend.' Violet began to cry, hot blinding tears streaming down her cheeks. Her loss returned, shuddering through her, with a violence that took her breath away.

Violet's fingers trembled as she tore at the envelope and pulled out the single sheet. At the cove, all that time ago, Claudia had said that she'd written to her, while Violet had been staying at Muriel's. Had the letter got stuck in the post? Dropped down the back of a sorting tray somewhere for all these years?

She read as she walked, for she must keep going to Jack, feeling staggered to see Claudia's beautiful handwriting, her friend's own singular spirit singing from the page.

Claudia wrote that she had seen Weston come to the farm, the evening of the soirée at Charlecote and shoot his dogs. She had run out to him, had comforted him. He had said he was a wicked person. That he had been beaten badly as a boy by his father. Pain and suffering had been his life. And this made him who he was. What he deserved.

Claudia had fallen in love with him in that moment, wanted to take care of him. She wished Violet and Jack every happiness, and love. She said how sorry she felt, for she never wanted this astonishing turn of events to come between her and Violet. They were friends, always.

Violet stopped, reading the letter over and over, letting the tears fall.

'Yes, we will be happy, Claudia,' she uttered, her smile curving over her face, but wishing, imagining, that her friend walked beside her. 'And look, this is where Jack and I first met.'

White roses, like drifts of snow in summer, filled the Rose Garden. But where, Violet wondered, have all the other colours gone? But, never mind. White roses were her favourite. And this was where he had been sitting, watching her, drawing her, and she didn't know... And, oh goodness, Violet thought, laughing in delight. She was not used to feeling this happy.

The sun shone sharply in Violet's eyes as she walked out from under the willow trees and she raised Muriel's parasol. Happiness formed a blissful bubble around her and her footsteps bounced over the springy grass, lush and green and spangled with daisies. Oh, the daisies that Aster found. Jack will be able to see them pasted in her journal when they went back home together to Old Trellick. Perhaps, all being well, they could take the night train.

'Jack, this is where you first saw me. Here. Right here,' she whispered to herself. 'This is *Violet in the Daytime.*'

I am moving through the park, under the dappled silvery shadow of willow trees; star-like daisies bright at my feet. My face is half in profile. My parasol is the colour of luminous water, protecting me, keeping me separated in my own world. My eyes, even in shadow, are lucid sea-green. As I walk, I am not aware of the artist as he sees me; just of the light that comes from below me, reflected from his direction, to illuminate me and set me apart.

Violet lifted her hand to her brow, to peer back along the path. The shocking ringing noise of hooves thundering towards her forced the breath out of her. The young couple, who moments before had been laughing and kissing, screamed and clung to each other, rocking from side to side on the buggy seat as the pony clattered on down the pathway.

Violet's limbs turned to dust. Her mouth opened, silently screaming. In her mind, she stepped neatly to the side as the pony and carriage bore down on her, as the screams intensified, and the hammering hooves kicked on. But there seemed to be no moment in which to save herself, for time had stopped. No time left at all.

Violet lay motionless, crumpled on the grass, as people ran from all directions towards her. Claudia's letter, released from her hand, lifted suddenly in the breeze and, along with Muriel's parasol, blew away across the daisy-spangled grass.

ACKNOWLEDGEMENTS

A walk across Regent's Park, a stroll down Parkway in Camden, and getting lost in the pinewoods at Lanwarnick, near Polperro, Cornwall, have all contributed to the writing of this novel.

The Imperial War Museum provided me, as always, with the facts and the background to this traumatic time, and military historian, Iain McHenry, put it all into vivid reality on a battlefield tour of Ypres and the Somme. I found inspiration at two particularly memorable places: Sanctuary Wood Museum Hill 62, near Ypres, Belgium, and Museum Historial de la Grande Guerre, Péronne, France, where I saw the hellish visions of trench warfare in the sketches by German First World War artist Otto Dix. Also from the books: *Forgotten Voices of the Great War* by Max Arthur, *The Great Silence* by Juliet Nicolson and *Testament of Youth* by Vera Brittain.

Thank you to my father Gerry for lending me his *Book of Wildflowers* and for passing on to me his love, knowledge and appreciation of the countryside.

And thank you to talented military artist, David Bryant, for his interpretation of one of Jack's 'trench sketches' which you can see on the next page. For more information, visit davidbryantart.com.

I'd also like to thank the team at Boldwood for giving me the chance to re-tell the story of Violet, Jack and Aster.

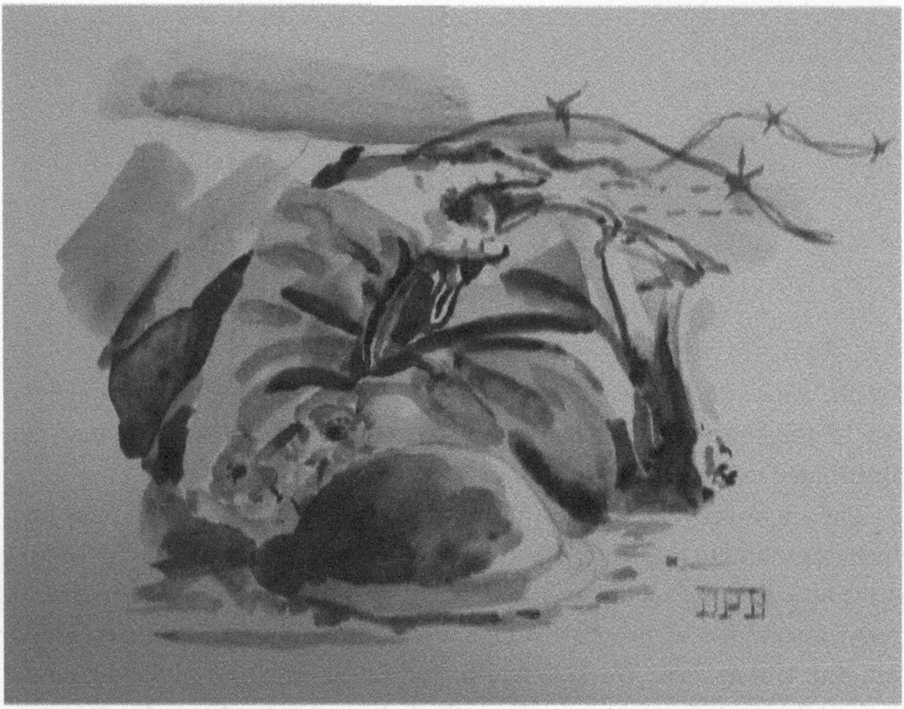

ABOUT THE AUTHOR

Catherine Law writes dramatic romantic novels set in the first half of the 20th century, during the First and Second World Wars. Her books are inspired by the tales our mothers and grandmothers tell. Originally a journalist, Catherine lives in Kent.

Sign up to Catherine Law's mailing list here for news, competitions and updates on future books.

Visit Catherine's website: www.catherinelaw.co.uk

Follow Catherine on social media:

- facebook.com/catherinelawbooks
- instagram.com/catherinelawauthor
- goodreads.com/catherinelaw

ALSO BY CATHERINE LAW

The Officer's Wife

The Runaway

The French Girl

The Code Breaker's Secret

The Land Girl's Letters

The Map Maker's Promise

The Artist's Daughter

Letters from *the past*

Discover page-turning historical novels from your favourite authors and be transported back in time

Join our book club Facebook group

https://bit.ly/SixpenceGroup

Sign up to our newsletter

https://bit.ly/LettersFromPastNews

Boldwood

Boldwood Books is an award-winning fiction publishing company seeking out the best stories from around the world.

Find out more at www.boldwoodbooks.com

Join our reader community for brilliant books, competitions and offers!

Follow us
@BoldwoodBooks
@TheBoldBookClub

Sign up to our weekly deals newsletter

https://bit.ly/BoldwoodBNewsletter

Milton Keynes UK
Ingram Content Group UK Ltd.
UKHW021552111224
452278UK00001BA/3

9 781837 516308